LORDS OF PARADISE

LORDS OF PARADISE

Lon LaFlamme

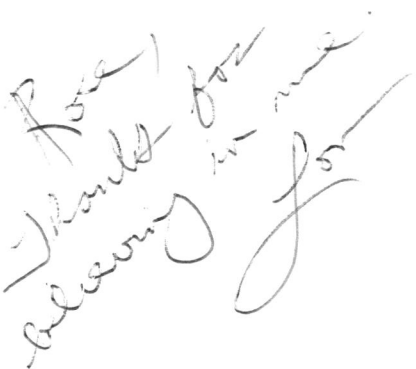

Writer's Showcase presented by *Writer's Digest*
San Jose New York Lincoln Shanghai

Lords of Paradise

Published by Writer's Showcase presented by *Writer's Digest*
an imprint of iUniverse.com, Inc.

For information address:
iUniverse.com, Inc.
620 North 48th Street
Suite 201
Lincoln, NE 68504-3467
www.iuniverse.com

ISBN: 0-595-09425-2

Printed in the United States of America

For Karen

AUTHOR'S NOTE

In 1890 polygamy was renounced by The Church of Jesus Christ Latter-Day Saints, commonly referred to as The Mormon Church. Since that time the Church excommunicates any member involved in any aspect of polygamy.

There are as many perspectives on polygamy as there are polygamists. Each experience is different; every perspective is personal. All have one thing in common—a belief that polygamy is God's commandment, a divine principle or higher law, the pattern of heaven. For them, polygamy is one dimension of paradise on earth.

The shrouded illegal world of polygamy in Utah and surrounding states hides unimaginable social dynamics used at their darkest as the foundation for this purely fictional story. While actual court proceedings, newspaper accounts and personal stories of alleged sexual abuse served as inspiration for the creation of *Lords of Paradise*, there was no intent to associate any actual persons, locations or events with this story.

This book is a result of many small inspirations, starting with the brave handful of women who, in March 1998, escaped their plural wife bonds along with their children and formed Tapestry Against Polygamy (TAP). Literally fearing for their lives, these women organized to help counsel and guide others to appropriate state services and support groups. The National Organization of Women selected the founders of TAP to receive the coveted "Women of Courage Award" for 1999.

I am donating a portion of the sale proceeds from the first edition of this book to Tapestry Against Polygamy in hopes they grow and lead more and more women and children to true personal freedom.

A special thanks to my ardent agent, Nancy Ellis-Bell; editor extraordinaire, Laurie Rosin; and gifted cover design artist, Kat. My supportive best friend and wife, Karen; along with Scott N. Howell, Mike Bodell, Ed Hammond, Steve Thompson, and iUniverse's Mike Johnson also deserve my gratitude.

Further, I am indebted to the following for welcoming me as an insider into Utah's top-notch criminal investigation departments:

Daniel Weaver
Salt Lake City Crime Lab Technician (and a favorite cousin)

George Throckmorton
Salt Lake City Crime Lab Manager

Kevin M. Patrick
Utah State Crime Lab Supervising Criminalist

Detective Kent W. Timothy
West Valley City Police Department
Forensics Services Unit

Terry Lamoreaux
Utah Chief Organic, Chemistry & Medical Examiner Toxicology

Gregory M Cooper
(One of the first members of the FBI's Quantico, VA Behavioral Sciences Unit)
The City of Provo, Utah
Chief of Police

FOREWORD

While *Lords of Paradise* is a riveting work of fiction, many of the events portrayed are, unfortunately, all too real.

Many of the elected officials in Utah have joined me in committing to enforce the Utah State Constitution prohibiting polygamy. Since 1998 State officials and private citizens have rallied to finance and create support services to victims of polygamy as they courageously escape from this unlawful practice.

It is our responsibility as elected officials to ensure that the rights of the Utah and United States Constitution and Bill of Rights are honored, allowing women and children freedom of choice and self-directed fulfillment.

Polygamy has just gone on too long. It is too convoluted, too immoral, and is hurting vulnerable lives.

Scott N. Howell
Utah State Senate Democratic Leader

PROLOGUE

Satan's bride.

The thought comforted the shadowed intruder with each stealthy footprint he punched through the deep crusted snow of the desert floor.

Barely a woman. What can a child understand of God's plans? Of course she can't. Satan's hot hands rubbing her body. Driving her mad.

Sensual tingles surged through his wildly pumping heart, and he suddenly found it hard to swallow.

He rolled his stooped shoulders back and inhaled the crisp midnight air, then expelled an enormous plume of mist, cleansing his mind of temptress delights.

His dull brown gaze scrutinized the long row of frost-laced windows, then came to rest on the yellow glow emanating from the last room on the second floor. He knew it had to be Sarah, even though all ten children's rooms were on the second floor.

She was alone in that bedroom. The thought again started red-hued images that threatened to cloud his singular purpose. His lips moved in silent prayer.

The key in the front door would make a small clicking noise—no problem in a fifty-year-old, wood-framed house that nightly hosted a chorus of creaking timber.

He moved the twenty paces to the whitewashed front porch verandah, with its freshly painted white wicker rocking chairs to the right of the front door and wooden gliding bench to the south. He pictured himself at twelve with his brother, hip-to-hip, playfully slugging each other, oblivious eyes to the isolated beauty of the distant purplish mountain range and endless pale blue sky.

The crouched predator crept to the twelve-foot windows on his left, stretching his steps to minimize the squeaks of the floorboards. Hand-made lace curtains framed a darkened living room, now only populated by drab, bulbous fabric-covered furniture, a long out-of-tune upright Lancaster piano, and tassel-trimmed lampshades. He lingered, studying the accent table crammed with framed photos arranged below a gigantic gilt-framed mirror. He used to primp in that mirror before his father huddled the brood into a circle for evening fireside sermons.

He crept to the north bank of windows and glared in at the dining room table with matching benches milled from one of the property's cloud tickling spruce pines ages ago. His granite face cracked into a rare smile, recalling that the house had to be built around a table that would seat thirty.

The dark man tugged off one of his supple leather gloves and fumbled in his black cashmere overcoat for the old-fashioned front door key. All would work out. His mission was in God's hands. He was a mere instrument of His needs and guidance. The thought filled him with warmth, purpose.

The dutiful wife has always slept deeper than a well-fed farm girl . He felt close to her. She was a godly woman who understood, and helped other family women do the same. If he was light afoot, she wouldn't wake. It was important she didn't wake. Even *she* might not fully understand his mission tonight.

He would start by being nice, quiet, gentle. Sarah would think he had had second thoughts about how she had been corrected and would willingly follow him to the barn where he had parked the four-wheel-drive for them to go home.

But they wouldn't be going home. Not yet.

Feeling safe as a child in her father's arms, the temptress would provide names. Names of others who might need correcting.

If the child had to be beaten into confession again, so be it.

God understood his weaknesses. The Bible was crammed with stories of prophets made vulnerable and even momentarily brought down by a female's deceiving charms.

But he wouldn't be tempted tonight.

Throughout the last hour of his trek to the ranch he had turned off the radio. He allowed his imagination to run undisturbed, flooding his senses with her cries of resistance, her delightful succumbing moans, her prayerful whispers in the darkness and the erotic inducements of her sobs for forgiveness for not being a good girl.

She could destroy everything. Like all women, she was a mystery that had to be resolved by a godly man's willpower. Yes, ultimately she would reveal herself, and the intensity of the experience would depend upon what purpose and secrets she possessed.

The anticipation was delicious.

1

C H A P T E R

Sarah Zimmerman's eyes locked wide open. Somebody was downstairs making heavy noises—the kind of clanking noises a man makes when he thinks he's being quiet. She felt her face instantly flame with heat. Her hands were shaking, clammy. *It could be him.*

The belt-beating bruise tracks down her shoulders and back still gripped her with white-knuckled pain. She quietly moaned with each movement as she rose.

The floorboards creaked and popped like brittle bones.

It couldn't be him. The drive from Salt Lake City is five hours. He wouldn't have turned around.

The well of her stomach wasn't buying it. It was him.

She made for the window and nervously parted the cotton drapes while envisioning his pasty white face with black holes for eyes. She rubbed the beaded ice droplets from one of the panes and pressed her nose to the glass. A hint of moonlight allowed a dark, flat view of the snow-laden treeless yard. She finally began to breathe again. No sign of the truck.

Sarah squinted to see the charcoal outline of the dungeon-like barn beyond the riding stables. Wind, rain, and sun had long laid down a silver patina on the barn's durable cedar siding. She absently bit down on one of her delicate fingers. That was where it had started.

~

Still no sign of a vehicle or movement. Her slight sigh of relief withered when she heard the creak of ascending footsteps on the staircase. In the back of her mind she heard a deep resonant voice.

You're a wicked child. A bad girl who needs to be shown how to treat a man.

She knew more pain had come to wake her at the midnight hour. The savage apparition from hell finally spurred her into action.

Sarah considered, then dismissed the idea of rebraiding her long silken ebony hair. She bolted to the chair holding her meticulously folded calico dress. The dark blue tights went on first, then the dress and sneakers. *No time for socks.*

Quiet, she silently ordered her banging heart. She needed to hear every sound beyond those nightly creaks and ceiling mice races that had filled so many sleepless hours since she had been forcibly taken to the isolated farm house. Bile rose in her throat as if molten lava about to burst through rock. The door had no lock, of course, so parents could enter a child's room whenever they wanted.

He's coming up the stairs!

Sarah dropped to her knees to climb under the bed, then stopped. There wasn't time to make the bed. He knew she was there anyway. *No safety in the room.*

She panted, sucking in great lungfuls, yet she couldn't seem to get enough air. The deeper and faster she inhaled, the dizzier she became.

Her peripheral vision alert to the doorknob, she focused on the window. She put her hands to her face. They were freezing, but her face was colder. For no reason Sarah could understand, she thought of her mother's beautiful face, as clear as the photograph of the two of them on her bedroom nightstand.

She shoved both palms against the paint-curled upper window frame and pushed with all her strength. It didn't budge. *He had to have heard that.*

She thumbed open the tarnished brass lock and with one adrenaline-driven thrust, rammed it open. A shattering coldness bit her face. She puffed her cheeks and climbed through the window frame.

Her right leg dangled inches above the foot-deep snow clinging to the ice-covered wood-shingled roof.

"Come on," she coached herself. She grabbed the window frame and let the other leg drop. The slashing pain of the rough ledge forced her hands open. She plopped onto the steep snowbound roof like a rag doll, then involuntarily rolled down and off, dropping twelve feet. She heard the cracking thump first, then saw a flash of white when her head smashed against a clothesline pole before she landed on the rock-hard ground. The arm she landed on tucked to her side snapped like brittle kindling on impact. She let out a shrill scream just above the low whistle of the freezing wind.

With her good arm Sarah examined her body. The broken arm was spilling blood onto her long-sleeved dress as fast as spilled milk on cloth. She winced as her fingertips touched broken ribs. The pain triggered flashes of memory—sudden, violent, blaring—a memory of pain so sharp, so intense, it took on qualities of sound and taste, the smell of fear, the presence of evil. Trapped air caught in her chest as if she were drowning then slowly seeped out between her teeth.

He would be coming now. And not to comfort her. No, he wouldn't make the pain go away. He was pain.

She glanced around, torquing ribs that demanded no movement. Her mother's loving face again flashed in her mind, and then crimson pain obliterated safe thoughts.

Run, she ordered her mind and body.

She slowly started for the stables, fully aware that if he saw her, escape would be impossible. She shuddered, more at the consuming feeling of being violated again than at the icy chill of night.

She smiled, a quivering smile that appeared and vanished like a nervous twitch. She had cheated him out of creating the pain without leaving marks. He hated lingering evidence of his punishing hands. Even he wouldn't shove her off the mortal ledge.

That's it, confess. Plead for God's grace. Maybe, he would help her after she promised to be a good girl.

She could suddenly feel his soulless, lustful eyes crawling across her bare skin. There would be no pity. He only seemed wise and calm. She had swallowed the poisonous nightmares too, and they were slowly eating her mind.

She dragged her broken body toward the barn. Maybe he didn't see her. She shoved open the door and gasped.

The truck!

Everything was getting hazy. She could hear him running to her now. He was a spearmint breath away from grabbing her. He always smelled of spearmint.

Although awake, Sarah felt as if she were dreaming. Her breathing grew less labored, and she suddenly felt the lure of sleep. The piercing pain in her side subsided long enough for her to take a shallow breath, then welcome the darkness.

At that moment Sarah knew she had won. No matter what her self-appointed torturer attempted to do to protect himself, she wasn't talking. Not tonight. Not ever.

"Bad girls get punished," she heard a soft voice repeat over and over as if she were going to respond.

CHAPTER 2

There were only two choices for people who worked in homicide: absorb the horror into the marrow of your nightmares, or cultivate a warped sense of humor.

Charlie Carver smiled, watching the whirling cloud settle desert dust over a 1994 metallic silver Ford as it roared to a stop. Whether it was for drama or expediency, the driver had hit the brakes as if a cat had run in front of the car, less than thirty feet from the taped-off scene of the serial killer's latest feast.

The bumper sticker on the van read, "When your day ends, mine begins." It had to be the coroner. Charlie liked him already.

~

Reed Smith was more walrus than man, right down to his drooping gray mustache. The hefty coroner stepped down from the van cab and inhaled a long raspy breath, collecting himself. He took in the familiar sounds of the remote murder scene, ambient two-way radios, the thunder of a circling news helicopter. He scanned the cluster of black and whites, suits, uniforms, cameras, the Suburban belonging to Independent Procurement Services, known to insiders as 'I Pickup Stiffs'. The standard drill.

"I love the smell of napalm in the morning," he said in Charlie's direction. Smith dragged his forearm across his brow as if he had already done his part. "Don't tell me, hemorrhaging on both sides of the larynx. Not a mark on the babe. Positioned like a Vargas girl—picture perfect."

Before Charlie could answer, Smith sauntered up to him and leaned in with a curious, squinting glare. "Hey, Ponytail, you the girl our boy's been giving phone sex to?"

Charlie ran a hand down his thick molasses hair and gave a deep appreciative chuckle. To him, Salt Lake City had about as much color as a Ku Klux Klan gathering. "I'm the guy." He hesitated, but decided not to elaborate.

"Glory hound, huh?" Smith rolled his red eyes. "Real sick puppy. How many is that now?"

Salt Lake Homicide's chief, Derek Strickland approached and caught Smith's arm. "If it's all the same to you, I'd like to tag her and bag her," he said. "Let's get the hell out of here before the media vultures contaminate the search perimeter." He jerked his chin at the hovering chopper, then turned to the black uniformed that had shadowed him. "Get on that son of a bitch's frequency and tell him not to land. He'll blow every cigarette butt, gum wrapper, piece of clothing—you name it—to kingdom come."

He faced the reporter, who, in his loose brown tweed jacket, wool turtleneck sweater, and baggy corduroy pants looked more like a Berkeley college professor than the city's only seasoned investigative reporter. "No offense, Charlie."

"No sweat," Charlie snapped.

"At least we're getting a good mold of prints and the tire tread," Strickland remarked. "I'd put him six feet or more, in a four-wheeler. Hope it's the factory tire." He shot a glance at Charlie, who was doing all he could to avoid viewing the body. "I thought you guys live for this shit."

"Yeah, right," Charlie said softly.

"You haven't had a peek at your friend's latest masterpiece," Strickland went on. "He's a real artist, the way he strangles without leaving a mark or print, then poses the naked bodies like *Playboy* spreads."

"Their sexuality torments him. It's his sick way of getting even," Charlie offered.

Strickland nodded. "You two sound really close."

Understanding the rise that Strickland was after, Charlie didn't bite. He replied mildly, "Yeah, I hope we get so close, I nail the bastard."

Tag-along reporters had burned the chief before. This case was worse, because the killer had flaunted his masterwork and brazenly directed clues and warnings to Charlie. Ten months earlier, the move of a prized *Chicago Tribune* investigative reporter to a one-off market daily had been trumpeted as front-page news. Once Charlie started burrowing under rocks and slaughtering sacred cows, the *Observer* had dropped his byline, but too late to avoid the attentions of new friends—and worse—new fiends.

Strickland started toward the corpse. "Smart, though. He's gotta know we can lift prints off of skin."

Charlie winced and glanced over at the crime scene investigator who was snapping close-ups of the seemingly unblemished naked body. Being a kid from the projects, Charlie had thought he had the constitution for a police beat. A twisted friend at the Chicago Crime Lab had regularly tested him by including him in horrors that would keep Stephen King awake at night. The worst was the butter body, where consecutively hot daytime temperatures melt the fat right out through the pores. A fire-cooked body. Only homicide detectives were supposed to know that smell. His sick friend had also demonstrated his favorite technique, extracting fingerprints from a butter body by scoring the wrist with a scalpel and slipping off the outer epidermal layer of the hand, then putting it on like a glove to roll for prints.

He had passed these tests with flying colors. Even the crime lab murder books, each one housing virtually hundreds of gruesome photos, hadn't gotten to him. Charlie was puke-proof.

Until it all changed. Her name was Charlotte Perry, daughter of his friends, Steve and Robin Perry. Charlie and Robin had found the body together behind a landscaping mound near the family's backyard pool. Charlotte was naked, raped, strangled to death. After Charlotte, a corpse was no longer an object for investigation. It became someone's wife, mother, sister, daughter.

"I'm not here to watch," he said to Strickland.

Strickland shoved his brass-rimmed glasses back toward his steel blue eyes and arched his back. He towered over Charlie. "What the hell good are these calls you're getting, if he only tells you he's planning another one?"

Like the department's sound and linguistic experts, Charlie had played and replayed all three recordings he had received before each murder. The killer prided himself on using his own deep voice, rather than mechanically or audibly altering even a syllable. The voice resonated like that of a seasoned speaker, stage performer, or radio announcer. He sounded middle-aged, and from his accent, definitely a homegrown monster.

"What color is her hair?" Charlie asked Strickland.

"Same as always."

CHAPTER 3

Rachel Zimmerman gazed vacantly at her beloved northern red shafted flickers maniacally pecking black oil sunflower seeds beyond the kitchen window between bursts of morning song.

"Who's lined up for a handout today?"

Rachel let drop the hand she had pressed tightly to her pursed lips. She welcomed the prickle of warmth at the sound of Ester's voice, her one friend who treated her as a person with uncritical, undemanding companionship. For seconds the friends stared at each other in a surrealistic, frozen immobility, Ester with deep concern, Rachel with a sense of bewilderment, as if she barely knew where she was. She knew swollen eyes were scarlet with dammed tears and fearful dreams.

Ester swallowed awkwardly. "Sarah," she whispered. "She's a remarkably strong child."

"Strong headed, you mean, Sister."

Ester's chin disappeared in the folds of her neck when she chuckled. "That too."

The bond between the sister wives had been instant since the day Ester's husband, James, had blurted out between spurting bites of a McDonald's Big Mac, plans to take his fourth wife.

Rachel glanced down at Ester's labor-worn and unadorned left wedding ring finger, then her own. She now understood the woman's selflessness in taking her ring off and offering it with God's blessings to a total stranger about to bed her husband. She had watched Ester's glistening auburn hair turn coarse and streaked with years from husband neglect and frequent barbs over a waistline that expanded with every belittling comment. Her face, once effervescent with inner purpose, had long since closed off, as if the curtain had been drawn over a view to a bright world.

The knockout punch to Ester's self-esteem had arrived in a lean, supple, baby blues package—Jessica. She was the fifth wife in the Zimmerman household and the last to wear the coveted ring. A collective sister wife sigh of relief filled the house when Jessica got pregnant, and most importantly, fat. Her transformation took some of the sting out of her theatrics that invariably followed a night of sex with the master of the house. The child would hint at, and then, if no response were received, detail unmentionables that, if the Father had heard, could have landed her behind closed doors at the ranch for a week or more.

A caved-in ceiling beam that crushed James' chest cavity as though an underfoot insect had ended sister wife rivalries and everything else, both strange and familiar. In the Zimmerman house the morning ritual of backbiting and silent treatment toward the lucky recipient of a night's attentions were replaced by edginess and displaced aggressions. Their anxiety was warranted. The five women and twenty-five children could be split into different families, or worse, used as barter with other polygamist group men who were primed with wealth and property, but short on attractive and willing wives.

Rachel scanned the school-cafeteria-sized kitchen to ensure she and Ester were alone.

"Did you see who took Sarah to the ranch?"

"You know, dear, Sarah's been troubled lately," Ester said, avoiding Rachel's eyes.

Rachel lifted strands of raven black hair from her forehead and clasped them in place as if she was taking her own temperature. She allowed a flash of anger to escape her cobalt blue eyes, then lowered her head and obediently nodded.

"Sarah was just being Sarah, I'm sure. Everybody knows she speaks her mind. That's reason to take her away without even a word," Ester said tartly.

"The Father knows what's in our hearts," Rachel whispered.

"I wish I had your faith," Ester replied. The mother of six retied her home-sewn pink floor length robe and adjusted her waist-long braid. She quickstepped barefooted over the blue linoleum floor to Rachel and draped a comforting arm around her companion.

"I wish I had your faith."

"It's only been two days, Ester. She'll be…" Rachel couldn't play charades any longer. "I got home from work and she was gone. Nobody will even tell me what she did to—to get corrected."

Oblivious, as always, Jessica stomped into the kitchen, stretched her arms straight up and yawned loud enough to command a lion tamer. She was flanked by fully dressed sister wives Carmen and Marion, both delicately slender, quiet, obedient, and totally lost without their husband's supervision.

As Rachel and Ester turned, Jessica rubbed her generous breasts, then bulbous stomach. "Breakfast ready?" she snapped. "We're starving."

She breezed over to the weekly schedule attached by magnet to one of three side-by-side refrigerators. "It's your turn, Rach."

She jerked open a refrigerator and gulped milk from the carton. Since the master of the house's demise four weeks earlier, rules were beginning to slacken and the ten-hour-a-day work ethic grew a bit wobbly, all under the disapproving eye of Mormon Fundamentalist Order patriarch, Donald Goodman.

"It's after six. The children will be late for school," Jessica said.

Ester rolled her eyes at the flippant remark from the schedule's greatest abuser.

"I need some help this morning," Rachel said, her panic subsiding. She rubbed her sore neck. "I've been up all night worried about Sarah."

Jessica huffed in surprise. "Telling the Father *she'll* decide who she's going to marry. And throwing a fit over the Father's announcement that you two are to be celestially married! Why? At the age of twenty-nine, it's an honor. I mean, Rach, with you constantly miscarrying, and the Father—"

Rachel wheeled on her. "Maybe it's none of your business."

Always the fast-talking calmer, Marion stepped between Jessica and Rachel's instant rage. "That isn't what Jessica meant. Nobody knows why it happens, but any of us could have a difficult time carrying a child to term. It's always been a problem in the Goodman family. We're high in death at childbirth, too. It doesn't mean Rachel can't ever have a child."

Jessica backed away with her hands up in surrender. "Fine," she said tightly and began helping the other women prepare for the stampede of hungry children.

The first of the brood to arrive in the kitchen was Carmen's oldest, fifteen-year-old Anna, with two towheaded little sisters lagging behind. She steamed through the arched kitchen doorway, elbows knocking her mother and a sister mother.

"That's mean!" she pronounced, her uplifted chin and scalding hazel eyes cutting through Jessica's uppity facade with ease. "Nobody should have to marry who they don't want, including a man as old as my grandfather."

"Heavens! Oh, good heavens!" Marion put a hand to her mouth in shock.

"Anna! That's enough," Carmen said. She stood protectively beside her child, her lovely makeup-free oval face strained and her eyes full of anxiety.

"It's not right." Anna turned her tear-filled eyes on every woman in the room. "And every one of you knows it."

Carmen slapped Anna across the face, then raised her hand again until the child cowered. "God will punish you for such blasphemy. And in front of your sisters, too. Now go to your room and pray for God's forgiveness."

Anna was used to her mother's quick-to-act hands and unquestioning black-and-white view of a woman's place on earth, but was caught off guard and almost fell backwards from the power of today's wallop.

"Father Goodman's going to hear about your attitude, young lady," Carmen said in a low voice and unforgiving eyes. "I don't envy your punishment."

"Like Sarah? I don't—"

Rachel clutched Anna's arm. "What? What did Sarah do? Why was she taken away? You know we're not allowed to call the ranch."

Anna tightened her lips, then lowered and shook her head.

An army of thunderous feet bound across the second level hallway and down the wide staircase, shaking the house like a badly tuned engine. Somebody was getting it, and the Zimmerman kids weren't about to miss out on the action. Wide eyes and giggles poured into the kitchen.

"Where's breakfast? Who's in trouble? What—"

"All right, children," Ester said. "Breakfast will be soon. Make sure your rooms are neat and you've said your morning prayers. Go on, get moving."

Ester took Rachel and Anna by the hand and led them into the living room. She turned her eyes to the child. "Anna, there's time for you to go on a little walk with your sister mother." She nodded toward the kitchen for Rachel to see Jessica was hovering in the doorway, listening to every breath.

Ester's smile remained fixed, perfect and glowing. There wasn't a thing classically beautiful left about her, except the glimmer of her trademark heartland smile so seldom seen now. Rachel didn't miss a beat. "Good idea, Ester. I think we—"

"I thought we had a schedule for a reason. Anna's got laundry to do," Jessica glowered in slit-eyed disgust at the child only two years her junior.

Ester smiled wickedly. "Don't listen to her, she said to Rachel. "She's been on a rampage ever since the Prophet's attentions turned to you."

Anna tugged free of Ester's loose grip. "I don't know anything!"

Ester threw up open hands. "Then just walk. Now go on, or you'll be late for school."

"I'll just be a minute, dear. Wait right here while I dress," Rachel said, trying to conceal any hint of desperation. On this Friday, like any other weekday, Rachel would be changing into her clothes to enter Babylon, the name the congregation used for everything outside the Goodman Compound.

~

The city's most obvious and opulent polygamist center was shrouded in mystery to those outside its seven-foot cement-walled world. The almost two hundred inhabitants, mostly children, lived like aliens stranded on a hostile planet. Just outside the walls they believed evil, deceit, and cruelty clawed at God's chosen like a soulless beast with an all-consuming appetite.

Since childhood, Rachel had believed Father Goodman's warnings about grocery store price bar codes translating to 666, Satan's mark. The congregation purchased food at Goodman owned and operated grocery stores to ensure nobody was poisoned. Thousands of followers in Salt Lake Valley did their purchasing, banking, and borrowing at Goodman-owned banks—and even cars from Goodman-owned businesses. The Goodman's hidden labyrinth of misleading company names and owners had saved a fortune in state and federal taxes since the early 1950s. They unknowingly kept God's oasis on earth prosperous.

Mormon Fundamentalists called their world of plural marriage the Order. If one word summed up life in the Goodman Compound, order was it. From compulsively cleaned garden tools used to shape and manicure landscaping and an acre of perfectly rowed vegetable gardens, to home cleanliness bordering on a hospital's intensive care unit standards, order prevailed.

The compound boasted one mammoth three-story Georgian colonial main house of cherry-red brick architecturally dramatized by an entry arc of crisp white Doric columns. The patriarch's home for fifteen wives and seventy-two children loomed at the center of a row of typical suburban brick homes built by congregation labor for Goodman's royal-blooded sons. The late James Zimmerman, whose father's fortune had earned him a seat on the Council of the Seven, had occupied the last compound home. Behind the homes, a modest one-story green plywood building served as church and school. Two grain silos, a chain link-fenced emergency power generating station, and a half-acre water retention pond completed the near self-reliant Goodman world.

Father Goodman fondly referred to the compound as his fortress. It abutted a Babylon neighborhood, under the shadow of a Rocky Mountain backdrop as ruggedly towering as the Swiss Alps. The daily parade of local and international downhill skiers, en route to and from world class Snowbird and Alta ski resorts passed the silent fortress without ever giving it or its seldom seen oddly-dressed occupants a second glance.

Polygamists? Impossible. The practice had been illegal in Utah since 1890 when the Mormon Church, under pressure from Congress, was obliged to renounce it as a condition of joining the Union.

~

Rachel paused before the bedroom door mirror and glared at herself in her wrist-to-ankle white cotton sacred temple marriage garments.

Lose weight.

Her eyes turned sapphire-bright with tears. What a waste. Since entering puberty she had secretly hoarded old magazines between her mattresses. In the glow of a late night flashlight, she studied every detail of Babylon women: their snow-white teeth and teasing smiles, their rapture with dreamy men their age, and clothes that boldly revealed curves, skin, and provocative femininity.

Vanity is evil. The conditioning thought didn't work when she was twelve and it wasn't working today.

~

Anna was hunched over with a grimacing nose-wrinkled expression when Rachel descended the stairs. The girl shrugged into her heavy wool coat and worked the thick plastic buttons into their moorings. "It's too cold for a walk. I told you anyway, I don't know anything."

Rachel could read Anna's expressions just as a meteorologist knew the sky's changing moods. She was acting as strangely as she had earlier at the mention of Sarah's name, definitely not herself.

Rachel nodded. "Let's leave the compound," she offered as a peace gesture.

Anna shrugged.

An inner voice urged Rachel to pace her interrogation. She scooted the girl out to the cement front porch of the Zimmerman home. The women walked on the sidewalk buried in a foot of fluffy, crunchy snow to the barred gates, already automatically opened for the throng of soon-to-arrive grade school students.

In less than a minute, the arm-in-arm women were away from the fortress and walking Babylon's suburbia. Rachel's peripheral vision caught what she always saw in Babylon, but would never stop shrinking from, curious eyes. The bony-kneed and mop-haired man in a bathrobe to her left paused while dipping down to retrieve the morning paper. Once before she had seen him plop down on the front steps, open the newspaper for cover, then peer over the top edge like a comical spy. She nudged Anna, who hadn't watched her feet in Babylon since she wore size fours.

"Take a picture. It'll last longer," Anna said, loud enough for the man and the neighbor woman lingering at the garbage can to hear.

Rachel's bleak, rueful expression lifted into a grin. "Gosh, Sarah—I mean Anna."

Anna shivered at the mention of her half-sister's name. The muscles in her body tightened and she visibly drew into herself. "If you celestially marry the Prophet, does that mean you still have to—well, you know," she asked.

"Anna, you're Sarah's best friend. I know you two talk about everything."

Anna halted her long stride. Her look was cold as steel. "I already told you—"

"I know, you don't know anything. We both know that's not the whole story."

Anna resumed walking at such a quick pace that Rachel nearly had to break into a jog to keep up. The child was holding back. There was something dark and forbidden, as if a sliver she couldn't quite get at just beneath the skin. "All I'm interested in is a reason why. What got her into trouble? Nobody seems to know."

Anna led Rachel back across the fortress threshold. It soon became obvious to Rachel that the sixteen-year-old ash blond boy hovering around the entrance, all-legs and teeth, was waiting for more than the bus to public school.

"You're not to mingle with the boys, Anna," Rachel said out of the young man's earshot.

"What are you talking about? Israel's just—friendly."

"You know the rules, Anna."

"The rules. I had to go to our dumb school instead of public school like the boys, and then got jerked out two years ago so I can learn to be the perfect wife, perfect slave for some old man."

Rachel put an index finger to her lips. "Hush, child. You sound just like Sarah. I didn't finish any further than the seventh grade, and now I'm a darn good court reporter."

"Israel gets to go to public high school and college. That's a gyp."

"A woman's role on this earth isn't an easy one. You know that every sacrifice you make on this earth—"

"I know, I'll get back tenfold in our Father's kingdom."

"Let's get back to Sarah."

"Talk to her yourself."

"You know we're not allowed to call the ranch."

Anna raised her voice an octave so the approaching boy could hear. "We're as good as boys, but do we get to hold the Priesthood? We're just slaves and I'm sick of it."

"Anna! That's enough. Keep your thoughts to yourself or Sarah's about to get a roommate."

~

Israel Goodman tugged on the fastened top button of his droopy flannel hand-me-down shirt. "What's going on with you this morning?" he said loudly. " I heard about the ruckus soon as I got up." Anna found his larger-than-life smile contagious and burst out laughing.

"I'm not supposed to talk to you, Israel, and you know it," Anna said.

Israel's dancing eyes shot a glance at Rachel, then darted back to Anna. "Who's talking? I'm waiting for the bus."

Rachel lightly squeezed Anna's hand. "You can wait with Israel for a moment, then get in the house. There're chores to do." Rachel turned heels in the pristine snow and left the two alone.

"I heard what you said," Israel whispered.

"I can't believe Father took away all our music."

The comment drew a peeved look from Israel. "Listen to the lyrics of *Smashing Pumpkins* or *Marilyn Manson*."

"Right. That's what I listen to—or used to. Give me a break. We've got no TV, not even music. He's trying to turn our lives into one big church meeting." Anna shivered her shoulders.

"How terrible. Love. Imagine love between two people the same age." She cut him a glance.

He wasn't much taller than her own five-feet-seven inches and had a build like an alley cat, lean and agile, with the restless energy to match. It seemed to vibrate around him as if someone had plugged him into a high-voltage generator. While his mouth was always hanging open, his face was finely sculpted, a mirror image of his father, Jacob, and grandfather, Donald Goodman.

Israel blushed and turned away. "You act as if everything that happens to you is my fault. You're going to get into bad trouble if you keep talking like this, and you know it, Anna."

She looked up at him suspiciously. "And you're going to tell on me?"

Israel listened to the crunching ice under his feet, the roar of a passing car outside the fortress. Every noise seemed amplified. The muscle around his mouth tightened ever so slightly. "No." He tipped his head up and blew a sigh at a playfully shaped cumulus cloud. "I've thought about some of the same things. But we don't have a choice, do we?"

~

The Zimmerman's solitary telephone trilled its high-pitched ring. The rarely heard sound ripped through Rachel like a shotgun blast. The fine hairs on the back of her neck rose when the phone rang again.

"Rach, it's for you!" Jessica yelled up the stairs.

~

The last call she had gotten at an awkward hour had come in the middle of the night when Father Goodman told her James was dead. Maybe Sarah had been found dead in some roadside brush like discarded trash. But to lose them both in a little more than a month? No, it couldn't be possible. Maybe it *was* Ida at the ranch, or even Sarah, wanting a ride home.

"Rachel Zimmerman," she answered, her voice taking on a hollow tone. Silence.

Her mind exploded with possibilities: all bad.

"Ida, is that you?"

No response. The caller remained on the line. Seconds clicked past on the round plastic kitchen clock. The breathing was raspy, familiar. Someone with asthma.

"Ida, is that you? What is it? Sarah? Has something happened to her?"

Not a sound.

Rachel slammed the receiver down. Her self-deception was made painfully clear by the way that she nearly jumped into Ester's arms as the phone rang again. She stared at it, holding her arms out as the warning for no one else to pick it up. It rang a second and third time before she gave herself a mental shove.

"Rachel Zimmerman."

"Rach, it's me, Ida. Sarah's vanished."

4
CHAPTER

Donald Goodman was a proud man, with reasons that stretched as far back as his Mormon pioneer ancestors who clawed out a living as coal miners. If not for his grandfather's vision while toiling in the earth's belly, Donald wouldn't have been a god on earth today with a half billion-dollar business empire and over ten thousand who were born, married, and died in his care.

He had followed in his father's footsteps as a prominent Salt Lake Valley corporate attorney. The two men were perfect chameleons. In Babylon, they were behind-the-scenes philanthropists for strategically self-serving charities and civic causes. Living in the Mecca of the Mormon Church, the practice of polygamy meant excommunication was easier than a non-Utahn might perceive. More than a handful of genealogically-tied community leaders in government and business were privately sympathetic, and even admired contemporary polygamist families and sects. Goodman kept dossiers on friends and enemies that even J. Edgar Hoover would have applauded.

While Goodman's business dealings were void of good whiskey, smooth talk and expensive cigars, the sound of his personal compound-based helicopter whirling overhead at unpredictable hours day and night gave his family a glimmer into his other world.

At the young patriarchal age of sixty-three, Goodman's destiny was coming along nicely. What self-indulgence he allowed himself was most evident in his cozy western style book-lined library—where he took his meals and whatever else pleased him.

~

Rachel had only visited the Father's sanctuary twice before, first when he commanded a discussion on the sanctity of marriage endowments, then days ago when she had nearly slipped off his leather guest chair at the announcement of their celestial marriage. His no-questions declaration had stopped her heart cold. She would be one of the chosen few the Father selected to wed and bed in this celestial bonding, still allowing her to take another husband of this earth.

At seven in the morning, Goodman's library was as cold as a horse barn. The Father had ordered the temperature never to exceed sixty-six degrees, and kept it even lower for sleep.

Rachel squirmed before her still-robust patriarch. She found herself holding her breath, expectation building inside her. The weight of his silence hinted at an announcement. Maybe Sarah's punishment was over and she would be back home before dinner.

She sat at the edge of one of the two ice-cold high-backed chairs opposite Goodman's desk. Rather than taking his chair, he had opted to slowly mill around her. In trying to sense his whereabouts, Rachel realized they weren't alone. The walls seemed alive with cowboys with clenched jaws and windblown hats; horses and buffalo charging at neck-breaking speed; a wagon train campfire with leather faces aglow in anticipation of the next tall tale; and of course, wedged between the oil reproductions, every Louis L'Amour paperback the Father could find.

Donald Goodman was a wanna-be cowboy, the lone gun defending the town from invading marauders.

Operating on too little sleep and too much stress, Rachel fueled her courage to confront the Father directly about her missing child.

She felt heavy and slow, as if the crisp air around her were as dense as water. She repeated her assertion that Sarah would never have run away.

The Father leaned down so close behind her she could smell his scented breath. "I was just telling Jacob." Rachel turned her head to a squeaking sound. The Father was rubbing down the seat of his prized 1894 Tombstone, Arizona saddle. He had official papers declaring it had once graced the buttocks of Virgil Earp, Wyatt's oldest brother. He dropped down into the side chair next to her, then lurched both body and chair uncomfortably close.

"Yes, I was reminding my eldest last night that royal blood courses through his veins. It's an awesome responsibility to directly descend from the Israelites."

Rachel tilted her head. Had the Father even heard her desperate plea for police intervention to find Sarah? "There's no way Sarah would have run away," she timidly whispered.

Goodman was mesmerizing. She had seldom seen the Prophet out of his black or midnight blue suit, crisp white shirt, and tie. Today he was clad in stonewashed denim. His western shirt was adorned with white pearl set in silver snap buttons. His pants were what the kids referred to as "butt huggers," set off by a silver and bronze belt buckle and spit-polished cowboy boots. His shirtsleeves were slightly shoved up his Popeye forearms, like a rugged mountain man's before he hoists an ax to down a tree. His western getup and brawny, robust body brought his oldest son, Jacob to Rachel's mind.

"The name Rachel is a blessed one, just as God has touched you with such radiant beauty."

Rachel glanced up into eyes beaming with appreciation. "Father, she's my only daughter. We have to get the police looking for her. She could be kidnapped or hurt."

He cocked one eyebrow and looked right through her. "Are you still throwing up your meals and exercising night and day to keep that fine figure?"

Rachel gasped and put her hand to her mouth.

His dark eyes thundered in delight. "Thought I didn't know about your little secret?" He closed his eyes and turned his mahogany face upward. "I know what's in your heart, too."

Rachel brightened with false hope. "I'll always work hard to—to stay attractive." She suggestively lowered her eyes. He was beginning to lose control of the conversation. She could feel it. If Plan B meant the man and woman thing, so be it.

"So I assume Sarah will be coming home shortly. Today, maybe?"

The Father reached over and rested one of his thick palms on Rachel's clenched hands. "I've prayed for Sarah more than once. She has always been a rebellious child."

A long silence bubbled up her fear.

"She'll come running home any time. Babylon is a terrifying place." He gave a fatherly pat. "Be patient."

She tried to put on a game expression, but it hung a little crooked, letting the worry seep through. "She didn't leave a note. Nothing. Sarah and I are closer than that. We have to do something right now," she murmured with her head down, her mouth twisting.

Goodman pushed his chair back and rose, straightening his belt buckle. He moved behind his desk and directly faced her, pressing his palms flat on its polished surface. "Haven't you learned a thing, child?"

Rachel's head jolted up at the sudden change in tone.

"Never a question," he said. "No police intervention. We've always taken care of our own. I'm not about to have outsiders snooping into every corner in the compound."

"And what happens when our own is missing? We just let them get ripped apart out there?" Rachel said automatically, now prepared to play devil's advocate.

Goodman stormed around his desk and gripped her arm. He made a rumbling sound in his throat. "How dare you mock me."

Rachel's eyes flared. "Sarah's still a child. She's all I've got."

Goodman combed his fingers through his thick curly hair and puffed his cheeks, then exhaled as if he was doing deep breathing exercises. His tensed shoulders dropped from an attack position. He sat down closed his eyes, and pinched the bridge of his nose. "You do realize that with the questionable possibility of ever bearing children again you could be subject to the procreation Law of Chastity?"

Rachel looked up in puzzlement. No doctor had ever told her she couldn't have any more children. Then again, she had never been allowed to see a Babylon doctor. She and Sarah didn't even have birth certificates or social security numbers. Father Goodman had some made up for her when he placed her in the municipal court job.

"Imagine never to be touched again by a godly man." His voice was soothing, his words cutting. "Here, I've gone out of my way to help you. Even though your husband was making a fine living, I understood you wanted more so I arranged court reporter's training and a courtroom job. All in less than a year."

Goodman again rose, slowly this time. He went to the door, scanned the outer library to confirm their privacy, and closed it.

"I understand your protective attitude toward your child. It's as it should be." He pulled the side chair almost against hers and placed his hand on her lower thigh.

Rachel felt dirty. "I just want my baby back."

"Of course you do. I can see I need to take action here. I'll send Jacob and Hyrum to Snowville to see if there is any more to learn about where she may have run off to."

"Can I go with them?"

"Better yet, we've got thousands of employees. If she doesn't show up in a few days, we'll send her picture out to everybody." He gently rubbed Rachel's leg, more like a suitor than a counselor. She cringed. His hand, minus a little finger, suddenly looked like the talons of a dangerous bird of prey. She had to remind herself he would soon be touching more than her leg. It was the Father's right.

Arguments tumbled around in her mind, in her conscience. An officer of the court had told her that with today's high speed scanners, a high-grade computer image could be created of Sarah, instantly transmitted to computers all over the country, and printed from those computers onto more fliers. She felt the minutes ticking by, and Sarah getting more distant with each hour. She resisted an urge to look away from Goodman's determined eyes to her wristwatch.

A family alert wasn't enough, and she knew the Father knew it. Until Sarah's disappearance, Rachel had never faced real adversity in her personal life. She had never acquired the skills necessary to cope with adversity. She felt out of balance and knew she was missing her husband's support. While they had never been a twosome team, to be without him was to suddenly become an amputee.

"I hate to be blunt, Rach, but I have to weigh the unlikely loss of a rebellious runaway to intervention that could tear our world apart."

A runaway? Her name's Sarah. One of your own.

She made no response. The voices of the Goodman wives and underfoot children rose and fell away as Rachel made her way out of the house and down the sidewalk to her home.

A childhood rhyme with a different twist flashed in her mind: sticks and stones can break my bones, but only God can hurt me.

5
CHAPTER

His eyes, bottomless black holes, tracked Rachel like dual rifle scopes all the way back to her house. The corners of his mouth turned up in a cold-blooded smile. He knew something she still didn't know. Something he would kill to protect. Little secrets that, if brought out of the shadows, could rip through the fortress like a tornado.

Sarah had paid for her sins, paid in full.

God's instrument clenched his teeth and released a low throaty growl that gave sound to those thoughts again. He could feel the heat in his loins. One image blurred into another. He imagined Rachel beginning to back away, but unable to resist his power, his God-given charisma. *Bad girl.* The words wrapped themselves around his mind like silk. His skin pebbled with goose bumps.

~

Sarah's unintentional killer was alive and not so well. The need was beginning to overpower the fear. *Rapturous Rachel* and *Luscious Little Anna* were beginning to dominate his dreams, asleep and awake. They were within an arm's length, teasing him with their seductive ways. The anger button started going off in his head. It quickly spread to his chest, his stiffening neck.

The other "him" would hide for a while, he decided. Unless, of course, Anna knew what Sarah knew. *Yes, better that way. Bad girl. You need to be shown how to treat a man. You two aren't like the others with beautiful spirits I brought to the light. You're dirty, soiled by Satan.*

Suddenly aware of a plume of morning mist and bone-deep cold, he drew jagged, short breaths. His pocket-jammed hands strained to curl into fists.

It had started years ago with a higher purpose. Or had it? He knew now that control—the essence of his being and life's purpose—had at some unknown moment mutated into an uncontrollable obsession. The child's death had been an opiate for a hunger that was sprouting up like a jungle over healthy thoughts of family and God's work on earth.

All pretenses were gone now. He hated himself. No, he hated women for luring his pure soul into Satan's parlor. He felt hollow, too empty to be one of God's shepherds.

What kind of control and planning had it taken to slip into the Zimmerman house after midnight and lurk like a rapist outside Anna and Rachel's bedroom doors? A meticulous search of every inch of their bedrooms and the rest of the house had choked up nothing. The dirty little secrets were in her head, and Anna was every bit as resistant as Sarah had been. Of course, an unannounced trip to the ranch might be just what the two of them needed. *No, what I need.*

He had heard about the obstinate child's blasphemy. Perfect timing. He didn't even have to create an opportunity. Nobody would be surprised if correction was in order. The only thing stopping him was fear of the evolving beast inside, hidden in the shadows of his own fantasies. He had controlled himself while invading their house that night, but waiting was growing thicker, heavier.

He tugged his hands out of the rough fabric of his pockets while his lips moved in softly whispered prayer. *Please God, stop this. I can't.*

6
C H A P T E R

She was scared. It was growing to be an odd fear, but was beginning to feed her strength and determination. A cornered girl would freeze up in a panic, but a cornered mother had it within her to roar in defiance, "Enough!"

Two weeks had passed since the Father had promised Rachel that a search party would act immediately. Her whispered rumblings were becoming more vocal by the day during the Father's absence on an extended business trip. Never one to use profanity, Rachel was creating new cussing words.

Repeated failed attempts to pry Anna's secrets off the tip of her tongue were driving her mad. She could tell from the teenager's avoidance of her eyes and brooding responses that fear, not lack of knowledge, was blocking even a hint of information about the disappearance.

It was early Saturday morning, and Mother Nature had dropped two feet of new snow on Salt Lake Valley. A blast of air had come sweeping down the canyon directly above the Goodman Compound to stir the snow to a ground-scudding cloud that limited visibility to a fraction of a mile.

The temperature, which had for weeks been teetering on the brink of tolerable, went over the edge and into a long, hard fall, taking with it the last of Rachel's spirits. School was canceled. The road leading up the canyon was closed, and the search for Sarah Zimmerman had been called off for lack of interest.

Rachel was brushing butter on loaves of bread just out of the oven when Father Goodman's youngest son, Hyrum, grabbed her narrow waist from behind.

"Gotcha!"

Rachel turned and her eyes widened in surprise. Black hair with a hint of red swung across his narrow brown eyes. Some deep instinct told her the thinnest and most handsome catch of the Goodman boys was out prowling for more than a baked treat. Since shortly after her husband died the Goodman boys had been ogling her like a chocolate éclair, none more obviously than Hyrum. Her face tightened into a veil of somber unhappiness. "Don't sneak up on me like that."

Hyrum's eyes swiveled from the three girls in calico dresses and braided buns that were coloring at the end of the long breakfast table directly to hers. "I've got an idea you're going to love."

She lifted her shoulders slightly. "I've got backed-up chores to do. Thank you anyway."

"Then just a walk. I need to talk to you about something important."

She sighed. "It's freezing outside this morning. I'm too busy."

Hyrum playfully snatched the pastry brush from her hand. "What I'm trying to say has to be said alone. Girls, go up to your room to color."

At an urgent and official-sounding male command, the girls gathered their crayons and books in a flurry and disappeared.

"I imagine it's better if I get right to the point." He motioned to a chair at the kitchen table. "Sit down. This is important." His voice was almost a tangible caress.

Rachel put down the brush, but didn't move. "I have a feeling about what's coming."

Hyrum shuffled close enough to be intimate.

"Please, Hyrum, don't do this." She started to hold up a hand meant to stop him in his tracks, or a foolish invitation for him to grab hold of her arm. Pulling the gesture back, she went to the chair and sat down. He gave her a crestfallen look that was ruined by the sense that he was more amused than affronted.

He arched a brow. "Oh, so you think you have an idea why I'm here?" He liked to catch people off balance. They revealed more of their true selves.

"Perhaps," she said coyly.

"Well, I've never been accused of being a chip off the old block. No one knows what's going on in his mind."

"Your brother Jacob's the same way. It took him over twenty minutes of hemming and hawing to finally tell me he wants me for his wife."

"I'll have you for my bride. All we…He said what?"

With her face suddenly hot, Rachel struggled for a reply that would be honest and not clumsy. It would not be kind to equivocate. "Your brother Jacob was just here yesterday discussing marriage. Didn't you know that?"

Hyrum turned so he wouldn't have to face her, but Rachel caught a glimpse of shock and hurt.

"Jacob already has more wives than he can handle and he's practically Father's age." He dropped to a bent knee like a fairytale suitor. "Rachel, you need a younger man. I've already discussed this with my father."

"And he agrees? The same man who's going to celestially marry me?" There was no lightness in her voice. Rachel had dared speak in irreverence.

"I've told Father how I feel about you, that's all. Jacob's already decided he wants a younger, fertile bride."

There was a note of embarrassment in Hyrum's last barbed comment. Rachel knew he had long admired her, but until she was widowed, had no chance to express long-held feelings. She had seen it all in his eyes.

"Thank you, Hyrum, thank you. Your intentions are genuine, and you touch my heart. But with my upcoming sacred sealing with your father, and my husband only gone a little over a month, it's all too soon." She let her breath out slowly. "Is that a good enough answer for now?"

He glared at her fiercely. She could see a violent emotion brewing as he weighed each word.

"You misunderstand," he said acidly. "You always have, Rachel. Father will pray over my request. If he blesses the union, you'll obey and be darn glad you weren't committed to another man nearly as old as Father."

"Oh, Jacob would love that." The silence stretched into a moment, then two. "I'm sorry," she said with genuine shame. "My thoughts were selfish. Can you please just give me a little time? At least until Sarah gets back and things settle down."

"Who says you'll ever see that kid again?" He glanced down at the pile of missing child fliers waiting to be stuffed into envelopes, then back to Rachel. She had curled herself into the chair, pulling her feet up onto the seat and wrapping her arms around her knees.

Just the sight of her seemed to drain the anger out of him.

"Of course you'll find her," he said gently. "Then Father will determine the timing of the decision." He nodded until she did. "And you'll obey."

CHAPTER 7

The just-opened Scott Matheson County Courthouse sat directly across the street from the restored county-city building that looked like a Disneyland castle. On a typical winter day in downtown Salt Lake City, Rachel would have felt a tingling awe at not only seeing, but working in the heart of Babylon.

She inwardly delighted in invisibly working alongside female prosecutors wearing pastel, curve-hugging business suits and three-inch heels, and self-infatuated attorneys in double-breasted Italian suits and two hundred dollar shoes. She imagined their faces, one by one, as she told them she was one of five sister widows with twenty-five children, with a sixty-three-year-old man about to wed and bed her while choosing and giving his blessing for her next plural marriage partner.

But this wasn't a typical day. She hadn't had one since Sarah had vanished.

She scurried around a swarm of reporters ascending the courthouse stairs like locusts. She would see them all again shortly in the same courtroom.

She rummaged through her purse for her little sin that in her world was as serious as being caught with a bag of heroin—Virginia Slim cigarettes. It was a nasty ritual she had started since Father Goodman had set her free in Babylon for a few hours a day. She coughed down one a day, shielded from detection in the courthouse ladies restroom.

A blast of wind powdered one side of Rachel's face with snow. She shuddered and tucked her chin into her black ankle-length wool coat, given to her by Father Goodman in celebration of her first—her only—job outside the fortress. The treads of her black rubber-soled, low-heeled shoes nicely navigated the ice-sheeted cement steps leading up to the booming city's most imposing government building.

Salt Lake City was on a roll, and even government buildings proclaimed its bullish prosperity. The lines of the eight-story stone and glass building were clean, crisply conventional, and yet contemporary. The interior, plush. The lobby, with its one-hundred-foot marble and glass waiting area felt more like a Hyatt Hotel atrium than a house of judgment for murderers, wife beaters, thieves, and teenage gangsters.

Rachel hadn't seen enough of Babylon to fully grasp modern interior design, and her outsider eyes registered many things as strange. Today she marveled at an orifice-ringed, parole-violating gangster wanna-be who shuffled along the high-grade emerald green carpet, then sat on an expensive fabric bench, warmed by the rich yellow glow of stylish art deco light fixtures. A uniformed court deputy, complete with gun and badge, seemed as out of place in the elegant interior as a nun in a nightclub.

Another reason it wasn't a typical day at the Scott Matheson County Courthouse was because of the lanky, bespectacled bookwormish man with alabaster skin, tar black hair, and an ill-fitting midnight blue suit being led into the courtroom by the deputy sheriff.

In her brief tenure as court reporter, Rachel had felt detached from defendants, from shiny-faced white collar offenders to rock hard habituals with dingy-alley masks for faces, lined with every atrocity done to and by them. So what made Jared Jacobson's final day of trial so significant she had to wedge her way past newspeople from around the world?

One word: polygamist.

The word, that if the blazing spotlight ever swiveled around to her, people would gasp aloud and mark her with the scarlet letter "P".

She slipped into her favorite bathroom stall and secured the latch. As Rachel sat down she gathered up the daily newspaper strewn at the base of the toilet. With no outside music, television or news allowed in the Goodman Compound, she felt doubly naughty. She scanned the front page while the smoke curled lazily around her.

"No!" she yelped as her eyes widened in terror at the headline. "Salt Lake Strangler Strikes Again." All the victims were Caucasian women between fourteen and thirty. All the women had long dark hair.

Sarah's hair is long and black.

Rachel leaped to her feet. Her cigarette plopped from her quivering lips to the open newspaper. She batted it to the floor and stomped on it, grinding her dowdy heel into the floor as if she were trying to erase the horror looming in her mind.

"Don't be ridiculous. She just ran away," she muttered to herself and left for her court reporter's chair before the judge entered.

Rachel winced at the booming sound as 1st District Court Judge Meredith Wheelright's gavel finally quieted the standing-room-only courtroom. The door led to a glimpse behind, what one network anchor called, "Utah's dirty little secret," was being pried wide open with a prize catch. All were poised to get a glimpse into the secretive Jacobson group, a seventeen hundred member polygamous sect that had an estimated one hundred seventy million-dollar business empire. The Jacobsons were in size and affluence second only to the Goodman sect in Salt Lake County and other parts of Utah, Arizona, and Nevada.

Rachel flexed her fingers like an anxious concert pianist. She tried to remain oblivious to the mass of eyes zeroed in on the freak polygamist, but sensed they were really staring at her. She glanced down at the overtly plain dress she was wearing, suddenly feeling it was as clear a giveaway as her other bland calico dresses.

Never expect the devil's own to care about God's laws.

Rachel absently nodded at Father Goodman's soul-healing words from one of his polygamy sermons. This *was* Babylon, after all.

Judge Wheelright cleared her throat. Show time.

Jacobson's attorney, Robert Schloeder, opened the proceedings in a bold, confident voice. He looked good before the lights—Republican, solid, conservative—from his Brooks Brothers suit to preppy horn-rimmed spectacles. His statement was brief and to the point. He intended to prove beyond a doubt his client's total innocence. With exaggerated pauses between whisper-soft sound bites, he said the decision that rested with the jury would be based solely on the word of one confused, wild child with a history for lying and trouble that warranted scrutinous attention. He concluded by saying he welcomed the child's testimony and her father's heartbroken rebuttal.

His client was accused of a lurid crime that had snatched international headlines, but Schloeder's out-of-courtroom televised assurances of trust in the system and trust in Jacobson's innocence rang with believability throughout the month-long trial.

Rachel decided that Schloeder would be the one to watch when a still deeply bruised and bandaged girl of fourteen took the stand and recounted being beaten with a belt at least thirty times across her back and thighs before losing consciousness. Would Schloeder even flinch when the teenager's pointing finger led to her own father who she blamed for nearly whipping her to death? It had been her third attempt to flee for her life from becoming the ninth wife to her thirty-eight-year-old uncle.

Even with the girl's testimony, Rachel knew there would be no easy conviction for a subject the state's courts, politicians and police had gone to extremes to avoid. If convicted, Jacobson could get fifteen years for felony child abuse.

Kipp Wade, assistant county attorney representing the prosecution, commanded attention wherever he applied his profession. He was young, sharp and relentless. His hair had the sheen of polished gold, the very precious metal he hoped to surround himself with from the international notoriety the case promised in spades.

Jared Jacobson didn't look like the kind of man who could be full of passion and rage. He took a seat with as much dignity as he could, considering the accusing electricity that filled the room. Rachel grabbed a last glance before being chained to her machine for every word of the proceedings. Jacobson settled his clasped hands gently on the smooth tabletop; pale hands with no scrapes, no contusions, and no suggestion of hands that could be the instruments of such horrors.

Rachel lifted her eyes to the posturing local and network news cameramen, and the sea of unrecognizable faces she assumed were working the periphery like circling wolves, ready to tear into pieces any story angles the networks failed to recognize. The local media had been thrown in with the big guys and were still trying to get their bearings— with one exception.

Rachel couldn't miss the boyish smile unquestionably intended for her. Her eyes dropped back to the keyboard, feeling the red in her face was spreading out to the tips of her ears. He was more than smiling. He was outright staring. Why her, when everybody else was riveted to Jared Jacobson and the showboat attorneys? *He knows.*

Between the attorneys' sparring remarks, Rachel tracked the still-beaming man madly scratching out notes between flirtatious stares. Her stone expression cracked while sneaking a peek at the way he dressed, like the kind of guy who would carry a sandwich in his pocket. From what she could see, he looked fit beyond reason, with hair a shock of rich chocolate tied neatly into a ponytail.

The judge seemed almost immune to the usual peacocking by the two attorneys. She peered over the rims of a pair of reading glasses perched on the tip of her nose that were more authoritative props than reading aids. Rachel had seen the gesture before. Judge Wheelwright never let glass stand in her way when glaring down at pews full of gawkers making distracting interruptions.

Now for the victory, the prosecuting attorney had sleeplessly been awaiting throughout the trial proceedings. He adjusted the knot of his Armani tie and took a last inspection of his Italian-made double-breasted suit jacket. He was more than ready.

"I call Debra Jacobson to the stand," Wade said.

Jared Jacobson leaned forward, his forearms braced on the table. His doe eyes remained lifeless as he watched his daughter rise from the seat next to the assigned matronly custody counselor from the Division of Child and Family Services.

Wade stood before the witness stand facing the teenager and the jury. "Debra, this is your chance to tell the court what your father did to you."

"Leading the witness," Schloeder said, bolting upright.

"Sustained. Please rephrase the question, Mr. Wade."

"Debra, please tell us in your own words what happened."

The zombie-like girl turned her full attention to her father's fixed eyes. "I beat myself up so it would look worse."

Wade swallowed his Adam's apple. "You what? No, no, Debby. It's all right, now. Nobody's going to hurt you."

Schloeder was back on his feet in a fury. "A slanderous inference and again leading the witness."

Judge Wheelright slowly slid her half glasses up her nose. "Sustained. Mr. Wade, you've been warned."

"Yes, your honor." Wade took a deep breath and wheeled around to Jared Jacobson in time to catch the man's wild glare at his daughter. "I ask that during Ms. Jacobson's testimony, the defendant be escorted to an outer chamber to get at—"

"Your Honor, that's totally unnecessary," Schloeder yelled from his chair.

"I'll determine what is and isn't appropriate in my court," Judge Wheelright said, then motioned for the bailiff to remove Jared Jacobson from the room.

The courtroom buzzed with the first juicy development.

"Quiet, or I'll clear the entire courtroom." Judge Wheelright pulled the prop glasses from her face. "My patience is running paper thin. Nobody has in the past, or will now make my courtroom a media circus." She paused, as if testing the silence. "Consider this a final warning." She watched Jacobson file past her podium and to the back of the room without even raising his head.

"Mr. Wade, please proceed with your questioning."

The county attorney smiled at the media like a movie star descending the steps of his private jet. "Thank you, Judge, for your sensitivity."

Debra Jacobson rubbed her tear-lined cheeks.

"I must remind you, Debby, that you're under oath. You know what that means?" Wade said.

"Yes, I do sir."

"Good. Now you are only being asked to repeat what you've already gone on record as saying. I can't imagine how hard this is for you. Would it be easier for me to read what you said, and with each statement have you agree or disagree with your earlier statement?"

The teenager nodded.

"No objections," Schloeder volunteered.

Here it comes, and the bastard deserves it. In Rachel's mind's eye she could see not Debra Jacobson's face, but Sarah's, bruised and battered, the fires of hatred and stubborn resistance burning in her eyes. *That's it, girl. Tell them. Tell them everything.*

Debra Jacobson eagerly accepted a tissue and glass of water from the bailiff.

"Go on, dear. Just tell the truth. It's as simple as that," the judge said.

"When I turned fourteen I had to marry my Uncle Jonathan." The teenager's eyes scanned the room for mothers and relatives. Rachel could see her desperation and fear.

"Keep your eyes on me, Debby," said Wade. "Like I said, you can tell it, or agree with what I read." He patted her hand. "Better if you tell it, though."

"They said it was a secret ceremony. I just wanted to go to high school and have a normal life."

Wade nodded. "And did your uncle have sex with you since this ceremony?"

The girl nodded. "Twice."

Judge Wheelright raised her gavel like a hatchet, hushing the rumbling crowd.

"And my father had sex with me, too!"

"I object!" Schloeder roared.

"Overruled," Judge Wheelright snapped. "Go on, child."

Rachel could hear her heart in the dead silence. Her fingers froze at the keys. *What happened at that ranch?*

"You didn't report that earlier, Debby," Wade said gently.

"I was afraid." The tears couldn't be ebbed any longer. She wiped the tissue across her eyes. "I remember him telling me…That before the night was over, I'd think twice before running away," she told the prosecutor.

"Him, being?"

"My father. The first time I ran away, my father brought me back to my uncle. He took off my…He made me sleep with him."

Wade gave encouraging nods with each revelation.

"The second time I ran to my mother, then Dad took me to our second home in Idaho."

"You mean where wayward Jacobson wives are taken to be punished?" Wade coached.

"I object. Hearsay and leading the witness," Schloeder shouted.

Judge Wheelright glanced at Rachel, then paused and stared at the normally stoic woman's distant teary-eyed expression. "Strike that from the record."

Rachel could feel the weight of the judge's curious gaze and felt compelled to act as though she had a head cold. She let out a pathetic cough and put one hand to her throat. The judge smiled compassionately.

"I didn't know where we were going, but kind of figured it out when we passed Ogden." The teenager fondled the end of her long braided hair. "When we got closer, Dad grabbed me by the hair and pulled me to him, then he slugged me in the nose and mouth. That's when he broke my nose. I could taste the blood. When we got to the summer house he dragged me from the car to the living room, where he beat me up until I passed out."

Wade pulled a manila envelope from his jacket. "I present these photos of the swollen, broken nose and deep bruises as Exhibit D to the court." He turned back to the teenager. "You're being brave, Debby. Please go on," Wade said.

"When I woke up the next morning I was the only one there. I walked for a long time until I got to a gas station and called 911."

Wade turned away from the girl to the jury. "What you did was just about a first. We all know polygamy in Utah lives and acts outside the law. By having the courage to come forward you've turned the world's eyes on acts and lifestyles that have to conform to the greater society's definition of right and wrong, good and evil, slave and master."

During cross examination, Schloeder attempted to paint a picture of the young girl out of control, who worried her parents by staying out all night, drinking, taking drugs and sleeping around, including the night before the beatings.

Rachel gasped, again alerting the judge, when the girl admitted spending a night with an older man at a motel, where they took drugs and consumed alcohol. Schloeder capitalized on the moment and declared the offense did not qualify as a second-degree felony but as a lesser Class A misdemeanor.

"If a parent slaps a child and the next week slaps him again, the child might have two bruises, but is the parent guilty of a second-degree felony? I submit absolutely not," Schloeder growled in his closing remarks.

Wade's rebuttal was equally persuasive. Now fully aware of Rachel's non-stoppable tears that only boiled up when the child was speaking, he turned to two women jurors who had reacted similarly to further boost his convictions. "The physical abuses this child of fourteen has bravely revealed, while literally fearing for her future safety, marks the beginning of the end of torture for all those children, teenagers, and women who have suffered in silence under the yoke of the illegal act of polygamy." His arm shot out at Jared Jacobson, returned to the room for cross examination and final summations. "That man inflicted methodical pain and torture on his own flesh and blood."

Jacobson leaped to his feet before Schloeder could stop him. "Is it really the truth you want, or a polygamy conviction? This isn't a trial about a fight between father and a wild daughter, it's—"

Judge Wheelright slammed her gavel to quell the new wave of clatter. "Sit down right now, Mr. Jacobson, or I will have you bound and gagged if necessary!"

Schloeder jerked his client by the arm until Jacobson sat, audibly mumbling to himself. The attorney snapped his briefcase shut. The show was all over, except for the jury's decision, and of course, the media firestorm at the heels of whatever verdict was read.

Rachel watched the defense and prosecuting attorneys leave, a sick heaviness resting as if a stone in her stomach.

It promised to be a long deliberation before the jury made a decision. Precedence would weigh heavily in the state's first major polygamy trial. Tugging on the string too hard could unravel a tangled mess that Schloeder had powerfully dramatized: raids like in Waco, Texas on compounds and polygamist communities, inevitable blood spilled, families torn apart forever, a bona fide constitutional first amendment nightmare.

Persistent thoughts of the pasty white man who stood only feet away from her, degrading her religion and purpose on earth, and of Sarah held somewhere with her face a palette of cuts and bruises made her light-headed and nauseous.

The media swarm had moved out the door with Jared Jacobson. Rachel scanned the courtroom for the smiling stranger as she gathered her notes. He was gone. Even though reporters would ignore or shove her aside, she hesitated to avoid the crowd. Considering the lingering chaos against the arrival of her bus, she trudged up the aisle separating the pews.

He stood just outside the courtroom door surrounded by reporters.

"Carver, have you received another call from the killer?"

"Did you know any of the murdered girls?"

At the last question bubbling up from the tight circle of light-beaming television cameras and notepad-carrying reporters, Rachel froze in mid-stride. She leaned in closer to catch a response.

"I'm not the story," the man answered. "Read about it in tomorrow's *Observer.*" Rachel swallowed hard as the reporter pushed through the crowd and strode directly to her. "Would a beautiful woman let me buy her a cup of coffee?"

Rachel shook off the comment as meant for someone else.

"Yes, Rachel Zimmerman, I mean you."

She twitched, feeling exposed, vulnerable. *How does he know my name*? His request held more confidence than she could muster to respond to without sounding foolish. She lowered her eyes and shook her head, then scurried toward the elevators.

The man stayed close behind, then reached her side, keeping stride with her pace.

"Sorry, I didn't mean to frighten you. Just a cup of coffee, really," he said. He advanced in front of her and walked backwards to face her. "There's a sandwich shop right downstairs," he gestured gracefully, as though he were a magician drawing attention to a stage trick.

The over-dramatized act drew out a smile.

"I knew you'd have a beautiful smile," he said, stepping closer.

"Please, leave me alone. I don't drink coffee." She sighed at the sight of the elevator bank and lurched to push the down button. He moved like a dance partner, never letting her get enough distance between them to diffuse the electric tension even she couldn't resist.

"I'm really not a rascal. Well, maybe a little bit." He held up a hand like a witness being sworn in. "I'm Charlie Carver, a reporter for the *Observer*. I've seen you in that courtroom for days, and I don't see a ring."

Rachel tried to project an image of self-control. *Charlie Carver.* She pictured his byline on the story on the Salt Lake Strangler. *Don't ask. He'll have too many questions.* She checked her watch for the fourth time, and still couldn't see the time in her nervousness. "I've got to get to my bus." She stared at Charlie Carver while every internal alarm in her being screamed shrilly in her head.

One corner of his mouth made a sly tilt up. "I've filed my stories. C'mon, I'll give you a ride. It's snowing like hell out there." His blue eyes twinkled with anticipation.

The elevator door opened and Rachel leaped in without a response. She jerked her head up and stared at Charlie Carver while every warning signal rattled in her head. Just as the metal walls closed over a smile that knew he was getting to her, she leveled a terrified gaze at the reporter that sent chills through him.

CHAPTER 8

The moment's respite from worrying about Sarah faded faster than bursting fireworks with Rachel's first step off the bus in front of the Goodman Compound.

Rules be damned, she was going to call the Snowville ranch house every day until she got some answers. The search party the Father had promised still hadn't set a foot in any direction. The sight of Hyrum and Jacob's trucks sitting idle in tire-high snow blasted apart the last of her patience. She stormed into the house past the twelve-year old twins tangled in a wrestling match in the living room, Jessica primping in front of the hallway mirror, and Anna and a younger sister cutting out calico floral dress patterns strewn across the kitchen counter island.

Rachel squeezed her eyes shut in silent prayer as she dialed. "Ida, is that you?"

"Rachel! Do you have Father's permission to be calling here?"

Rachel's braided hair had come loose from its twist in her flurry to make the call. Even the top button on her proper dress was unbuttoned. Her lifelong armor to ward off temptation was coming undone. She couldn't decide who she was becoming at that moment: Rachel Zimmerman, the protective mother, or Rachel Zimmerman, the earthly facilitator to God's master plan.

"Have you seen or heard anything from Sarah?" she demanded.

"Everything will be fine," Ida announced, though it clearly was not, and it was obvious in her tone of voice.

"I don't need comforting, Ida, I need some answers."

"Look, Rach, we've had girls run away before. You know that. They always come back when they get out there with no money, and no skills to make any."

Rachel shook off the reply, frowning. "It's been three weeks and not a word. I'm done waiting, Ida." She reached for fortitude to insulate her from the bottomless list of dos and don'ts that she had gagged down since before entering puberty. "I deserve answers right now!" She slammed down the phone, showing a glimpse of herself she never would have unveiled if every instinct hadn't finally force her to admit her daughter was in danger.

Jessica sidled into the kitchen for more tidbits to report.

"Everything's under control," Rachel announced while combing trembling fingers through the free-flowing strands behind her right ear.

"You aren't allowed to—"

"I'm a grown woman, Jessica, unlike you. I'll decide what's right when it comes to finding my daughter."

Jessica shrugged, ignoring the bite in her words.

Rachel grabbed her by the arm. "I'm sick of being afraid. Sarah needs me." She tightened her grip until her knuckles turned white. "Now where are James' keys to the truck? You're the only one he let drive it." She released and pursued her infantile sister wife across the kitchen, into the living room, up the stairs and into the master bedroom. Jessica seemed to sense that further display of righteous indignation or reprimanding would unleash a fury she had never seen in Rachel. She pulled a denim jacket out of James' closet and fished out the heavy ring of keys.

Rachel fingered each key without a clue as to which one fit the Chevy Suburban.

"You don't even know how to drive it," Jessica said.

"I've driven," Rachel answered, wagging a finger in her face. "When I was younger James used to let me drive." She clasped her hand tightly over Jessica's. "If you don't shut your mouth about my taking off, I'll make your life a hell on earth. You think I don't know about you and Hyrum? Sex is for procreation in marriage. The Father would be furious."

The scant few inches of air between them seemed to thicken. Jessica tugged her hand free and stepped back. "That's a lie!"

"Imagine how Hyrum's wives would take it. And you're eight months pregnant." With that she stared her nemesis in the face, then walked out on her for the first time since the child became her husband's fifth wife.

The Goodman congregational parking lot was a rough sea of ice and hardened snow crushed into jagged ruts by truck tires. Rachel let out a plume of breath when she spotted the lone truck twenty feet away from the two shiny grain silos. Since his death, James' Suburban was being used to pick up polygamist school children in the Valley. Clouds had swallowed the daylight early, and snow was beginning to fall. Large, intricately patterned flakes floated like down feathers from heaven onto the unforgiving ground.

Rachel stepped a little closer to the truck. She hadn't seen it since James' death. The empty dark green hunk of metal suddenly seemed as eerie as his bedroom, still left undisturbed as though the master would be home at any moment. James' absence now felt as if a loose end she could tie up and move beyond as soon as Sarah was home to fill in the spaces. She jostled the frozen door lock, then hopped onto the driver's seat, bone-chilling despite its Indian blanket cover. Her body growled for lack of fuel, but the thought of food turned her stomach.

As she watched the fortress in the rearview mirror, she nodded, knowing there would be punishment. She accepted, even welcomed it as a physical manifestation of her pain.

~

The whisper was thin as Mylar, barely above a thought. "Rachel took the truck and nobody knows where she went?"

Jessica cast a glance out of the Father's library window. Even without the blinds drawn, the light was fading to black outside and whirling snow started to glaze the glass.

"She was talking crazy. Making up all kinds of stories about me just to scare me off from telling you." Satisfied with her plan, she dug her shaking hands into her coat pockets and sat down before her prophet.

"Where do *you* think she went?" Each word had smooth rounded tones.

Jessica's eyes danced around the room that had been illuminated by a full moon and naked writhing bodies less than two weeks before. Hers, and the Father's son, Hyrum's. Even though her husband's body had hardly grown cold in the ground, she just hadn't been able to resist Hyrum's delicious invitation to brazenly make love in the Prophet's most private room. The wind swept in down the canyon, wrapping its powdery white self around the contours of the house.

"I know where she went, Father."

"Well, come out with it, child. She could kill herself out there with weather like this."

"She went," Jessica winced, "to the ranch." She scolded herself for what would happen next.

Goodman didn't move at first, then sprang up from his chair. "How dare she!"

Jessica flinched in terror at the outburst.

Goodman narrowed his eyes, rubbing his chin with his finger-missing claw hand. "And what does she expect to find there?"

"Sarah," Jessica answered meekly.

Goodman made a mad dash for the door. He spied Beth, one of his wives, framed in the light of the kitchen. "Beth, get Hyrum and Jacob right now. Tell them to meet me at my truck in fifteen minutes."

CHAPTER 9

Charlie found at least one redeeming value in being the paper's only spook hunter: he didn't have to conform to the New World of work teams.

Bottoms-up management and the business buzz-phrase of the early nineties, "empowerment to the people," had swept through organizations so deeply, even the newspaper business had gotten the bug.

The endearing, goofy, eclectic menagerie of oddballs who gravitated to a business whose reward for horrible hours and public service wages was a front page byline were long gone, replaced by preppy hunks in suspenders and well-coifed women who looked more like television anchor people than cynical, crusty reporters.

Charlie was old school, a lone crusader of the Woodward and Bernstein vintage. At thirty-seven, he wasn't about to change colors. All for one be damned.

There had been one redeeming feature, only one, in his rash decision to move to the Promised Valley—city editor, Theron Liddle. A real newspaper man with hot type and ink pumping through his veins.

"Hey, hotshot!" The voice wafted over Charlie's fabric-covered cubicle wall.

Liddle always called Charlie *hotshot*. What the early-fifties newsman was missing in physical presence he made up for with electric hazel eyes, thick wavy prematurely white hair, a year 'round tan from skiing and hiking that George Hamilton would envy, and contagious enthusiasm.

He popped into Charlie's vacant side chair. "Here's how I see it. The wire just sent over a story about the serial killer that's got your name plastered all over it." He stood and tapped Charlie's shoulder. "You're definitely back in the byline business for good, buddy."

Charlie shrugged. With an explosive polygamy story brewing in the back of his mind he was thinking the same thing. He could even smell a best-selling book in it.

University of Utah intern Robin Fogle timidly cornered Charlie's cubicle and brushed back locks of chestnut hair over one ear. "Oh excuse me, I'll come back—"

Charlie flapped his hand for her to join them. "Theron, Robin's doing a hell of a job. You ought to know that."

Liddle swiveled his chair around. "A little more than you bargained for young lady, with this serial killer running loose in your head."

Charlie jumped in. He had watched her fresh, clear-eyed start less than a month ago wither to running on will after exhaustive research and repeated rewrites under his tutelage. "She's going to be Salt Lake's first *real* home-grown investigative reporter," Charlie boasted. "The inside stories and balanced angles Robin's fleshed out on the Strangler's victims has resurrected these poor women from dead naked freaks to real people."

"Thanks, Mr. Carver, for giving me such an important assignment."

"It made sense," Charlie said, reaching out for the three-page backgrounder on the twenty-six-year-old advertising account executive found on the desert floor like a discarded animal carcass. "You can really put those psychology classes you've taken to task on this sick son-of-a-bitch."

"Has the Strangler ever tracked down your home phone number?" the city editor asked.

Charlie shook his head. "I can feel him at times as though he's following me," Charlie said, thinking out loud. "This guy's no idiot."

"You gotta gun?" Robin asked.

Charlie shook his head, half-disgusted. "Of course not."

"Ever notice he only calls when you're in town?" Liddle said. "If I had a serial killer tracking my every move, I'd bend my principles just enough to fit a.38 under my pillow."

The shrill ring of Charlie's phone made them jerk as if someone just jumped out of the closet at them.

Charlie pressed the police-provided recording machine and picked up the receiver.

"I'm sorry. I can't stop myself," the rich, deep voice said.

Charlie's eyes narrowed as his index finger popped up to alert Liddle and Robin. She balled a tight fist and put it to her mouth.

"The only way to stop is to give yourself up," Charlie said without a hint of surprise in his voice.

The line hummed in silence. "Please forgive me. She's such a beautiful child."

Charlie knew the voice. It gave a new sound to his nightmares.

"You know what I'm going to do to her, don't you?" The air was thick with evil. "Such pretty skin. I'm not going to rush any of it this time."

"I'm not your priest." Charlie's brows shot up as a new approach rushed through his mind. "You're damning yourself to hell, but it's not too late. Let her go and confess to God right now!"

Silence. The caller hung up.

"Shit! I thought it would work. I know damn well one side of him needs to be punished."

Liddle slowly nodded. "But the other side's winning."

10
CHAPTER

The truck stop cafe glowed silver and pink under a ten-foot neon coffee cup.

With the wind at her back, Rachel scooted into the dimly lit feeding stations for regulars and nomads passing through. The aroma of dirty bubbling lard wafted corner to corner.

Careful to hold her ankle length dress in position, she kept her legs together while walking to an empty booth for four. A furry, rumpled man of thirty, with the belt overhang of a fifty-year-old watched Rachel's every move as she hung her overcoat beside a booth's grimy green plastic seat. He sauntered over and blew out stale liquor breath toward the acoustical ceiling before settling in on his prey. His drink splashed a puddle on the table as he flopped into the empty bench seat. "Order anything on the menu." He slowly poked a finger at his chest, as if a curve ball coming into center plate. "My treat."

"I appreciate your kindness, sir, but—"

"Skipper. Just call me Skipper. Never been to sea, but I got me a good strong rudder." He curled his fingers around his Jack Daniels double and took a deep swig, then winked and released a pirate's grin.

She weighed her answer. Her impulse was to get up and leave, but he would likely fall in step behind her into the black of night.

The lazy-eyed waitress inhaling a non-filter Salem down to her toenails didn't even lift a brow. Rachel tried to signal her with an exaggerated head tilt, but got no response.

"I'm not really hungry," Rachel said, rising.

Skipper reached over and touched the long braid of satin-black hair while brushing a thumb across her nipple, then gingerly tugged her back down to her seat. "Well, if it's not food, how 'bout a little drink?" he drawled.

"Really, please, just leave me alone."

Again playing the rogue, he rose and slid in beside her as if a prowling tomcat. His eyes locked on her heaving breasts as she fought to catch her breath. The sole rim of his hard boot brushed across her bare ankle. He made a phlegm-clearing sound and pulled a cigarette out of the pack in his shirt pocket. Just as he was about to strike a match, Rachel nudged against his hard thigh to move.

"Let me go. I need to leave right now!"

"What if I said I get lonely and just want a little company?"

"I'm a married woman."

He shook his head. "You're married all right." She could see the venom in his eyes. "With me, you'll be more than just one in the herd."

She glared at him. "What do you mean?"

"You think I don't know a plyg when I see one?" He eased out with a flirtatious smile. "We got a pile of 'em round here." He stared at Rachel's starkly black hair and light topaz eyes. "You're a dead ringer for Elizabeth Taylor when she was young." Rachel's barriers lowered for a flashing moment in the madman's web.

He perked up, as if he was about to turn the moment to his advantage. Instead, he tossed down the rest of his whiskey and set down the glass. "Never hear sweet words like that from your lord of the roost, do ya?"

Her shields came up again. "I don't know what you're talking about."

He glanced at her ringless left hand. "I knew you was one of 'em the second you stepped your purdy little ass in here. You girls don't wear rings."

"I need to go," Rachel mumbled.

Skipper narrowed his eyes at her, then anchored the palm of his hand on the table, blocking her passage. "Tommy, we got us a little plyg here."

Three booths down a bull-necked redhead stood on the tiptoes of his scuffed cowboy boots to see the catch. Rachel's captor stood up and away from the booth long enough for her to quickly slip out and dash for the exit.

Rachel tunneled her vision, walking past a table of two sympathetic clean-shaven faces nursing coffee cups. The balding one rose as she whisked by. "Don't pay any attention to that idiot, ma'am. He'd chase a female elephant into hell if it'd even bat an eye at him. No insult intended, of course." He began to stammer out apologies to the giggling delight of his friend, who grinned at Rachel and tipped his head.

"Just get along, ma'am. I'll buy Skipper another round. He won't be bothering you."

Rachel caught her breath. Outside the Goodman fortress, everything bothered her.

11
CHAPTER

By one in the morning, Mother Nature had dumped nearly a foot of new snow on Central Utah. A blast of northern wind stirred the air with a blanket of white that limited driving to a crawl. Hyrum Goodman knew his father was never much for small talk, especially when it came to discussing his desire to wed and bed Rachel Goodman.

Hyrum squirmed while glancing at Donald Goodman's owl eyes and insistent expression. "Rachel is a fine looking woman, but hardly suitable for your wife, Hyrum."

"She's good enough for you to celestially seal yourself to her for all eternity."

A hint of angry color stained Father Goodman's cheeks. He tugged at the too-tight knot on his midnight blue silk tie. "She is not suitable for a young man, and that's final."

"You mean, she can't have any more kids? We don't know that. A lot of our women have had miscarriages."

"Three in a row?" Father Goodman snapped. "James told me she hemorrhaged terribly with the only one she didn't lose. Just about died. I've prayed long and hard in considering the law of chastity, but there is a slight chance she could conceive. I don't deny it. "

"Why would *you* take her then?" Hyrum snapped. "You don't understand." The closest he came to an apology was a twist of his mouth. He turned toward the passenger door window as though there was more to see than snowflakes illuminated by Jacob's headlights. They passed the Snowville exit sign on the freeway before Hyrum cracked the silence.

Hyrum sat forward in the truck seat and braced one arm on the back of the rest. "I want to marry her father. I love her."

Father Goodman leveled a scorching look. "I've had big plans for you and Jacob, but you worry me Hyrum."

The late twenties son silently shook his head. Nothing new. He had always disappointed his father.

"I can appreciate that you think you love her, son. She can be a real tease when she wants to." He paused for effect. "I've been thinking about Anna for you. You've always been attracted to younger ones. You were sealed to all your wives before they were eighteen."

"I want a real woman."

The truck swerved to the side of the road and slid to a stop. Jacob's Jeep Cherokee was close behind. Father Goodman yanked Hyrum a breath away by his black suit. "Don't you ever, *ever*, question my judgment again!"

Hyrum ripped away from his father's grasp. He was too old to draw his body into the tight ball he had as a child, arms wrapped tight around his knees, back pressed up against his locked bedroom door. He had tired of his own tears years ago. He squeezed his eyes shut. There were so many things his father didn't know about him, and never would.

Fornication was considered a breach of the faith, and the Father could even order it punishable by expulsion from the family—or worse. While other bug-eyed campfire listeners were riveted by stories of the mad killer with a hook for a hand, children of the Order were whispered stories of unmarked and never-found graves hidden under sagebrush at the Utah and Arizona borders. Tales of blood atonement for those who betrayed, degraded, or challenged the Prophet's word loomed over children's nightmares as if a dragon's shadow.

In his mind, Hyrum opened the door to his secret place and went inside, where Father couldn't hurt or frighten him. Where only he was ruler. Where only he could touch.

"Something happened to Sarah, didn't it, Father?"

~

Every creak in the floorboards, the musty, mothball smell at the top of the staircase, the endless row of bedroom doors down the narrow second-story hallway, all slapped Rachel with mixed memories of both corrective and non-punishing summer visits to Snowville.

"I can't imagine what got into your head, Sister," Ida muttered. "Father's really upset with you."

Rachel paused at the doorway to the room where Sarah always stayed. She steadied her shaking hand on the doorknob. She was holding it together with what little strength she had left, but barely. On the drive down she had imagined throwing open the ranch house front door, sweeping Sarah into her arms, and rocking her, as much to comfort herself as to comfort her wayward daughter. Now she found nothing but a ghostly calico dress draped across the back of a wooden rocking chair by the window and an overnight case with last minute toiletries left open on the ivory pedestal sink. Sarah's private possessions suddenly seemed precious: toothbrush, a half-squeezed tube of Crest, and a plastic bristle hairbrush, roll-on deodorant.

Rachel winced at the thought of what wasn't there, something that was always there when packing wasn't a red alert. Dental floss. Sarah was a fanatic over flossing and did it as a ritual every night before bed. Rachel's throat burned, tasting sour as if battery acid was leaking into her stomach. Sarah had vanished from the ranch without taking a thing.

"She didn't even leave a note."

Ida stood with folded arms and an inspecting drill sergeant's scowl. "Nothing. I told you that on the phone. Just up and ran away."

Rachel pursued Ida back downstairs. "When? When did you know she was missing?"

"Who said missing? *I* never said missing." Ida opened her arms enough to shake a pointing finger in front of Rachel's nose. "That girl of yours is bullheaded. You know darn well, Sister, she has the spit and vinegar to up and run off without a word." Ida shook her head. "I sleep sound as a baby. When I got up shortly after seven, she was gone. Simple as that."

"She left her suitcase! Even her toiletries behind! It's ridiculous, Ida, and you know it!"

Ida shot her a scathing glare. "You're going to be doing some time here yourself."

Rachel was done talking to Ida. She threw open the door to the entry-way coat closet. A tiny voice in her head prayed it would be empty. The sight triggered an automatic convulsing response. She went rigid and her mouth went dry. "And what do you call that?"

Ida's tacky rubber soles squeaked as she moved to inspect Rachel's discovery. Sarah's winter coat, hanging neatly among the others on thin metal hangers. Her voice faltered. "I never thought to look there."

Beyond the kitchen a door opened and closed with the sounds of Father Goodman and sons coming in through the mudroom. Rachel's eyes widened. She snatched the coat off the hanger and started for the front door. Father Goodman broke into a run and caught her by the arm. In one dizzying move Rachel found her back to the entryway wall and Donald Goodman leaning in on her, his face inches from hers.

"Where do you think you're going?"

"She's my daughter. I have a right to be here."

"You will *damn* well listen to me," he growled. "I get my power through God. Do you understand, Rachel?" He tightened his grip. "I told you she ran away. There's nothing more to be said about it. Satan whispers in our ears, and it's up to us not to listen."

"And you're saying Sarah listened to Satan and deserves to die?" Rachel whispered.

He held her gaze, his expression explosively intense. He slowed his speech to roundly pronounce each word as though it was being recorded for posterity. "You're jumping to unwarranted conclusions. I'm saying I never gave you the authority to call, to come to this house, or to ever challenge my word."

She could see it in the cesspool of his eyes. He wanted her. That was the bottom line. She couldn't argue with his mixed signals. The reckless foolishness of unveiling his passion for her permeated the room like incense. It wasn't just sex; sex could be easily had with any of his wives or other women in the congregation with the simple act of declaring celestial marriage. Women had always come to their Lord's bed willingly and thankfully. But that wasn't his need. His need was for control, something he had never gained over Rachel Zimmerman. She knew at that instant that if she gave it to him, he would suck the last of the life out of her like a ravenous vampire.

"Take your hands off me," she said steadily. "I'm not some child you can scold. Don't you want to find Sarah?"

He released her with a dramatic springing motion. A stark, haunted look crossed his face, as if he was afraid to give her an answer. The expression touched off fear in Rachel that she couldn't afford to allow. Not right now. Not when Sarah's survival depended on it. "I won't stop until Sarah's safe and at home again."

~

Hyrum stepped forward and lightly pulled his father away. Rachel saw a hand rising, then white light when the thudding blow to her face made impact. "You never talk to the Father in that tone again. If that child of yours dies in some ditch, she put herself there."

Jacob, always the one to contain confrontation, grabbed his brother's punishing arm.

Donald Goodman's glare at Hyrum took on a razor's sharpness, though he didn't raise his voice a decibel. "It's not your place to interfere in these matters, son. Rachel has made a mistake." He turned and aided Rachel to an upright position, her hand still clinging to her burning cheek. His brows popped up at the sight of Sarah's coat in her arms. "She's worried about Sarah, like a mother should." He put a comforting arm around her and led her to the front door. "Get your coat on and we'll go on a late night walk. The crisp air will do us good."

He was wasting time. Again. She clutched the coat and shook her head. "I don't want to do anything but find her."

Father Goodman nodded, reading her every thought. "That's exactly what I want to talk about, as well as a few things that need reminding."

"I didn't mean to yell, Father," she said calmly.

Goodman glanced at his still-fuming son. "Everybody got a little out of control tonight. Let's just slow things down a touch so we can figure out the right action."

~

Strolling on the ten-acre ranch property, Rachel pressed ice-cold hands to her cheeks and willed herself not to cry.

Father Goodman gave her shoulder a sympathetic squeeze, then blew out a sigh of frustration. "There are two words you and Sarah don't begin to understand—everlasting and unchangeable."

Rachel slowly nodded. *Sarah means nothing to you.*

"God revealed laws to Moses and us Latter-Day prophets not to have them change with the seasons, but be timelessly honored with every breath we take."

He was close enough that she watched his nostrils flare in sensual delight. His unabashed gaping at her made Rachel feel shamefully naked.

He had made it obvious he wanted her long before James Zimmerman took her for his bride. It gnawed at her that he carried no outward burden of guilt over her husband's death and his uncontrollable lust for her. At the funeral Hyrum had whispered in her ear, "Father Goodman knew Tunnel Thirty-two was unstable and closed, but he ordered James to have it inspected anyway."

"I have sacred responsibilities that aren't always easy to bear," the Father continued.

He was too close, his cuddling arm too tight on her upper arms, his mouth just inches from her ear. Despite spending her life in awe and humble appreciation of the Order, Rachel had managed to hang onto a piece of herself that demanded respect, even from her patriarch. Deep inside—since puberty—she could feel his sexual hunger. She writhed at the sudden thought that God was punishing her for the shameful vanity of her compulsive exercise and bulimia. Beauty versus fertility.

She coyly tried to move away by feigning a coughing spell. "I know, Father, how afraid we *all* are of getting the police involved, but I can't see any other way of finding her. She took no suitcase, not even her coat."

"We do need to expand our search. With your fliers getting Sarah's picture out to Goodman employees across the state, we've made a good start, but it's clearly not enough. We can, and will do more."

Her rage and pain were boiling near the boundaries of her control. She turned her back on him and pressed her mitten-covered hands to her face, furious with herself for her blasphemy. She thought she was certain of her commitment to God and the Father, if nothing else in all the madness. The prospect of losing the very purpose of her existence felt terrifying and raw. "Thank you, Father. I won't forget that you got the police."

Goodman watched her struggle to reign in her feelings. Her back was ramrod straight, her shoulders straining against the impulse to quiver. "No, no, not the police," Goodman said quickly. "I'll have Hyrum and Jacob take a couple of weeks off and search everywhere until we get some answers."

Rachel stepped forward on the moonlit snowpacked trail. She blurted her response with no thought as to how to address her prophet. It felt liberating. "That's not enough."

12

CHAPTER

Charlie Carver sat in the gallery toward the back of the courtroom in his favorite vantagepoint. On the left-hand side of the aisle opposite the spot where, a week before, four plump, Kmart blue-light-special-looking women wearing 'Women Against Polygamy' purple ribbons had hung on every word of the Jared Jacobson trial.

The jury had caucused only three hours and returned with a guilty verdict of second-degree felony child abuse.

With only he-said-she-said evidence proof of incest and marriage, and the teenager's admitted wild antics, the sentence had been reduced to one year suspension with a $10,000 fine and community service to be assigned and overseen by the Division of Family Services.

Charlie had followed up on the Jacobson girl. International attention had garnered her an all-expense paid ticket to any private college she could earn grades to attend. Her benefactor, a middle-aged Scarborough, England retired stockbroker, had read a series of articles in the *London Times* about Debra Jacobson and acted even before the verdict. His stipulation for the endowment was the requirement that the state allow her to safely sever all ties with the Jacobson clan and be placed into a non-polygamist household. Charlie had learned where the teenager had been placed with a new identity, but decided to not even let his city editor in on his potential front-page scoop. He was saving his ammo for a history-making battle.

It would take an outsider to rekindle the blaze from a brush fire to a raging forest fire. He was the outsider; Rachel Zimmerman could be the match to ignite the blaze.

~

His ticket to a Pulitzer was back in her court recorder's chair, stoic and beautiful as a marble Greek goddess. Charlie was confident enough in his charms to lure the woman into opening the Goodman gate. She wasn't the problem. Charlie's city editor wasn't buying his brainchild of getting the inside dirt on one of Utah's wealthiest and most noted corporate attorneys. He wasn't buying anything that included the word polygamist. A trickle of resistance from the publisher had become a waterfall of blockades on the subject. In the face of such resistance his interest turned from fascination into obsession. It was black and white: polygamy was illegal, but even the State Attorney General was back peddling in interpreting and acting on the law.

Charlie tipped his head back and looked up at the courtroom's tiered ceiling, then refocused on the drama unfolding at the front of the courtroom.

"We don't know yet what the blanket will prove," the well-worn county-appointed defense attorney said. "Nobody knows yet whose blood is on it. The lab has a rush on it, but there's a problem, Your Honor. Once the dry blood is again dampened, it has to remain so to retain its DNA integrity. I understand it dried out again at the crime lab, making it inadmissible. I ask the court to allow for now that Ms. Benitez is telling the truth about her role in Mr. Avery's death. She states she bought the car from an ad in the paper less than a week earlier and the bloodstained blanket was already there. We might well have a red herring here, throwing us off the trail of the real killer that night."

Charlie shook his head. The case concerned a gorgeous exotic dancer accused of bilking more than a cool million out of a middle-aged building contractor with a wife and six children.

He stops paying for her silence; she turns his body into a blood sprinkler. Sex, murder, and not a network prima donna in one hundred miles. But Debra Jacobson lured the media from New York to London.

A trial date was set with bail far beyond reach. A bullet-headed jailer came in from a side door and led the exotic dancer through the door to the cellblock. Charlie was one of only ten people in the courtroom watching the show-stopping beauty exit the room.

Throughout the graphic descriptions of the stabbing, Charlie had watched Rachel's expressionless face. She had been somewhere else, as always.

He waved to her the moment she looked up at the first recess. He followed her out of the courtroom, sniffing at her like a hound dog. "You'd better go in the restroom and wash up a little longer."

She side glanced and pursed her lips.

"The smoke. I can still smell it."

She kept walking, frowning as he moved just in front of her, walking backwards. She stopped, tipped her nose down to her shoulder, and sniffed. "Do you?"

He nodded like a schoolboy. "I do. I'm from Chicago, but from what I understand about your Word of Wisdom, smoking's a no-no." He hesitated, then advanced on her. "Even with polygamists, Rachel."

"Who *are* you and what *do* you want?" Rachel demanded. "What makes you think I'm—what you said?"

"A closet smoker?" He took his wallet out and flipped it open to his license. "Name's Charlie Carver. See right there? From Chicago, less than a year ago."

~

The elevator doors jolted open. It was empty. Rachel turned to take the stairs when Charlie lightly took her arm. "Don't be afraid of me. I'm one of the good guys."

Rachel manufactured a smile, so he released her arm and the two entered the box.

"How about I give you a ride to the Goodman Compound so we have time for a cup of coff—chocolate in the cafe here?"

"And if I say no?" The timber of her voice registered a yes.

"Hmm." Charlie assumed a contemplative expression. "Yes, well I guess I would have to write a pretty dark story about the Goodman Clan without the benefit of your input."

The door opened to the bustling courthouse lobby.

"You're trying to frighten me."

"I'm sorry." He offered the apology sincerely. "I couldn't think of any other way to talk to you."

Rachel bit down on her lip. Her look was stormy.

Charlie tried to open his mouth to continue the charade, but something about the vulnerability in her azure blue eyes stopped him. He shook his head and broke eye contact.

Rachel looked around before speaking and lowered her voice. "What are you going to do with what you've found out about me?"

"I'm an investigative reporter." Warmth swelled within him. The immediate attraction was only partly sexual; creating a torrid of confusion in his mind that made it hard to think. "You're not the story."

The cafe would have better been described as a cafeteria, featuring food as bland as the colors, and stark contemporary design. Charlie motioned for her to claim a table in the narrow, empty room.

He soon returned with two hot chocolates, topped with tall pointed mounds of whipped cream. He wanted the story badly enough that he knew he could get it without her cooperation.

He could investigate or write it from a dozen different angles. But he wanted Rachel Zimmerman in the center of it. If possible, in the center of something even more.

"I'm only drinking this stuff because of you, you know." He chuckled. "Especially the goop on top."

"You're a reporter, and you'll do what you have to to get your story," Rachel blurted.

Charlie nodded. She was absolutely right. He knew better than to get his emotions tangled up in a source. Crossing a line he was ordered to retreat from, especially with a married woman, was a double invitation to disaster.

"I want a behind-the-walls exclusive. I won't color it any way but how you people see it and live it everyday."

Rachel was clearly unimpressed with his bag of tricks. She had probably dodged supposed outside do-gooders all her life. A new tactic was in order.

Charlie narrowed his eyes. "You're one of how many wives?"

Her fingers tightened around the cup handle. Impulse told her to throw the scalding hot drink in his face. "What do you reporters use in place of a heart?"

His mouth twisted into a thin smile. "Never heard that one before, but you got me where I live."

"Would it surprise you to learn that most women who live in plural marriages are happy and fulfilled beyond anything someone like you could put into words?"

She looked down at her ring finger. "And I'm a widow with one child." A tear slipped along one of her cheeks.

"I'm sorry. I seem to be stumbling all over myself," Charlie said.

She nodded, frowning. "It was terrible. What happened to that girl? Her father beating her."

The thought seemed to touch a raw nerve beyond empathy. There was something more, something hidden. He could feel it. "That's why I thought a story to balance the headline-bashing that your people have been getting for weeks would appeal to you."

"His face never moved when his daughter told the court how he had…Oh, that poor child," she sighed. Her inner struggle to defend, yet destroy her own world clouded her eyes. Charlie had seen it all on her gorgeous face from the moment the defense attorney called the child to testify.

He rebounded with the undaunted resilience of a young beat reporter. "No reason to have it end like this. Power, incest, money. Where there's evil, there has to be good."

He waited for her answer. Even a sound bite. He could feel her about to open up when the muted ring of the cellular phone in his sports jacket pocket shattered the moment.

"Excuse me," Charlie said, never taking his eyes off hers.

"Carver here."

"Where? I'll be right there." He flung shut the phone and cursed, then remembered his companion's sensitivities. "Sorry. That son-of-a-bitch just killed another girl!"

She looked as if he had just stomach punched her.

"Am I missing something here?" he asked. He sat wide-eyed watching her flounder. "Yes, Rachel, tell me your story. I can tell you *need* to do it. Every day in that courtroom you were right there with that girl, going through every punishing blow."

Rachel's face contorted with every probe.

Charlie reached over and clasped her hand without even considering the impropriety of such a personal gesture. "I've got to go."

"How old was this—person?"

"The victim? He didn't say. I can tell you she had dark hair."

He could see the comment shoot through Rachel as if a poison-tipped arrow. She was doing all she could to ebb a mounting pool of tears.

"Would you please call them back right now and find out the girl's age?"

The question why entered Charlie's mind. He didn't ask.

"The body wouldn't be at the ME's yet. They figure it's been less than a couple of hours. Even if they've got an I.D., it'll be hours before the crime team notifies the parents."

Rachel set her cup down and turned away from him, only half listening. "I need to know right now," she mumbled.

"Somebody's missing," Charlie said just above a whisper. *A beautiful child*. The strangler's last telephone call made his heart pound.

With her head still turned, Rachel nodded.

"A family member. A child?" Charlie stated gently.

Tears lined Rachel's cheeks when she turned to face him. "My daughter. And she has black hair."

Charlie could hear the pounding in his ears now. "How old?"

"Fifteen."

Charlie whipped out the phone and dialed Salt Lake Police Department dispatch. "Give me Phil Jensen, public information officer, please." Charlie blew out a breath. "Phil, it's Charlie Carver. Yes, I know. What was the—What was her age?" Charlie gave Rachel a pained smile. "I'm not asking for the name. Just about what age. I *really* need it, Phil."

Charlie nodded. "I'll be right there." He hung up, unable to curb the fear in his eyes.

Rachel's shoulders strained against the need to shake. "What? How old?"

Charlie clasped both his hands over one of hers. "There's less than one in a million chances it's your girl." He squeezed tighter. "She is guessed at this point to be around sixteen."

"Her hair? Her hair color? Was it—"

"He only said it was long and dark, like the rest of them."

Charlie watched the woman opposite him struggle to rein in her emotions. "Can I go with you?"

"To the crime scene?" Charlie shook his head. "You don't want to do that."

Rachel pulled his hand away and bolted to her feet. "I do! I need to know."

~

While the strangler's body disposal sites were always unpredictable; they were getting more public with each new corpse. His latest unblemished, naked masterwork was posed atop a piece of crimson velvet by a water fountain on the grass of the State Capital building. The body lay provocatively on its side with one leg pulled up against the other, and arms behind the head. He made the victim look as though she were a World War II bomber pilot pinup girl by a fountain at a downtown city park. Crime lab investigators were still dusting for prints and popping flash photos when Charlie and Rachel wove through a sea of onlookers and uniforms to get to the body.

Rachel broke away from Charlie's guiding hold of her arm and stood over the body trying to breathe.

"Is it her? Your girl?"

Rachel turned with her hands over her tearing eyes and shook her head.

Charlie pulled her into his arms and rubbed her back. "I knew it wouldn't be. You shouldn't have seen that." Charlie turned his eyes to the brooding sky. "It's getting dark and cold as hell. Let's get you home.

An onlooker, a head taller than the crowd around him, leaned in close enough to the taped off crime scene to smell the horror. *What's wrong, Carver? Don't you appreciate my work anymore, you bastard? Who is that angel with you?* The onlooker zipped his red down parka up to his chin and paced behind the reporter and accompanying angel, whom he instantly decided looked more like a whore. *His* whore soon. "Thanks again, Charlie," he whispered just above the low whistling wind.

~

The air was thick with half-said sentences and unstated thoughts on the drive to the Goodman Compound. Until Rachel exposed a raw, terrified vulnerability, she had just put a picture-perfect face on a great story.

When his dead-end story stepped away from his Jeep, turned, and gave a timid wave goodbye, he took one long last look. The usual noise in his head fell as silent as the drifting snowflakes.

13
CHAPTER

"Called off? The search never damn well started," Rachel said, shaking uncontrollably, tears leaking the same as broken plumbing.

Ester gasped at the profanity, uncommon as a rainbow in winter at the Zimmerman house. Her finger rose to scold, but instead she dug a clean handkerchief out of her cooking apron's front pocket and offered it to her heart mate. Rachel reached for it but made no effort to use it, crumpling it in a white-knuckled fist.

Rachel poised to leap out of her chair, but her sister wife pressed her back down. "Let's be calm. There's nothing anybody can do. Just wait for her to come back."

"Ester, Sarah's been kidnapped or—" Nobody seemed to grasp what she was trying to tell them, as if she was speaking in tongues. "I've got to do something right now!"

Jessica watched the scene from her position by the door. "And what are you going to do, call the police?" she snapped while rubbing her swollen stomach.

"Jessica, this is none of your business," Ester said. "Leave us alone now."

If I don't call them, nobody else will. The sense of failure and guilt pressed down on Rachel. She had to pause and wait until she could breathe again. The mother inside her couldn't rationalize or wait any longer. She tightened her hold on the handkerchief and pushed the words out of her mouth. "If I have to leave here for good to find Sarah, I'm going to do it."

A fresh wave of tears washed down her cheeks and fell like raindrops onto the lap of her calico dress. She doubled over in sharp stomach pains, wanting to curl into a fetal position while images of her dead daughter tore at her mind.

Ester leaned closer and stroked her hair. "Well, honey, you'll just have to follow your heart."

Rachel's mind replayed the debate she'd been hearing from the moment that Debra Jacobson opened her mouth during the trial.

Get Sarah's picture to the sheriff's department and the highway patrol. I can't do that. Father Goodman would be furious. What would he do? What could he do? Anything he wants.

Jessica took a half step back and laid one hand on her stomach. "I heard them talking about it last night at Hyrum's." She took her time. "They said Sarah's possessed by the devil and won't come home until he lets her go."

Rachel arched a brow. "The devil seems to pop conveniently into the picture whenever a woman says 'boo'. It's just an excuse, Jess. I knew it before I was twelve, and I'm sick of it! Sick of it!" She sprang from her chair and drew inches from Jessica's startled face. "I didn't even get an hour's start for the ranch before you were running and tattling to Father Goodman."

Rachel planted her hands on Jessica's shoulders and forced her to a stool at the long breakfast bar. She squeezed unconsciously and shut her eyes tight against the onslaught of more tears. As scalding as acid, they squeezed out and ran down her cheeks.

I'm losing my mind.

"Tell Ester about you and Hyrum making love upstairs, less than a week after James died," she said with forced calm. "Go on, tell Ester."

"Rachel!" Ester yelled. "That's enough." Her eyes madly darted around for listening ears. "You should be ashamed. And Jessica, in her condition. Speaking about Brother Goodman like that? He's a man of God."

At the humbling tone of Ester's voice, Rachel broke free of her trance-like attack. She released Jessica and dropped her shoulders.

"What about me? What about how she's talking about me?" Jessica asked. Her hand went up to her mouth, afraid an answer might come out she didn't want to hear.

Ester draped her arm over Rachel's shoulder and led her to the entry staircase. "You go upstairs, kiddo, and lay down for a while. I'll get Jess to help peel the potatoes and set the table."

"It's up to me, Ester."

"Oh, Rachel." She patted Rachel's hand resting on the stair rail. "No, it isn't, dear. It's up to God. You go on now and pray for Sarah, and maybe just a little one for you, too."

Rachel's face hardened. "Prayers aren't going to get her back."

14
CHAPTER

Angering Hyrum Goodman was no different than poking a hungry lion with a stick. Rachel's tongue lashing of sister wife Jessica and her sexual romps with the patriarch's son had him pacing his Goodman home office in a threatening rage. She stood hugging the archway, ready to bolt if he started to get physical.

"Rebecca," Hyrum said over Rachel's shoulder his fourth wife lingering in the hallway behind Rachel. "Get us some hot cider." The nineteen-year-old flaming redhead nodded and scurried away to the kitchen.

Hyrum took Rachel by the arm and jerked her inside the room furnished with a desk and three chairs he had pilfered from the Goodman school. The walls were bare of books, pictures—any sign of interests or life. "There are some things I need to get straight with you right now."

"Talk? Why in heaven's name aren't you and Jacob trying to find Sarah like Father promised you would?"

Rachel cringed at Hyrum's darkening expression. The cold that she suddenly felt filling the room had little to do with the bitter chill of night. He lurched for Rachel, wrapped his arms around her and held her tightly by the waist. "Imagine becoming a Goodman. When I become patriarch, I'll be worth millions." He ran a hand lightly across her buttocks. His lips brushed her cheek. "All I need is a yes."

Her heart beat a little faster, seeming to rise at the base of her throat until she felt she couldn't breathe. Somewhere in the distance a helicopter passed overhead. Father Goodman was home early. "Hyrum, your wives are right outside the door."

"So?"

"I told you—" She broke off and sighed, then tried again. "I need time."

"Too much time's the problem. Cooking up some story that a madman grabbed your daughter." He went to the window and glared out at black nothingness.

"I talked to an officer at work and—"

Hyrum wheeled around and gaped at her, feigning shock.

Rachel reeled back as if he had struck her across the face. "Oh, I didn't tell him about Sarah. Nobody even knows I'm—was—married. I pretended I had a cousin whose son ran away."

Hyrum returned to the desk chair and scowled. "You are a talkative little thing, aren't you? Always spouting off the first thing that pops into that beautiful head of yours."

"He said the boy's description could be sent out to all surrounding law enforcement agencies and entered into some national crime information center. He'd be registered as a missing child all across the country. I was thinking—" Rachel couldn't bring herself to finish the thought. She moved toward the closed door and put her hand on the handle.

Hyrum nearly jumped over the desk to get to the door. "Where do you think you're going?"

Tears began to roll down Rachel's cheeks. At his rough touch a warning shot through her. "There isn't anything more to say, is there?"

"There's a lot to say." He pulled her tight to his chest. "You drive me crazy. Marry me. I'll give you nights you couldn't even imagine."

His hands cupped her shuddering breasts. "And you're right," he whispered. "You have nothing to say, about anything."

Rachel squirmed until he released her. "You're making love to Jess out of wedlock one minute and telling me you love me the next?"

Hyrum stared at her, incredulous and offended. "I'm a little angry with you right now, but we can get past all this in one night together."

He reached out again, but Rachel jerked away. "Father wants me to marry Anna. I don't need another child." He clasped her hand as if a beau about to pop the question. "You'll be my golden girl." His hand slid around her slim waist. "If you need to be angry with someone, be angry with God for letting Sarah listen to Satan's whispers."

"Because she had the courage to want to go to high school and college? To love a man that, heaven forbid, is her age?"

He again stepped back, gave her a rueful look, and shrugged. "It isn't a woman's place to make those decisions."

"Anna? He promised you our Anna?"

Hyrum cocked a brow and nodded.

"She would kill herself first!"

"If there was the slightest chance of the family helping you find that brat, you just killed it!" His yelling resonated beyond the closed door, spilling into the ears of three of Hyrum's wives huddled by the door. Rachel could hear the name "Anna" bubbled up from their chatter.

"I'm sorry, Hyrum. Let me go. I'm so sorry," she murmured. "I won't say another word about Jess."

He released her slowly so she could sense that he was in total control of when and if she could leave. "Now you're going to tell me exactly what you said you saw."

Rachel crumpled like a broken toy. Even the slightest retort could mean, at a minimum, time locked in her room. "With Sarah gone, I must have been confused. I guess I didn't see anything."

The door flew open without even a knock. Hyrum stared at his third wife in silence while she set the tray down on the empty desk. "Can I get you anything else?"

"You can leave us alone!"

"Yes, sir."

The rebuke brought Anna's future to mind, renewing Rachel's resolve to break with her strict conditioning.

Once the sister wife was gone, Rachel deliberately turned her back on him, then turned around in calculated forethought. She blew out a long breath. Fatigue pressed down on her as though a millstone. "I'm leaving."

"I'll tell you when we're finished!" Hyrum bellowed.

Never make eye contact unless invited. She shoved the thought into an abyss.

She didn't know what terrified her more, Hyrum's clawing and threats or the sense that her life's bearings were shattering no different than a skiff in a wild open sea. Her eyes narrowed directly on his. "No. I'm leaving the family. I'm getting out and taking Anna with me."

"Keep talking back like that and you're leaving all right. For the ranch. I've heard about the fits and swearing coming out of Anna. You set a terrible example Rachel." He grabbed and mercilessly squeezed her arm. "Go pack something warm right now! Pack for Anna, too."

They both stopped talking at the sound of overhead helicopter blades beat the stillness of the icy night air. Father Goodman. His mood turned black.

"Where are we going?" Rachel asked.

"I just told you. You're both going to the ranch, before you infect the rest of the women with your blasphemy."

"Leave Anna out of this. I won't say another word about you and Jess."

Hyrum pulled himself back, his face spread with suspicion and disgust. His eyes said it all, and it terrified her. He wanted to wrap his hands around her regal throat and shake the devil out.

"Think I'm kidding?"

She blinked back tears. Defeat began overtaking opportunity. "Only Father says who goes to the ranch."

Since the blush of womanhood she had known she had power over all the Goodman men, regardless of her less-than-godly behavior. Power, at least, below the waist. She filled her mind with Sarah's face. She had turned a numb heart to dreams of the kind of love she had only read about. Hyrum wasn't a lot different than her dead husband. One sexual movement or inviting glance, and he'd transform back into that devouring lover.

Not tonight. Not any night.

"You and Jacob must be having the same dreams about me." She batted her long eyelashes flirtatiously. "And that's all they are, Hyrum—fantasies."

He shook his head. "You're incredible. One minute you're acting possessed, the next you tease me like a cheap whore." He automatically shot a look in the direction of the closed door. "I'll make sure you enjoy your time away."

She could see it in his eyes: crazy thoughts. Irrational thoughts.

He stepped aside and waved a hand to the door. "Leave me. You won't be going back to work. There may be other plans I want to discuss with Father."

Rachel bolted for the door and whisked past a swarm of women with another thing in common besides sharing Hyrum Goodman as their husband. They were all smiling.

15
CHAPTER

Charlie overslept, dreaming soft, sensuous dreams about Rachel Zimmerman. As he slowly pried open his eyes, the warm feelings made the thoughts of touching her flawless skin and forbidden fruit even more gratifying. The feel of the contours of her narrow waist, her hips, his mouth exploring every inch…

He rolled over to the digital alarm clock, dimmed by the morning light, and struggled to break free of the vision of her body pressed to his in the tangled sheets.

He wondered if she had even given him a second thought since he had made a fool of himself over a mug of hot chocolate. He had always operated under the belief that whatever he felt, the feelings were reciprocal. Were the temptations of their bodies bonding in wild passion hanging around her like the lush heavy cloud that filled his sleep?

With each waking moment, his thoughts jelled from possibility to the disappointing fact that they were mere fantasies. She was supposed to only be a lead to an inside story. But every instinct and alarm in his groin wouldn't let go that easily. He had glimpsed more in her eyes, the tempting vulnerability and sensuousness of a woman who desperately wanted to be kissed, kissed by him. She was full of mystery, living a forbidden life in a hidden world.

The thought drove him out of bed and into the shower. Finding Rachel Zimmerman in her court reporter's chair before anybody else entered the courtroom was as dependable as Wall Street's opening bell.

He let the water beat down on him in an attempt to wash away a morning hangover. His head felt as heavy as his dumbbells. Even his eyes were pulsing, as if they had their own migraine. Five hours of sleep in forty-eight wasn't enough, even for an investigative reporter.

At the ring of the phone he hopped out of the shower and groaned as the noise exploded in his dizzy head. "Charlie Carver."

"I hate to wake you from your beauty sleep, buddy, but we've got a deadline to meet. Kinda works that way with morning papers."

Charlie ignored his city editor's jab. "Hey, Theron, I've been thinking about that story on the Goodman—"

"Goodman? Will you drop that polygamist thing? It's old news. Nobody wants us parading their dirty laundry when there's nothing to hang it on."

"You don't call a guy worth a mint running his own illegal world right in our own backyard an exposé?"

Charlie waited, finally hearing a long deep sigh. "Look, I can appreciate a Chicago boy would have a hard time understanding this, but that's not news. Polygamists have been around here for eons. We leave them alone, unless a crime forces them into light."

Charlie bit down on his temper. "Unless some poor girl gets beat to death, right?"

"See you in a few minutes. Phillips just got nailed wiretapping. Get the senator against the wall before everybody else beats you to it."

"The Goodman story could tie in to the killer."

The line was silent. "Your killer? He call you again?"

"One of the Goodman women has a daughter missing. She never filed it with the police."

"Of course not. They don't get outsiders involved in anything. They're living illegally, remember?"

"There's more to it. I can feel it. Her daughter had dark hair."

"So do half the white women walking around town." Charlie could hear Liddle's mind computing. "You think your friend's holding out on you, maybe not telling you about all his girls?"

Charlie momentarily hesitated before responding. "Maybe he didn't kill her yet. Maybe he's enjoying himself first."

"Come on, Charlie, let's move on here."

"Why are you shutting me down on this, Theron?"

"Hey, buddy, we've got a serial killer out there who's stepping up his appetite to twice a month. Focus on that."

"I am," Charlie snapped and hung up.

Charlie was on his way out the door when the phone rang again.

"I told you Theron, I'll be right there."

"Shut up and listen, you sanctimonious pile of shit."

Charlie thought the same word every time he called. *Surreal*. He blinked several times, trying to collect his thoughts to prolong the conversation so his line monitor and recording equipment could trace the bastard.

"I like your taste in women," the caller said slowly as though savoring every word.

"What are you talking about?" Charlie snapped.

"My next masterpiece will be close to home. I suspect you'll see her today, then I'll get to see her tonight."

Charlie flashed on Rachel's face, but shook his head trying to imagine how the Strangler could get at her from behind the Goodman Compound's seven-foot walls. "Who? Who are you talking about?"

"I was there—at the Capital. What did you think of my latest work? Don't be shy. Tell me, what was the first thing that ran through your mind when you saw her sprawled out on that piece of velvet."

"I pitied you for being such a twisted monster who probably can't even get it up."

"I've helped put your career back on the radar screens. I've opened my soul to you and all I get back are insults."

"I didn't ask to be part of your nightmare."

"Oh, Charlie, you haven't been—yet."

16

CHAPTER

The January evening was more raw than cold. Robin Fogle could taste the pollution, growing worse by the day. The Salt Lake Valley temperature inversion had locked murky, fog-like air to the ground with no sign of lifting.

As the tall handsome-faced twenty-year-old intern exited the *Observer's* double glass entrance doors, she turned her eyes upward to the pale sliver of a moon. Looking up made her feel dizzy. She started across the side street parking lot, navigating steadily toward her late eighties Honda Civic a hundred yards away.

The brown suburban was parked next to her, among the last of the cars and trucks belonging mostly to the paper's printers and cleaning people. She noticed it because of the man in a bright red parka seemingly lifting something in or out of the back of the truck.

As she passed near the truck she pulled her key out of her purse and before she used it she looked back. The man beside her was arching his back and letting out a loud moan. "My back!" the man bellowed in a strained voice.

"Are you all right?" she asked.

"It goes out two or three times a year. Would you mind helping me lift this box of books into the truck?"

"Sure."

At her distance she couldn't see the gleaming eyes inspecting the flowing clean auburn hair and shapely figure that even her long wool coat couldn't hide.

He reached in his coat pocket with one of his latex glove-covered hands and pulled out an ether-laced washcloth. When she drew close enough he grabbed her from behind and smothered her mouth and nose until the body flopped in his arms. Once he had her inside the truck, he delicately removed her clothes then taped her mouth and secured her hands with strands of nylon to floor-anchored metal rings.

"Careful now, my beauty. We don't want to leave any marks."

"Good girl," he said, as she started to wake and squirm while he tugged off her panties and added them to the rest of her neatly folded clothes.

"We'll want them nice and clean. Everything's got to be picture perfect," he mumbled before saying a prayer. "Nod if you agree."

The girl's bugged-out eyes belied her nodding head.

"It *will* be perfect. You and I will soon become one right here in Charlie Carver's parking stall."

17
CHAPTER

Anna hasn't heard.

Rachel had no desire to announce Hyrum and the Father's marital intentions for the girl as she passed Anna and Israel, glowering at her from the living room couch. With no man in the house and the Father out of town, the two were braving being seen together each day. She prayed that she alone had seen them wrapped in each other's arms at dusk the night before.

"Israel, you know you're not supposed to be here," Rachel said unconvincingly on her way to the kitchen. They sat in silence for a moment. Anna shrunk down, heat rising in her cheeks. Israel leaned forward, his bony elbows on his knees. One word from Rachel to his father, Jacob, and it meant a week's grounding. She had watched the relationship bloom like a crocus rising out of winter snow. Though she couldn't say a word, it was the only spectrum of bright color in her darkening world.

Once the two knew Anna's fate, both would be mute witnesses to another marriage conceived and blessed by Father Goodman. Rachel stubbornly clenched her jaw. She wasn't about to destroy their last moments of innocence. Rachel could feel new awakenings rolling through her in waves. Sarah and Anna had barely dared say aloud what Rachel's heart and mind had held silently captive for years.

Temptation was too difficult to resist, so she slipped into the shadowed recess of the hallway to pluck out bits of conversation.

"You do not!" Anna said to Israel, her lips a feminine bow set in a fine-featured oval face.

"I do. I believe a woman should have the right to marry whoever she wants."

Rachel leaned back against the wall, fearing the couple might sense they were being watched.

"There are things we have to accept," Israel said.

Rachel could see, even from a distance, the shakes going through him like the tremors before an earthquake.

"What in the world are you trying to say, Israel?"

He released a long, slow breath. "I heard my father talking to Uncle Hyrum last night."

Anna shoved back wispy pieces of her fine ash blond braided hair. "What are you trying to tell me?"

Rachel watched the nausea swirling through the young suitor. Suddenly Anna looked vulnerable, a word Rachel had never associated with the girl in her life. Strong, intelligent, bull-headed, and equal, but never vulnerable. She could never imagine Anna living as a foot servant to some man.

The words came out at gunfire speed. "You've been committed to Uncle Hyrum. He's marrying you whether we like it or not. You know, that's how it works."

"What?" she whispered almost to herself.

"Uncle Hyrum was going to tell you tomorrow."

Anna bolted to her feet, shaking as if a palsy victim just as Rachel rushed into the room. "Uncle Hyrum's—" She choked on the words. Rachel had seen it time after time: family girls committed without even a tender word or warning. Uncle Hyrum was only one of the tall shadows standing over her life.

Israel's chin quivered. Scarce tears lined his cheeks. "I shouldn't have told you."

Anna's pleading eyes turned to Rachel. "It isn't true, is it?"

Rachel rushed to the frantically blinking and disheveled girl and took her in her arms. She automatically kissed her hair and ran a hand across her tightly woven braids.

"Shh," Rachel crooned. "Israel, please go home now."

She held Anna fast in her arms, feeling as useless as a glass shield to protect her from tomorrow. "I have a plan. We need time to talk—alone."

18
CHAPTER

There was nothing arbitrary in where to sit at all Goodman Compound dinner tables: women and children in assigned seats in the dining room, the Lord of the house served a better meal in a private setting.

Israel never ate much whenever his father settled into his chair at the head of the blond oak dining room table that seated thirty. He picked at the crispy brown noodle edges of his reheated tuna casserole, freshened up by the women with the addition of frozen peas. Shame washed through him as though an icy mountain runoff.

Sister mother Elizabeth had been forced to move down two chairs by her twelve-year-old-son, full of himself for having entered the Aaronic Priesthood. Israel had never abused control over his mother once he had assumed his religious rights of manhood. He had silently watched how brazenly his brothers asserted their powers over the women of the house with their father's blessing.

Jacob devoured the last bite of his gravy-covered rump roast, leaned back and cleared his throat, silencing all dinner conversation buzz. "I wasn't home five minutes and Lord above, I couldn't believe it. Rachel Zimmerman was raising Cain again."

Israel stiffened, anticipating what would come next.

"Israel, I understand you've been socializing with Anna Zimmerman. Is that right, son?"

He surveyed the sea of small and large faces, finally homing in on his father's demanding stare.

"Out with it, son. You *know* the rules."

"He's been kissing her," little Jacob Paul spouted out, then got a sharp elbow in his ribs from one of the sister wives.

"Well?"

A hoarse, tortured sound wrenched out of Israel's throat. The feelings ripped loose from their chains. He clamped a shaking hand over his mouth, trying to swallow back his words. He couldn't let them loose, or things would never be the same with his father. Praying silently for God's help, he summoned the strength to quiet his screaming heart. He was the son of the oldest son of the Patriarch. Conflicting urgings flooded his mind. *Deny, better yet, destroy the feelings. Make your father proud.*

"I'm talking to you, Israel. I hope what your brother's saying isn't true. Father has decided that Anna Zimmerman will marry Hyrum. These aren't matters for children."

Israel forced his eyes away from the inquisition to the blackness outside the dining room window. His memory wouldn't let go of Anna, laughing, teasing his tongue with hers. The horror in her eyes when he dripped the poisonous words into her ears. *If I'm a child, what's Anna?* He almost set the thought free, but resisted.

"I love her, Dad." He felt hollow as he stared out at the drooping jaws and dead silence. He felt so alone he ached. At that moment he desperately wanted a different last name, to be somewhere else, someone else.

Jacob rose like a pistol-shot grizzly from his chair. "Did I hear you right?"

The question was perfunctory. At this point, there was no turning back. Israel nodded, his stomach turning in anticipation of his punishment. He drew himself up. His eyes narrowed at the lynch mob stares. "I can't help how I feel."

His father bolted around the table and yanked Israel's quivering frame out of the room. He stared defiantly at the silent heads he knew would be listening, first for the sound of a slamming door, then for the number of yelps and screams to follow each belt whipping.

19
CHAPTER

Live by the rules or pay the price. Rachel had always held on to the belief that good was good and bad was bad. Gray areas were for the poor souls in Babylon. *Sacrifice today for a heavenly tomorrow.* She had actually believed that, which now seemed a long time ago.

Anna's desperate pleas for any punishment but the ranch echoed with danger warnings in Rachel's mind. Her mouth twisted in a sad parody of a smile as she glanced at the teenage girl snuggled asleep against her shoulder. Like her, Anna was a victim of one of God's crueler jokes, the intoxicating effects of unharnessed power. Living under male domination was a truth she had tried to flee from since childhood, but had found it too blinding a light since Sarah's disappearance. The realization that she had willingly joined in the third generation of Goodman women to be duped into demeaning servitude, and was allowing Anna to be the fourth, made her feel nauseous.

She kissed Anna's golden chestnut hair. In less than an hour they would be at the ranch. In the back of her mind, she could hear Sarah's honey-sweet voice calling for help.

Rachel told herself it didn't matter. Not another day would slither by without answers that led her back to her baby.

The voices of the Goodman brothers in the Suburban front seat had softened to whispers. She studied Jacob and Hyrum from her backseat vantagepoint. They looked freshly clean-cut, like missionaries in their dark suits, with fanatical beliefs as unbending as the starched collars of their white dress shirts. She wanted to laugh, not with humor, but with the energy of her new understanding and determination.

Jacob lifted his arm over the back seat. "Pretty quiet back there. Thinking about things?"

"Yes, sir. Thinking about things," she answered with a bite in her voice.

A lingering headache began pounding to the beat of her heart. She reached up and rubbed her temples with two fingers.

Jacob's scolding eyes melted briefly into something personal. "I know it hasn't been easy, with Sarah running away and all, but you just can't act like this."

Anna stirred, licked her lips, and settled back into slumber. "You'll wake Anna," Rachel whispered. "And Sarah didn't run away."

Jacob rolled his eyes. "Believe what you need to."

Her gaze fixed on his smirking face, and a strange heat crept through her. In the dashboard panel glow he looked and sounded just like his father. She put it down to exhaustion, sat back, and closed her eyes.

Jacob turned back to conversing with his brother, raising his voice. "She's one stubborn woman."

"You got that right, Brother. Hopeless. Dry as a Kansas cornfield and still acts as if we're supposed to kiss her feet. Pretty obvious where Anna got her smart mouth from."

Jacob grunted in agreement. "The sooner we separate those two, the better for everybody."

Hyrum turned sharply onto the snow-caked dirt road that wound for three desolate miles to the Goodman summer home. Both men heaved a sigh once the ranch was in sight.

"Wake up, girls, and I mean that in more ways than one," Hyrum said.

Sarah's image floated up in Rachel's memory, and she blinked it away before it could undermine the focus she would need as her daughter's sole champion.

"How long do we have to stay here?" Anna got out between a stretching yawn.

The rugged lines on Jacob's face were set like stone, deeply etched from a life of determination. He looked at both women sideways.

~

"Why talk about the end, when a new understanding is just about to begin?" He shook his head a little in self-amusement, pulled a roll of mints from his pants pocket, and thumbed one off. "Want one?" Both women shook their heads.

"I'll have one of those. I love spearmint," Hyrum said. He gave Anna a wry look. "The last thing I need is a loose cannon for a bride."

"I'm not marrying you!"

Hyrum's backhanded blow to her face was swift and harder than any from her mother.

"Don't," Rachel ordered, reaching out as if to hold back his arm.

The gesture was dangerous, and she caught it and pulled it back quickly. No need to incite a beating before they were even out of the car. She stared after the two men as they stomped away through fresh fallen snow. "Be smart Anna. Keep them off guard or we'll never escape," she whispered.

"Jesus, Mary, and Joseph," Donald Goodman's first wife uttered when Rachel and Anna traipsed in behind the men. "What have we got here?" She glared at the two women as if a drill sergeant inspecting raw recruits.

"Father said he'd call you," Hyrum said while sloughing off his overcoat and gloves.

Jacob pecked his natural mother on the cheek. "How you been, Mom?"

"He did give me a little idea about all the fuss going on at the compound." Ida turned dark eyes on Rachel. "Heavens be, you've got everybody upset, girl."

Rachel scrunched her face into a look of utter disgust as she took off her coat and helped Anna do the same.

"You're here so it doesn't happen again. Least that's what Father told me."

Anna sniffed at the appealing smell emanating from the kitchen.

Ida gave Jacob a hardy hug. "Gotta take care of my boys here." Rachel watched her pull back to enjoy the expected look of delight in her son's widening eyes.

"Don't tell me. Swedish meatballs, mashed potatoes and string bean casserole."

Ida beamed and hugged him again. "Your favorite."

"Good, I'm hungry!" Anna said impulsively.

A smile of wry amusement curled up a corner of her mouth. "I only made enough for the boys. You two go up to bed now. We'll begin in the morning."

Anna winced. "I'm not really that hungry anyway," she said as the two women headed up the creaky staircase.

"Rachel, you're in the first room to the left. Anna's two doors down," Ida said.

Rachel looked into her eyes; her gaze was predatory. She was tempted to snap off a sharp retort, but nothing formed in her dry mouth. She moved too slowly. Her muscles tightened and her face muted out her thoughts.

20
CHAPTER

Through the long hours of the first three days, Rachel gained a new respect and sympathy for the life sentence of isolation Ida had endured for six years. Never did she utter a word of complaint. The woman had nothing to live for but prayer, short summers and even shorter winter visits from family—and finally, God's work.

The house smelled of furniture polish and liquid cleaner from compulsive daily cleaning. While Ida mostly grunted and paced, her scorching silence spoke volumes to Rachel. Ida Goodman's singular purpose had narrowed down to shepherding the Goodman family women along the path leading to the celestial kingdom. Who better than her knew how narrow the path.

Rachel tightly wrapped the bottom of the floor-length flannel nightgown below her knees and knelt on the grave-cold wood floor near the hearth of the living room flagstone fireplace. She signaled for Anna to do the same.

"Our heavenly Father, please cleanse the souls of these two wicked women." Rachel quickly closed her eyes when Ida popped one eye open to see if she needed to pounce on either of her captives for not closing theirs. "Their souls are full of lust, perversion and deceit. Their hearts and dreams are filled with adultery and fornication. As a child of the great nation of Israel, I lay at your feet these matrimonial offenses to—"

Anna opened her eyes and rose to her feet. "I didn't do any of those things."

Ida clamped a pinching grip on the nape of the child's neck and drove her back to the cold floor. Her legs buckled as her strength and resistance drained away. Anna might have fallen to the floor if not for Rachel's guiding hands. She slid an arm around her waist in an instant, catching her on the way back down. Anna turned her face into Rachel's shoulder and wept, the tears soaking the shoulder of her sister mother's gown.

"Shame on you, Ida, for praying such lies!"

"Move an inch, and Father Goodman's belt will keep you on your knees."

Rachel couldn't offer Anna protection, only comfort. She let her cry it out, guiding her hands back into steepled fingers, and gently pressing her eyes closed. The last thing she needed was any of the Goodman family interrupting her now, when answers felt within reach.

Ida edged away from the two, lifting her face to the heavens.

"Our heavenly Father, the sins of these two liars are like ripples in the pond, reaching out and touching the other Goodman women's lives with evil thoughts and actions that could send their souls to hell. I know thou can't forgive them, God, until they release themselves from Satan's power. They've turned to the world outside for answers to a woman's role on this earth. Help me. Through thee, bring back their faith and understanding of thy eternal plan. Release them from blasphemous questioning."

White light beamed in from the living room window. The three were gathered in the amber rectangle, providing the first bit of warmth to Ida's damning words.

"God, thou hast revealed to us through biblical law and Latter-Day revelation, that thou, too, are a polygamist—and without sin. Please give each of them understanding and strength to follow thine example and principles set forth by my husband, our own beloved Patriarch. I say these things in the name of Jesus Christ. Amen."

The fire went out of Rachel abruptly. She heaved a sigh and continued in silent prayer. The maddening noise polluting her thoughts as if an advancing brain tumor began to subside. In hot tears, she pleaded for God's forgiveness. Donald Goodman's first wife walked away and slowly ascended the stairs.

"Hurry up, girls, there are chores to do." She paused and locked both hands on the wobbly rail. "After you read your scriptures, clean the house."

"We've cleaned the house for three days. There wasn't a speck of dirt to begin with," Anna said.

"After you clean the house," Ida's unforgiving eyes fell to Rachel, still on her knees in prayer; "You two can start cleaning the barn. There's enough crap in those stalls to keep you busy for at least a couple of days."

"I've had it with that bitch," Anna said flatly.

Rachel broke free of her trance. She took Anna's temper and language in stride. It was nothing new to her. At her age, those would have been her thoughts a little less colorfully stated.

Three hours of scripture reading and two hours of prayer had been centering to Rachel, but she could see they were stirring Anna to the breaking point.

Anna shrugged off her sister mother's attempt to comfort her. She sniffed and swiped at her dripping nose with the sleeve of her nightgown. "If you knew what I do, you'd—" Anna whispered.

"Say it, Anna, for heaven's sake, tell me."

Anna shook her head.

"What are you afraid of? What somebody would do to you?"

The teenager dropped her head into her hands and sobbed.

~

"Anna," Rachel said softly, patting her shoulder. "Does this have anything to do with Sarah?" She pressed her fist against her mouth preparing for the answer.

"I…I think so."

"Let's try this another way," Rachel said evenly. "Did you and Sarah share a secret that could get you both into trouble?"

With her face still hidden in her hands, Anna nodded.

Rachel gave her a narrow look and lowered her voice. "You're going to tell me that secret right now!"

Fresh tears glazed across Anna's eyes. "I can't or the same thing could happen to me."

"What same thing?" Rachel felt horrified at the inference.

Anna lowered her hands as if closing a black curtain. She gritted her teeth and looked into Rachel's crazed eyes. "I don't know what happened to Sarah."

"But there is something you do know, damnit!" Rachel lurched and grabbed Anna by the arm. "Now tell me."

"Close that dirty mouth right now!" Ida bristled from behind Rachel, then whacked her on the back of her head. Rachel whirled around to her attacker. Heat flared in her eyes, and she shot up a finger in warning. "Don't you dare hit me again, or I'll knock you right on your head!"

"No. You *listen*, you child of Satan," Ida said, stabbing Rachel in the chest with a forefinger, backing her to the wall. "Get upstairs and get dressed right now!"

Rachel's brows knitted. She bit down on her lower lip. Her expression turned from shock to apologetic.

"You'll go to the barn and shovel crap until it's jammed under your fingernails."

Father Goodman isn't far behind.

The eyes staring at Rachel were made of glass. She could obey every humiliation a little longer. Anna was ready to talk.

21
CHAPTER

Sitting at his oval glass kitchen table, Charlie stared unseeing at his calico cat licking at the edges of her saucer half filled with cream. The fear in Rachel Zimmerman's eyes played back in his head. She had missed work for days without telling a soul why, or if she was even coming back. One man could give him an idea if she would be back, the man who got her the job, the man whose voice was as deep as the Strangler's—Donald Goodman.

~

The telephone rang just as Charlie's hand closed over his front door knob. He felt his heart in his throat all of a sudden. Intuition turned him around. He picked up the receiver as if it was filled with nitro, and stiffly sat down in his living room reading chair.

"This is Charlie."

"I had a Technicolor dream last night. Do you want me to tell you about it?"

Charlie felt his face flush with heat. "You're calling me at home now."

"Unlisted numbers are child's play to uncover. I see you're not a believer, are you?"

The caller spoke quickly, but without a sense of urgency, so his deep rich monologue came off so smoothly Charlie never wanted to interrupt, especially with his line bugged.

"What don't I believe in?"

"You don't believe in a higher power that directs good and evil. Running around with sluts and atheists…I don't know why I'm even calling you."

"And what I don't know is what in the hell's going on in your sick mind!"

The line crackled with only the sound of inhaling a slow breath. "Do you want to hear the dream? I've scrambled your signal, so you can't trace this call. Just shut up and listen."

Strategies banged around in Charlie's head as if a pinball.

"Good. She looked directly into my eyes. Oh, Charlie, the woman's soul was absolutely beautiful. She'll make a great companion."

"Soul? What are you talking about?"

"You don't listen!"

"You'll have to explain." Charlie's tone and pace was deliberately slow, but not demeaning.

"I have many wives and lives inside me."

"You're collecting souls? You're a polygamist?"

"And true to our prophet's teachings, I'll soon be a God. My clay jar was empty. I've had to refill it with heavenly spirits. I carry their essence inside me."

Charlie squinted. "Will you ever fill the jar and not need to kill any more?"

"You have been listening. Too bad you understand nothing—but you soon will."

Charlie's eyes popped open and enlarged. "You never call unless—" He felt sick. He tried to recapture a sound that was both fearful and respectful. "You're telling me you've killed or are going to again, until your soul is filled with these…Spirits? How many more?"

"I'll know. God will tell me when we're ready to join Him. You've violated her. Now I'm going to save her."

Charlie raised his eyebrows. "Who are you talking about?"

"I prayed for God's intervention or enlightenment until the sun came up." The caller sighed. "It's been so painful. I know God's got a purpose in all this, but sometimes it's hard."

"You keep talking about God. That's bullshit. You're raping and killing children."

"What are you talking about?"

"You know damn well what I'm talking about."

Charlie felt the draft-like silence.

"Children are closer to God."

"You're insane."

"You think I—or you—control our destiny? You are *so* naïve. I'll really enjoy taking my time with the next one. Knowing she was one of yours will make it even better."

"I want a front row seat when they fry your ass."

"The difference between you and me, Charles, is that I believe in something. I can even summon God's power and harness it when I have to. *You're* the one who's going to burn—in hell."

"If I do, you'll be there to see it," Charlie snapped and hung up. He reached for his phone directory as his mind scrambled through the relationships, the lovemaking, and the three women he had to warn.

"Marsha, it's Charlie—Charlie Carver."

"Charlie, it's been months. I'm on the air in thirty minutes. Can I call you back?"

"No it can't wait. The Strangler's still calling me."

"You told me you didn't want the news to cover that."

Charlie's face was hot. "Listen carefully, Marsha. He's threatened to kill one of the women I've dated. There have only been three, starting with us, since I moved to Salt Lake."

"I'm too old for that pervert. He goes for young blood, doesn't he?"

"The oldest we know about is twenty-three."

"I'm pushing thirty-three. Thanks for the warning. You should see the sick love letters and stuff I get from dirty little minds in dark corners. It comes with being in their living room every night."

A momentary silence assured him his warning was computing.

"Are you seeing anybody right now?" she asked.

"That isn't why I called. Just please be extra careful until we catch the monster."

"I've got to run Charlie."

~

The second woman, his personal fitness trainer until he landed a date, had gone bohemian and was last heard of sharing the back of a Volkswagen van with a sculptor in Santa Fe. She was out of the picture, leaving only the inaccessible Rachel Goodman.

CHAPTER 22

Charlie slowly blew out his breath and ran his hand along his hair all the way to the end of his ponytail. His eyes lazily traveled around Donald Goodman's mahogany paneled law office waiting room. He expected no less of the offices of Goodman and Tate, occupying a third of the top floor of the prestigious Eagle Tower building complex.

He was running a little low on adrenaline after using his day's supply on a stammering Senator accused of dipping into the wrong honey pots.

Rather than blankly rifling through the usual waiting room *Forbes*, *Business Week* and dog-eared *People* magazines, he rested his eyes on a stark empty marble and glass coffee table. A fortyish wisp of a woman, whose caved-in cheeks and pointed features resembled a just-hatched sparrow, neurotically tapped her pencil with every incoming call. The shifty-eyed receptionist seemed the size of a child at the high reception desk.

"Now tell me again why you're here, Mr. Carver," she asked.

"I just have a couple of issues Mr. Goodman could help me clear up," Charlie returned too sharply. His tone revealed a certain hostility when his instincts told him to reveal nothing at this point. He mentally kicked himself for the tactical blunder and studied the built-in bookshelves lined with aged maroon and sand-colored books. He squinted, seeing the words "Constitution" and "Utah Laws" jump out on every shelf. He knew he looked restless, edgy.

"I need more than that," the receptionist said, tapping the eraser tip of her pencil to her lips. "Mr. Goodman has to be in court in less than an hour. He can't meet with you."

Charlie rose from his seat and slowly sidled to the desk to allow time to think of a motivating reason for the interview. For the first time Charlie noticed the ego wall directly behind the receptionist, covered with certificates and commendations. Donald Goodman was formidable.

The bird woman watched Charlie carefully. Her brows popped up jack-in-the-box style at the first recognition that the reporter before her had a ponytail. It had to mean trouble.

"It's a private matter. I know he'll want to see me."

"Please, enlighten me." Her lips drew into a tight smile.

Charlie rested folded arms on the reception counter. They squared off, staring at each other no different than a pair of gunslingers. He glared at her sharp facial angles, and even sharper eyes that narrowed through horn-rimmed glasses as if she had x-ray vision. Pride and anger flooded his chest. He loved this part of his job.

"Then the story will run without him even getting to comment." Charlie shook his head. "That isn't something he would want, now is it?"

Like a cornered animal, she sat stiffly as the walls she was to protect around her employer. "No, no I don't think he would," she said.

"I think you're lying," the receptionist snapped, stubbornly daring to take a step onto that proverbial thin ice.

Charlie shrugged. "Okay, just thought I'd extend the courtesy." He turned on one heel and headed for the door.

"Wait!" He slowly raised his head with a heavy-lidded gaze. The feeling of control was intoxicating.

Within less than a minute she was on her feet, ushering him past a row of closed doors until they reached the double nine-foot doors leading into Goodman's office.

Donald Goodman sat in the leather executive chair behind his desk. His office was dimly lit with ambient light from sheer, drawn curtains. A standing lamp bathed his face in shadow highlights, giving his chiseled chin and foreboding eyebrows a haunted look that seemed appropriate.

Everything about the office was modern, sophisticated to the smallest detail, everything but the hidden practices of the man before him.

Charlie stared down at his open notepad, wondering what was driving him to such a reckless and probably pointless confrontation. Suddenly his beeper went off. He fished the cellular phone from his pocket and punched in the number.

"Just one moment, Mr. Goodman."

Goodman's brows tugged together, digging a deep furrow into his forehead. "I have to be in court in less than an hour." He glared at the phone. "You've got five minutes."

Charlie made a helpless motion with his hands and pushed the end button just as his city editor picked up his receiver.

"I'm doing a story on polygamy and wanted to get your opinion on the outcome of the Jacobson trial," he said, gazing at Goodman, whose mouth was pinched tight.

"Why should I weigh in on that?"

"Let's not play games, Mr. Goodman."

Goodman bristled and gritted his teeth. "It's you who's playing games, Mr. Carver. I think a little conversation with your publisher is in order."

Charlie managed a wry smile. "I'm not here about the Jacobson story," he confessed with a man-to-man look. "I'm here for *your* story. You can either give it to me from your point of view, or I'll dig it out."

Goodman scowled. "What's this shakedown really all about?"

"Polygamy, Mr. Goodman. I don't need to tell you it's a pretty hot topic right now."

The attorney was clearly incensed. "I don't believe you." He reached for his Rolodex and thumbed through the alphabet, then punched in the number without looking up.

"Mr. Bartholomew, please. Yes, this is Donald Goodman." His eyes rose long enough to give Charlie a narrow look.

Charlie watched stone-faced, his expression giving away none of the tension that was tightening inside him like a watch spring. Goodman's deep broadcast-quality voice seemed vaguely familiar. "Go ahead. I don't need the publisher's approval for a story," he said smoothly. His city editor's demands to drop *any* story pursuit relating to polygamy reverberated in his mind.

Goodman sat motionless awaiting the connection, his face as dark and somber as his clothing. He looked younger than his sixty-two years. Silver flecks were still dominated by thick curly brown hair. He was the rare kind of man whose opinions and counsel were seldom, if ever, challenged.

"Yes, give me his voicemail then. Glendon, this is Donald Goodman," he said. "I'm looking across my desk at one of your reporters here, a Charlie Carver, who claims he's got clearance to dig up whatever tall tales and dirt he can about me and my family. I think he wants to throw holy water on me to see if steam rises," he said and after a moment's silence nodded and smiled. "Get back to me soon, will you? I'm sending him on his way."

"I'm just doing my job," Charlie said evenly. "I don't draw conclusions. I just let the facts lead me to whatever form the story takes. If you hold polygamy as a sacred belief, then what's the harm in sharing a bit of your beliefs with the public?"

"Polygamy is illegal, Mr. Carver. Go crawl under another rock. This interview is over. No sound bites today." He rose from his chair, picked up a legal brief and walked back and forth behind the desk with his head buried in thoughts that didn't include Charlie Carver.

"If it makes you feel any better, I plan on talking to the Governor, too. I know there are hordes of people in this town who want the Church's founding doctrine to go away and get back to normal." Charlie scratched the trace of stubble on his chin. "Problem is, I don't define normal quite the same way you do."

Goodman's eyes sparkled at the prospect of crossing intellectual swords. "Normal. Here's a little defining thought. Polygamy is legal in sixty-five percent of the countries on this planet."

"I didn't know that," Charlie confessed.

Goodman shook his head. "You see. You thought you came here with all the answers, when you don't even know the questions. Goodbye, Mr. Carver."

"And as the lords of your paradise on earth, your job is to keep your flock and multi million-dollar empire all headed in the right direction?"

Goodman's eyes flashed at such blatant insolence. "Do I need to throw you out myself?"

Charlie couldn't help but smile. "Sometimes I affect people that way. I'll see myself out."

Goodman turned his back. His head dipped into his legal brief.

"Rachel Zimmerman."

The attorney's head jerked up similar to a marionette's. He slowly turned his expression somber. "Yes?"

"Where is she? You got her the job, and nobody at work has heard from her in days. Is she coming back?"

Goodman nodded with a knowing grin. "So we finally get to the point after all. This is all about a woman you're attracted to."

Lacking a good comeback, Charlie strode to the open office doors. He gave one quick glance back at the man whose facial expression was melting back into grim. He knew he couldn't afford to harass the power broker any longer, but that familiar feeling always preceded a great story. "Then she won't be back?"

"I doubt it. I understand she'd rather stay at home with her children," Goodman said.

Charlie cocked his head. "I understand she only has one child—and she's been missing for weeks."

Charlie watched Goodman's face tighten. "Once again you've been misinformed," he said and shut the double doors, inches from Charlie's face.

23
CHAPTER

The day had beaten Rachel down physically and mentally more than any since she had arrived at the Goodman Ranch. Constant praying and sober introspection under Ida's steely glare wre wearing her nerves and patience to the breaking point. Daylight was fading to black, and Anna was still not back from shoveling out the last stall in the barn.

Frantic searches to try and find something, anything that would spark a connection to Sarah's disappearance had led her nowhere. Anna had stopped talking altogether. Her marriage to her uncle seemed inevitable and more than her psyche could harbor without shutting down.

"Heavens be, what's taking that girl so long?" Ida spat out between bites of homemade bread dripping with raspberry preserves.

"I can't imagine. We were all but done an hour ago." The homey smell of the just-baked bread wafted over to Rachel, but she knew better than to ask for anything that wasn't offered.

"I'll tell you what. You two aren't going back to Salt Lake until that job's done. And done right."

Rachel mulled over the most recent threat, sitting back in the kitchen chair and crossing her arms. "It must get painfully lonely out here," she said.

"What?" Ida asked, arching one brow. "Sure," she mumbled, giving her attention over to the last bite of bread.

"Why you? Why should you have to live here all alone?" Rachel mentally kicked herself for prying open a box of dynamite.

Ida took a gulp of her milk. "You think the world's supposed to turn on your command, don't you?" she snapped.

"I was just—"

Ida launched into another sermon on a woman's heavy burdens in life and how they should be viewed as opportunities to humble oneself before God.

Rachel could see in Ida's wounded look that she wanted to slap her on the face to make her stop staring—and hit her again for being young and beautiful. The old woman's hand tightened around the milk glass so hard that Rachel held her breath waiting for it to shatter.

"You've got *other* things to worry about," Ida said.

Rachel heard the front door slam and listened for the sounds of Anna shedding her coat and stomping into the kitchen to report the job finished, ending their week in purgatory. No Anna. No announcement.

Ida stormed out of the kitchen to the base of the entry staircase. "Hey, Anna, you ready to have me inspect the barn?" She clucked her disapproval of the teenager's coat draped on the entry floor, only a few feet from the coat closet. Rachel quickly scooped up the jacket and righted the home's perfect order before the old woman could get out a word.

"She's just exhausted. It looks great. You'll see."

"We'll see," Ida said. She tugged her down-filled parka off its hanger and headed out the door.

Rachel climbed the stairs and slipped into Anna's room, feigning calm at the sight of the trembling, ash-white girl.

"Should I draw you a hot bath?" Anna sat as though she was hypnotized. "I bet you're freezing. I'm still trying to warm up." Rachel sat beside her and brushed a hand tenderly over her braided hair.

Anna turned and looked right through her. "I'll be a good girl. I'll be a *real* good girl."

"You already are, dear." Rachel dutifully leaned Anna back and yanked off her muddy, manure-caked sneakers, then her jeans, soaked from the knees down. "You should have left those shoes—"

"I'll do everything Uncle Hyrum says," Anna said to herself, nodding. She turned her face up to her sister mother, her big brown eyes swimming in tears. In a thin, trembling voice she said, "Do you think it will be enough?"

Rachel held her breath. "There's nothing to be afraid of, dear."

Anna wrapped her arms around Rachel's waist and held her tight. "I, I *can* be a good girl."

Each word sounded like a dagger, driving deep as the child's soul. It was what every Goodman man wanted to hear. The words coming out of Anna's mouth sounded dirty and pathetic.

"He'll kill me," Anna murmured.

Without allowing herself to question the wisdom and sickening feelings of where her questions were leading her, Rachel knew the answer might save both of their lives.

"Who, dear? Who's trying to kill you?" She could hear Ida ascending the stairs. She knew she was standing outside Anna's door. She put her index finger to her lips. "Shh, she's out there."

Anna made a drugged nod. "I can. I can be a good wife. A good mother. A good—"

Rachel tenderly put her cupped hand over Anna's mouth and whispered in her ear, "You'll always be safe with me. No matter what." She pulled the closest person to her own child against her chest and rocked her harder, blinking back hot, stinging tears. "No matter what, you'll always be safe." She kept rocking her until she stopped her compulsive quivering, the tears ran out, and she fell asleep. Rachel tucked her under the covers, then went to the kitchen, sliced off a hardy piece of Ida's forbidden homemade bread, covered it with butter and jam, and took it and a tall glass of milk to Anna's nightstand. She sat there with loving eyes and aching heart, watching Anna sleep.

She would protect her.

The way she had never had the courage to protect Sarah.

The house had been silent for a long while when Rachel eased away from Anna and slipped out of her room. She left the nightstand light on in case she woke up with the same blinding fear that drove her to the escape of sleep.

The loud ticking alarm clock on Rachel's bedside table read twelve fifteen. Besides the predictable creaking and popping moan of the house, everything was dark, including Rachel's thoughts.

Her fears grew deeper with each corresponding deduction. She dragged herself out of bed, went to the closet, pulled out her still-drenched jeans and pulled them on. She was aware of their icy contact on her warmed legs. Her eyes strayed to the window, where just beyond the glass her dreams had been punctured by the looming vision of where Anna had come from before becoming a human zombie—the barn.

24
CHAPTER

He glared at Marsha Gallenson's long, lean neck as she gulped down the last of her vodka martini. "You know what I mean by a little party," she told him, then laughed that sensual, deep laugh of hers again.

"I have to get up early for work," she said without even a hesitating step as he guided her to the garage under the Walker Towers Building. She was trying to show him that she was different from the stiff, plastic smiling robot she projected on television at six and ten every evening. She could be playful, teasing, and adventurous. Her efforts weren't going unrecognized. He got the message. The chance meeting at the popular sports and media watering hole had been no chance at all. She was even exceeding expectations. Although still above par, her speech was getting a bit slurry. It made the television woman more human, touchable.

He insisted they take his truck, even though the tingling invitation was to her American Towers condo, just three blocks from the downtown nightclub. He slid in without reacting to a pounding impulse to pull her close, taste her mouth and put his hands around her elegant, pulsing throat. He could wait. This was going to be the best.

Marsha kept talking rapid-fire, a classic overachiever response to even a moment of silence. She needed to feel in control. He understood the compulsion completely. It was nice to have something so important in common. He caught himself liking her for just a moment. She was going to be different than the others: informed, intelligent, electric.

"I really do have to get up early," she said, stroking, then tucking a shock of dark chocolate hair over her ear. "You said you move money around. What does that mean?"

His smile was warm, genuine. "Back on the beat again?"

"I'm sorry. I'm a little nervous, I guess." She impulsively giggled. "I don't know what got into me. I'm really not—you know, nosy."

It's wearing off. Didn't use enough. Toxicologists will still find traces.

"I guess I'm a little nervous myself. I hate dating, don't you?" He sighed. The statement was partly true. "Tell you what. Let's fix a great breakfast together, then I'll leave."

She led him up the winding metal staircase to her master bedroom loft. They weren't going to have breakfast, and they both knew it before they got out of his truck. The bedroom had canvas colored walls, and matching peach tapestry bedspread and drapes that accented a near floor-to-ceiling window overlooking downtown Salt Lake City.

"This place is my little hideaway from the world," she said in a tone as soft and fluffy as the sheepskin rug spread in front of the gas fireplace opposite the king-sized bed.

He quietly surveyed her work area. Laptop computer, HP printer, tabletop copy machine, a small television with a built-in VCR, brass-framed photos of family, celebrities, and friends, and inspirational and motivational gems of wisdom.

Such a full life. But you don't trick me. Always teasing. Torturing. You like torture, don't you?

Marsha paused and stared into his eyes. He could see a danger alert cross her face. Something more, too. The edginess excited her.

"Let's go fix that breakfast," she said.

He lightly grabbed her by the arm. *I still have a little powder left.* "Great idea. I'll make the bloody Marys." He followed her slightly swaying hips down the staircase. *Trying to give it to me, aren't you, you little tease?*

She turned, perhaps to see if she was imagining what she thought she saw in his expression. He rolled his sparkling emerald eyes and an inviting little half-smile appeared. Even though he was twice her age, he knew he still had it. He was a master at this, if necessary. "You're absolutely beautiful." He continued to beam. "I really mean it."

Marsha swooshed her hair back as if she were a Revlon makeup model. "Thanks."

"I should leave and let you get some sleep," he said just above a whisper.

He could see she was disappointed at the suggestion. She needed genuine talk and feelings in her life. Like all women, she had needs. He had needs.

Marsha made the first sexual gesture in the dance. He loved it when they took the first step into the darkness.

Knowing his eyes were fixated on her generous chest, protruding, invitingly out of her skin-tight wool turtleneck sweater, she breathed heavily and drew close to him. She lifted his suit jacket high enough to place her long, flawless arms around his waist and used her hips to grind against him ever so lightly. Yes, she loved control. She was without question the most desirable so far. He felt himself instantly grow rigid down the right side of his trousers. It wasn't the anticipation of sex driving him wild. He planned something more orgasmic, at least for him.

No more powder. Let her take us there.

"I think I changed my mind," she whispered in his ear. She leaned back and started to undo his belt buckle. "Let's go back upstairs," she purred.

He kissed her neck. Not a freckle, a blemish. A woman had never undressed him. She had no pretensions. Apparently she always got her own way, even in the bedroom. He could wait.

"Now there's a great idea!" Marsha said as she slowly unbuttoned his white, starched shirt. She rubbed her palm back and forth across his firm maleness. She pushed him away just as he began to respond and whisked up to the top of the staircase. "I'm going to put on something a little more fun. Don't come up until I tell you."

Who's raping whom?

Marsha unbuckled and pried open the silver metal button of her curve-hugging black jeans. She slid off her sweater and arched her back with a teasing smile as he looked up at her in the loft. He gave her the salivating response he knew she was after.

"No, not yet. I'll tell you when."

No, I'll tell you when.

He still had his trousers on when he ascended the stairs at her breathy command. She wore three-inch heels and a purple sheer nighty with matching thong panties. She lifted her arms in a come hither position. "I'm ready."

"Perfect," he said, kicking off his shoes.

He scooped her into his arms as if she weighed no more than a child. Maybe it was a mistake to go for an older woman. Young girls were easier. She was beginning to trick him into thinking she was different than the others. She wasn't different. It wouldn't be different.

"You're really strong," she sighed, joining him in kicking off her shoes.

He carried her over to the spectacular view out the expansive bedroom window. He felt as if he was holding up his most prized trophy. He squeezed out invading sentimentality. The fact that he liked her just made their eternal soul sharing even more precious. He sauntered over to the bed. With her still cradled to his chest, he bent down, allowing her to pull back the covers. He set her down gingerly on the champagne colored satin sheet, took off his pants, and rolled on a condom. Semen is no different than blood in a DNA analysis. She giggled when he playfully pinned her arms down. "My turn," he said.

Marsha writhed to his hard-edged ravishing of her body and even harder pounding when he entered her. "I'm in control now. You'll do what I want," he whispered. He pleasured that Marsha was too engulfed in moaning ecstasy to begin to understand.

"Keep going," she got out between moans.

He lifted himself off of her, reached over the edge of the bed and poked around in the pocket of his trousers. When his arm rose, he was clutching a pair of black nylons.

"What in the—"

He gently took her arm and knotted the nylon around her wrist.

"Oh, I like that," she cooed.

He secured both hands tightly to the brass bedpost rails. He leaned over again and pulled out a pair of latex surgical gloves. In the yellow glow of the firelight she watched him slowly cover both hands without a word of explanation.

"What's this about? I don't—"

His voice was deep, rich. "Do you think you have a soul, Marsha?"

She shook off the last of her carnal playfulness. She had lured a monster into her bed. He watched her eyes darting from hand to hand while searching for the right answer. An answer that wouldn't upset the man straddled on top of her.

"Please! What are you doing?" Her eyes popped wide open. "You're—him?"

She stretched and twisted, sobs of horror catching in her throat as she gasped for breath.

"Please, get off me right now!"

His hands whipped in position around her throat. Marsha clawed at the muscle-taught forearm that was squeezing the air from her lungs. Wild creature sounds of distress escaped from her throat as she kicked her legs to no avail.

"Strong right to the end," he whispered. "Hold still, damn you." He tightened, then loosened his grip.

"Please," she managed to choke out while still trying to buck him away. She couldn't budge him. She couldn't hurt him. She was going to die—slowly.

~

"Listen! You do have a soul." Then he gentled his tone and cinched his grip again, his eyes bulging with each millimeter of closure. "Mine needs it."

He began feasting on her eyes. A woman could tell you anything. Lie, cheat with other men, anything. But their eyes never lied. Time slowed to an illusion as he watched confusion, then horrifying awareness that she was dying. Just before he plucked out her essence, he loosened his grip again for a split second. Her eyes were lifeless as a porcelain doll. "Isn't it terrible to lose control?"

25
CHAPTER

"Bartholomew's going to skin me alive and make lamp shades out of my hide if you ever write another word about polygamy, Goodman, or even a side-bar on that Jacobson girl," Liddle said.

Charlie paced the length of the glass box conference room, shaking so much that he couldn't hold a coffee cup. It had been that way since he received Homicide's call at his home before his alarm clock rang.

The Strangler's latest victim, thirty-two-year-old television anchorwoman, Marsha Highland, was found dead in her downtown penthouse condominium shortly after 5 a.m. An anonymous caller, matching the voice of the Strangler had alerted homicide to the murder at 4:30 a.m. The body was found naked, provocatively propped up by pillows on the bed in the victim's master bedroom. High-heeled black boudoir slippers accented by tufts of black feathers at the toes were placed on the feet to further choreograph the intended effect. A dated Chicken of the Sea magazine ad featuring Charlie the Tuna had been presumably placed by the killer in the corpse's lap-positioned hands. The ad tagline "Sorry, Charlie," was circled in black ink.

"You're story's the Strangler, now more than ever," Liddle added with a hint of reservation.

"Somehow I think they're connected. Rachel Zimmerman is my lead to one mammoth stick of dynamite with Goodman's name on it," Charlie said.

Liddle rose. "You got the wrong name on it, buddy. Don't touch it."

Beyond words, Charlie could only gape at him. Then he looked away, rubbing a hand across his forehead, muttering to himself. "I guess I should have expected this kind of thing in such a one-note town."

Liddle shoved his half-lens reading glasses up his nose and cocked a brow. "Just what do you mean by that?"

"I mean, this paper just doesn't get it," Charlie snapped, wheeling back around on him. Every muscle in his body was clenched in anger, his hands balled into white-knuckled fists at his side. "Investigative reporting is about going where no one else is, going into dark hidden corners with a flashlight."

Liddle stood in front of Charlie with his feet braced apart, shoulders square, stomach sucked in, ready to blow. "Spare me the Woodward and Bernstein crap. I was a junior at the U of U when the Feds raided Colorado City to break up hundreds of polygamist families."

Charlie was in no mood for rebuttals. "Times change."

The city editor forced a sharp, unpleasant smile. "Do they? We've got over thirty thousand of them by most counts, probably more. Imagine the Division of Family Services and the Feds breaking down doors and ripping babies and children away from their families." Liddle stopped a foot from Charlie's workstation. "Some of them are armed to the teeth. They make Waco look like an opening act."

Charlie's jaw set in an uncompromising line. "It's illegal. It's abusive. And worst of all, nobody seems to give a damn. I can't stop the Strangler, but I sure as hell can blow the lid off polygamy while we're trying to find the son-of-a-bitch."

"It's a paradox. Some woman claim they love the arrangement, that it's righteous and moral."

"Right, tell that to the Jacobson girl."

"Somebody gets beat up, raped, or killed and we'll be all over it," Liddle said in a deadly quiet voice.

Charlie shook his head in disbelief. "And how in the hell are we going to know about it, when I can't even stick my head an inch inside the tent?"

"There was nothing I wanted more than to see Jacobson hang by his nuts for beating that kid, but buddy, we've got to take them as they come to us. Leave it alone. End of subject."

Chin up, Charlie walked past Liddle, wondering if there was any hope of even marginally recreating the fertile story environment he had walked away from at the *Chicago Tribune*. He had no friends. He had no chummy associates. He suddenly felt as deviant as the victims of his stories.

Once Charlie pounded out his last deadline piece around midday, what-ifs started spinning around in his head. He needed to put his thoughts back on track methodically, one by one. He knew the first step was to call Sid Burback, his Chicago city editor, whom he hadn't spoken to since his spur-of-the-moment announcement that he was quitting to ski and write a novel in the Rocky Mountains.

Like an idiot.

Compromising his career for what? Small town bylines and a regular paycheck before he had even finished the first draft of his mystery?

Other reasons whispered through his mind, excuses and half-formed ideas as to why he could never seem to juggle all the pieces of what the world defined as a balanced life.

~

Charlie let out the breath he was holding. "Okay, Sid, give me hell," he murmured and dialed the number from memory.

"Charlie. How you doing out there? Got any religion yet?" The fax machine behind Sid beeped.

The familiar sounds of chaos made Charlie smile.

"How are things going at the paper, Sid?" he said on a sigh.

"Been reading your polygamy story off the wire. Running it, too. Unbelievable."

Charlie shifted in his chair, his expression half scowl, half holding back. "Yeah, too bad about the verdict."

"You skiing out there? Bet the snow's great."

"Not bad," Charlie said wearily, rubbing his temples, falling momentarily silent.

"I'm glad you called," Sid said. "We moved Suzanne over to investigative reporting, but it really hasn't worked out. She doesn't have your nose for dirt."

Charlie perched at the edge of his chair. His heart was racing. "What are you saying, Sid?"

"I knew you had snow blindness when you bugged outta here, but it's numbed your mind, too. What do you think I'm saying?"

Charlie had long since pushed aside the hope of correcting his impulsive career-crashing decision. "If I considered it, I would want a raise and car allowance." Enthusiasm hummed in his voice.

"I wouldn't rule out a pop in salary, but car allowance?" Burback's chuckle turned to a raspy smoker's cough. "I don't even get that anymore, since they took away the tax incentives."

Charlie started to say something, but cut himself off as a hand from behind rattled his shoulder. "Charlie, get off the line." Theron Liddle stood so close behind Charlie that his washboard stomach almost rubbed against the back of his chair.

"Got to run, Sid. Sounds interesting. I'll call you back." Charlie slammed down the phone. "What the hell is it, Theron?"

"Somebody just blew a little West Side business to smithereens."

"So?"

"So, it was the temporary offices for that group of ex-polygamist women that formed a political action group last March." Liddle smiled. "You're back in business."

"Anybody killed?"

Liddle's eyes sparked behind his gold rimmed spectacles. He nodded ghoulishly.

~

If there had ever been a banner or hand-painted sign for Women Against Polygamy, there was no evidence of it left at the smoking, one-story cinder block building. The two-alarm fire was overrun with grime-covered firemen, law enforcement, media parasites like himself, and strip mall neighbors who had come to gawk.

Charlie cussed to himself. Less than thirty minutes since detonation, and he had missed the ambulance.

There would be no open-coffin viewing of the two co-founding women who had been idly chatting only feet away from the bomb when it exploded.

Charlie and his stubby photographer were still on a buzz from the giant cups of 7-Eleven coffees they had drunk en route. As he expected, the place was still in utter chaos, but settling down from madness to process. He stooped under the yellow crime scene tape and sidestepped through shattered glass and strewn pieces of tattered furniture. Even without the explosion, the office had a sickly hue that went well with the pee-yellow linoleum and moldy custard-colored walls.

At the annihilated front of the building a woman with a mammoth chest and even bigger hips was clearing the area of contorted hunks of metal frame, shards of glass, and other shattered pieces of her world. Lydia Pearson, mother of eight, ex-polygamist and founder of Women Against Polygamy had been Charlie's most articulate and credible background source throughout the Jacobson trial. She held one hand to her side, unsuccessfully trying to stop her long plaid skirt from whirling up in the wind. With the other hand she was shoeing away *Valley Tribune* reporter Rod Becker. Becker's smudged and crooked horn rimmed glasses, shoved as usual against a face as putty soft as his body, cheap wrinkled jacket and baggy trousers never failed to bring a smile to Charlie's face.

Sid would have gotten a gut-busting laugh over his former prize-winning reporter ducking out scoops with a man who looked more like a withered farm-town chemistry teacher than his only major daily newspaper competition.

Decker's eyebrows crawled up his balding forehead. "Could you have ever imagined this when you started WAP?" Nearby cohorts perked up at the question, as if rodents sniffing fresh food.

The question seemed perfunctory. Charlie surmised Lydia had gone through the same thing with the television reporters moments ago. Her makeup was scant and did nothing to hide the years of deep sadness. She shot a look at Charlie's familiar face.

"Save it for the press conference, Ms. Pearson," Charlie advised warmly, then elbowed his way past Decker and body-shielded her from further questions. The camera crews were rolling tape, not willing to miss anything. Strobes flashed as the newspaper photographers, including Charlie's, captured the fleeting moment of high drama.

~

"Thanks, Charlie." She drew herself up, but couldn't put on the game face. "I don't...I just don't know if I can do this right now. I can't think."

"Then don't."

Lydia gazed gratefully at Charlie's heartfelt expression while a cameraman circled her for a close-up.

"There's a right time to make your points." Charlie shook his head. "Trust me, this isn't it."

He saw two more camera crews shoving past people to reach Lydia. He hated nothing more than being scooped by anybody, but he instinctively felt protective. "Go ahead and tell everybody you're going to hold a press conference right here tomorrow morning at nine. "It'll give you time to collect your thoughts."

"Where were you when it blew?" a television reporter shouted.

Charlie raised his hands to draw the fire away from her. His face was bright with anger. He drew a bead on the blond local network reporter with drop-dead GQ looks. "The press conference is off until tomorrow."

A microphone was shoved in Lydia's face. "Is this the end of your organization?"

"Of course not," Lydia ground out between her teeth. She focused her attention on Charlie. "I'll be making a full statement tomorrow morning, right here, at nine o'clock."

Charlie shrugged and turned to the gathering crowd. "Guess that's it."

Once alone, Charlie watched Lydia's shaking hands struggle to open a purse and thumb off two chewable Maalox tablets. "With all the press coverage, we never thought they would dare come after us."

Charlie watched weakness wash through her as she teetered on the back of her low heels. Charlie lurched forward and braced her up.

"You're in no condition to drive. Let me take you home," he said as he guided her away from the scene and in to his forest green 1993 Jeep Scout.

Lydia dropped her tensed shoulders and let out a long sigh. "I know everybody's going to expect me to do things like organize prayer meetings and make arrangements for the funerals." She put her hands to her face and ran the fingers down slowly as melting butter. "I don't want to be weak after all we've tried to do, but I can't do it alone."

Charlie studied the courageous woman. She was spent as a fired gun shell. "That bomb changed everything," he said gently. "You've got recruits now, and I'm one of them."

She turned to him. Her eyes were bright with tears that wouldn't fall.

"Don't worry about what anyone else wants from you," Charlie said. "You don't even have to do that press conference tomorrow. Just do what you have to do to get through the funerals. Let tomorrow take care of itself."

~

Lydia reached across the gearshift and patted his knee. "People like you are keeping us going."

Her comment ended Charlie's back-of-the-mind intention to get an exclusive. It was enough just to be there for someone who needed him. The feeling was fresh, liberating. He wanted to tell her not to worry, that nothing was going to happen to her now that the police were on alert. But he couldn't make any of those promises, and he hated his inadequacy in leaving her alone with her children.

Her modest red brick home was only blocks from the bombsite. By the time Charlie tugged on the parking brake, her tears had dried.

"I could have walked, just as I always do," she said.

"You don't have a car?"

Lydia shook her head. "Everything's close—groceries and the kids' schools. We manage fine."

Charlie scanned the street for anything suspicious. "Mind if I walk you in?"

~

She guided him into the two-bedroom house where eight children and an adult were jammed into every livable inch like hobos in a boxcar.

Charlie inadvertently smiled at the two-foot-wide paths on the scarred wood floors, serving as the only space to navigate from one room to the next. The walls were covered with the latest family artistic endeavors, from a bright purple and electric yellow finger painting of three butterflies in flight, to a number of promising caricature charcoals. Charlie easily recognized Brad Pitt. Another twenty-something face looked familiar, but he didn't know the name. Not surprising, he thought. He hadn't even discovered Seinfeld until a year before the series ended.

While the living room looked like random chaos to Charlie, Lydia scrutinized the household for even the slightest shift of a sleeping bag on the floor, the changed tilt or movement of piled children's books.

During the silence of the room-by-room inspection, Charlie could see beads of sweat popping out on Lydia's forehead. Finally she heaved a sigh that there would only be two coffins for the moment. She led her guest to an open spot on the living room couch, and not finding a suitable place to sit, folded her arms and stood in a military "at ease" position.

"They've tried everything to kill my organization, even got a rich old geezer to propose to me in hopes the money would lure me away from our mission." She rolled her eyes and grinned. "The old fool kept leaking his died-in-the-wool fundamentalist beliefs before I even saw his wallet."

"What is your mission?" Charlie asked.

Rage filled Lydia. "To survive."

"You mean it's over?"

Scowling, Lydia stalked around the piles. "It's not about me or them anymore. I've got to protect my kids."

Her answer brooked no disagreement. Charlie said nothing as he watched her battle her newest adversary by herself. He wanted to help her, join the cause. His thoughts rang of commitment beyond headlines just when all was lost.

At the sound of the telephone ringing, they both jumped as if a slasher had leaped from the shadows. Lydia hesitated, then shuffled into the kitchen.

Charlie leaned forward, resting his elbows on his knees. He scanned the titles of a stack of books, with the paperback polygamy biography bestseller, *Secret Ceremonies,* atop the pile. He rifled through the polygamist biographies and related reading, then turned his attentions to a yellow legal notepad filled in blue ball-point cursive so meticulous he assumed it had to be from Lydia's hand. He inched the pad to the edge of the table, and craned his neck for surreptitious reading.

I can remember being suicidal as early as when I was eight. Mix a box of rat poison with a quart of milk? Hang myself? Jump in front of a car? Every new idea felt a little closer to freedom.

"Holly shit," Charlie muttered to himself. These thoughts were private, as hidden as Lydia Pearson's life—if that was her real name. He tingled, anxious as a five-year-old on Christmas morning. As much as he kept telling himself he shouldn't read it, he knew himself better than that.

I lived as a wallflower, an observer, trying to make sense of a life that never would make sense. I had seen girls in our organization marry men they didn't love, made worse by the necessity of sharing them with other women, having a baby a year, and living in poverty. At the age of ten I knew it all awaited me.

I tried to understand this strange God everybody always talked about who made me wear odd dresses and braids to school. The boys pulled my hair and called me a "plyg".

I desperately wanted to be normal, cut my hair, wear pants, celebrate Christmas—instead of lying about what I got, when the only present I ever received was one cheap doll I still sleep with. I wanted to have a special day of my own—my own birthday with a cake, candles, and a present or two.

None of my dreams ever came true. I was pulled out of public school at the age of eleven and taught at home. My parents said the world was evil and would corrupt me.

I could make a dozen loaves of homemade bread, bottle thirty wide-mouth jars of peaches, sew, and fix all three meals for twenty-five people—all besides school.

I worked harder and harder, trying to be a child worthy of love and protection.

Daddy gave me love, bad love, but no protection.

At thirteen, I ran to my mother in the kitchen after washing with lye so hard my hands looked sunburned red. I told her that my brothers had held me down and touched me all over and I hated it. She said she would go with me to my father and talk about it. I said, "No, not him!" She went to the bedroom alone with him to tell what I reported. My father then ordered that I tell him every detail. He said nothing. No comforting words. Not even a response.

Early the next morning my mother came into my bedroom and told me something I would learn applied to every man in my life. "You have to let him be who he's going to be. It's not your place to complain."

Those feelings came back again recently. I prayed every night when I was fourteen God would take me before daylight.

It's a prayer that still crosses my lips in bad times.

Charlie was so deeply mesmerized he didn't hear Lydia slip back into the room. "I thought you were different!" she hissed.

His face instantly turned crimson. "I was…" He closed his mouth and sighed, lost for words.

Lydia snatched the pad off the table and clutched it to her chest. "How dare you!"

"I shouldn't have," Charlie blubbered, fumbling in the pocket of his baggy corduroy slacks for his Jeep keys.

"I'm the flavor of the month for you too, huh?" she demanded.

Charlie could see her response was pure reaction. She didn't want to believe what she was saying.

"Just stupid," Charlie said in a quiet voice. "I promise, I won't use a word of what little I read." In shame, he couldn't meet her gaze. "I don't blame you for not believing me." He stood up and jangled his keys to announce his departure.

"Don't you dare pity me!" she said through her teeth. She had nowhere to go with his tenderness. She backed away from him, jaw set, her mouth pressed into an uncompromising line. "I'll survive," she huffed, swallowing back tears. "And so will Women Against Polygamy."

She paced the room, her arms wrapped around herself, too wired to sit, ready to explode into a rage.

"The phone call, right?" Charlie asked.

She took measured breaths. Her words were slow, overly even, as if she was going to hyperventilate. "I just got a call from an ex-fifth-wife whose former husband just bashed in her front door with a sledge hammer, nearly beat her to death, and took their five kids back to his polygamist house."

"Did she call the police?"

She shook her head. "He'll find a way to kill her if she brings in the outside."

"Unbelievable!" Charlie said.

"Women have a way of vanishing."

"I can't believe the police didn't help."

"I never had a birth certificate. No social security number. Was never allowed a credit card. I was enrolled in public school with a phony name," Lydia said. "How could the police help me? I don't even exist—and I bet she doesn't either."

26
CHAPTER

A soft knock sounded on the door, startling Rachel.

Anna poked her head into her temporary ranch bedroom. "Ida's not up yet," the girl said, seemingly unsurprised that her sister mother was already up before first light and dressed in cleaning clothes. "I brought you some hot chocolate," she whispered, using the excuse to let herself into the room.

Anna's offer went in one ear and out the other. Rachel had been sitting for hours so bone-deep terrified she didn't have the strength or courage to trek to the barn alone in the cold black of night.

The teenager entered, eased the door closed and placed both cups on the nightstand.

Rachel felt the fine hair on the back of her neck rise. Her fingertips rolled against her sweating palms. "You have something to tell me, don't you?" she said. She looked expectantly at Anna; too weary and too worried to even try to smile. "Go ahead, tell me."

The teenager frowned as she stared at her own clasped hands. "I just imagined seeing something. Probably nothing."

Rachel rose slowly and clutched Anna by the hand. "Let's go see this 'nothing'—right now."

Anna could barely draw a breath to respond. "I…I don't want to."

"Right now!" Rachel clasped Anna's arm and steered her toward the door. Anna struggled, trying to tear away and flee to her room.

"March," Rachel ordered, pointing to the stairs. "Straight to the mud room. And be quiet so we don't wake Ida." She wiped her sweating palms on her jeans.

The women slipped on their dirty work parkas and gloves. Rachel grabbed the closet flashlight and began wedging open the creaking door. Her hands trembled on the round brass doorknob. Her heart beat a little faster, seeming to rise up to the base of her throat as if villainous hands were trying to choke her.

They both swallowed a throat-freezing gust of blinding snow. Arm-in-arm they leaned into the wind and stealthily trudged to the barn, slid the door closed against the bitter sub-zero chill of the storm. Rachel pried her arm loose from Anna's and stepped back so she could face her.

"There's nothing here. Really!" Anna whined.

Rachel ignored the obvious lie and began her own investigation. "I've been over every square inch of this place," she said, then crouched to the ground like a sumo wrestler, and beamed the band of light into the first horse stall. "Come on, save us both the time. If there's something here, I'm going to find it."

Anna began to silently cry; her filthy gloved hand pressed to her mouth. "It's not in the stalls," she said.

The word "it" stung Rachel as if it were a snakebite. She turned the particle-filled stream of light on the teenager's face and flinched at the horror in her eyes. Anna's arm rose slowly as if she were a zombie, pointing to the far-left corner of the barn walkway.

Rachel's hand shook violently as she directed the light to the designated spot. Her first thoughts were of the bitter cold, wondering if Sarah was dressed warm enough, or if she was hiding in fear.

She ran towards the back wall, the light bouncing up and down, revealing nothing but smooth raked dirt. "Sarah!" Her loud whisper shattered the silence. "It's me, baby. You can come out!" Her ears ached with the silence. She got to the spot where Anna had pointed and breathed deeply. Nothing. Her daughter was stolen, kidnapped by a faceless stranger. Suddenly the thought shot bile up her throat. *Is she still alive?*

"There," Anna's high female voice whispered from the shadows. Rachel turned the light on Anna. Again she was pointing—to the ground. Rachel's eyes raced back to the spot. "What? What?"

"Nothing, probably. The—ground is soft. It was already cleared and raked over when I got to it."

"So?"

"It was about Sarah's size."

Rachel shook her head. She folded herself in two and dropped to her knees, anticipation racking her body as though a coroner was cracking open her chest. She ripped the gloves off her fingers and began clawing the soft reddish-brown earth. "That doesn't mean anything." Her mouth was moving, but someone else was talking. Someone else was on their knees scratching through dirt for their dead daughter. She was barely aware that the person beside her had left and returned with a shovel in her hand.

"Here, use this," Anna said, struggling to scrape even a word out of her throat.

"No, it could cut her," Rachel heard some insane woman inside her say. With each pawed handful of dirt, Rachel was beginning to let relief and belief seep into her ravaged mind. "See, she's not here. Nothing."

Anna nodded and put a shovel to the dirt. "Could be anything," she said tentatively.

Rachel sprang to her feet and grappled for the shovel. "I told you not to use it!"

Her resolve to remain hopeful disappeared when she looked into Anna's startled face. She handed the shovel back to her and motioned to dig. Anna violently shook her head. "Please. I can't."

She bit her lip until she tasted blood, then she forced the shovel back into Anna's hands. Once the digging got underway Rachel squeezed her eyes shut and held her breath.

Dear God, You wouldn't take my only baby. You wouldn't do that to me. You're all I've got left to keep us safe. She's your child, too.

In her mind's eye she could see Sarah's beautiful face with shy downcast eyes and a slight endearing smile. Her suspended serenity was interrupted by a sharp huffing noise. She turned the flashlight from the dig to Anna. They both stood there waiting, silent.

Anna's breath caught in her throat. She didn't need to say a thing. It was all in her face.

"You found something," she said evenly.

27
CHAPTER

Worst scenario—manslaughter.

The thought rested in his stomach as well as arsenic.

Since the morning after he had blindly buried the body, questions had grown from fledglings to monsters in his finely honed legal mind. Had he dug deeply enough? Sure, the body's decay was dormant now, but what about spring? Even worse, could the stench of rotting flesh be contained under only two feet of dirt in the heat of August?

I wore gloves. No prints. I raked over the gravesite and general area to hide footprints. Tire marks. Got them, too.

~

A peanut-brained typical killer might sleep well with such precautions, but not an undergraduate in criminology with a personal passion for forensics. He felt as jumpy as a psychology major that develops every phobia he reads about. He recalled one of the central tenets of the application of science to crime—exertion leaves evidence. In his mind's eye, the crime site investigators, dressed like archeologists in safari shirts, were sifting for days through sandy soil, brushing off the body like buried treasure, looking for that microscopic thread of fiber, button, or hair follicle. He could see his friend Kevin's face in clear orange goggles as the chief state crime lab investigator, running his Supermax luminescence wand over Sarah's clothes in search of semen, urine, or saliva stains. He sighed with relief that he hadn't mixed sexual pleasure in with the beating earlier in the evening—this time.

Accidental death. I panicked and buried the body. No evidence of pre-meditation or criminal intent. No posing of the body. Too bruised and messy. What would the Strangler be doing way out here? Damn, I had my hands around her throat with no gloves. The crime lab can lift fingerprints off skin.

Other grisly cases from other places paraded through his mind. Tales of bodies bubbling up from shallow drainage ditches, bodies dismembered and thrown—a leg here, arm there—in the woods like breadcrumbs for scavengers to feed on.

It had been a mistake. He should have hidden the body where no human, or even animal, could find it. Southern Utah's Canyonlands came to mind, plentiful in moonscape and Mars-like formations, and black-as-midnight nooks never seen by man or beast.

He had known it was a mistake from the moment Rachel's screams over the single ranch telephone had sounded the alarm. Circumstances now dictated one logical solution. He cleared all emotion from his mind, disassociating himself from his kin's death just as a coroner would handle an unknown.

Disappearance was the operative word in his solution: one dead Goodman disciple now, and soon, two more.

A smile edged up one corner of his mouth. Even God understood when violations of his sacred "higher principles" warranted blood atonement. Moving the woman and child to step across that unforgiving line wouldn't even begin to tax his mental processes.

He took another bite of the thickly layered roast beef sandwich his women had prepared on demand, and began to craft his plan.

28
CHAPTER

Rachel quivered with dread at the anticipation of seeing Sarah's marble-still face emerging from the earthen floor of the barn.

Anna released the shovel and dropped to her knees. "I need light," she muttered."

"I can't see anything!"

"It's not her," Rachel heard herself say. She beamed the light onto the young woman clawing through the dirt. The ground was stingy, only giving of tiny handfuls to her frozen, cupped hands.

"Down here!" Anna said, her voice hardened and chilled.

Rachel mechanically responded to the command. The glow crawled closely down Anna's shoulder, to her arm, then her dirt-filled hand. Then to the uncovered arm, draped in a pastel floral long sleeve. "Jesus!" The circle of light trailed to delicately splayed fingers. Rachel squeezed her eyes shut and prayed the image wouldn't be there when she opened them again.

"It's Sarah!" Anna's declaration hung in the air as if a monstrous ghost.

Rachel's nostril's flared and emitted twinjets of steam. She turned a steady beam on the arm, up to the partially revealed shoulder and from one end of the turned earth to the other. Then she tore out of the barn and broke into a run for the silhouette of a house with one guiding light from a small latticed window.

"My baby's been murdered!" Rachel lurched forward and wrapped her arms tightly around her wide-eyed woman prison keeper.

"What's all this?" Ida whispered, all alert, while rubbing her palm up and down Rachel's back.

"Sarah's—" Wrenching, immobilizing pain at the back of Rachel's throat wouldn't release the words.

Rachel ripped away from the old woman's warm embrace. "She's dead! Do you understand me?" Something inside her burst and the words came rushing out—screaming out. "She was murdered! Buried like a dead animal." Her arm shot up, pointing toward the barn. She turned back and looked up at Ida Goodman, expecting to find something stoic or smug in her expression, but the eyes were bright, worried, and moist with sympathetic tears.

"Murdered?" Her eyes darted around the room. "Heavens!" She dropped her voice to a whisper. "They...They could still be here."

~

Anna watched the scene from her unnoticed position at the front door. "They're gone," she spit out matter-of-factly.

"What?" Ida snapped.

Anna leaned back against the door. "It wasn't strangers."

Rachel could see it in Ida's eyes. Her mind was racing faster than a crooked bookie. A fresh wave of tears washed down Rachel's cheeks. Her stomach wrenched while sharp claws ripped through any protective denial. "We've got to call an ambulance." She paused at the insanity of the remark. "The police—yes, I'll call the police."

"No!" Ida yelled. "We need to calm down." She clamped a hand on Rachel's shoulder and forced her into the living room. "Anna, close the door and get in here!"

Rachel was too disoriented to not back down. Once the two women were seated on the living room couch, the old woman's demeanor and tone turned dangerously soft. "I'll call Father. He'll know what to do."

Anna shot out of her seat. Something hot and red flared behind her tear-brimming eyes. "No, don't! Don't call *him*." She wheeled around to Rachel and without warning grabbed her arm and pulled her up. "We've got to get out of here right now!" She turned her fiercest stare on Ida. None of them spoke. Each looked to the other for the next move.

~

Ida slowly turned, then darted for the phone on a living room side table and dialed at lightning speed. She shielded the phone with her body, stiffly tucking the receiver under her chin.

"Ruth, it's Ida. It's an emergency." She eyed Rachel and Anna warily. "Hello, Father. Rachel says she found Sarah buried in the barn. She says it's murder and she's trying to call the police." Ida paused, then her voice turned sweet and light. "Rachel, Father needs to speak to you."

"Don't do it," Anna interjected, flinching at the sound of the name.

A chill shot through Rachel. It suddenly occurred to her that nobody but Anna knew who the murderer was and he might be on the other end of the line. She leaned close to whisper, "When she hands me the phone, get between the two of us. I'm going to call the police. Stop her any way you can."

~

Rachel jerked the phone out of Ida's hand and gave her a hard shove into the armchair. She needed to lash out at someone, and Ida Goodman was the closest target.

Ida stared at her, incredulous and offended. "You're a bad woman, Rachel."

The anger flared inside her, turning listless pain into focused fury. Suddenly bad sounded good. She shot a glance at Anna. "She moves from that chair and I'll beat her to a pulp." Then she spoke into the phone. "This is Rachel. What is it?"

"I can't believe what I just heard. Now, what did you find?" Goodman said.

"Sarah's been murdered. That shouldn't come as a surprise, should it?"

"Good heavens, child, this is horrible. Don't do anything or call anyone until I get there. It could be dangerous. You girls need to come home right now."

Rachel's hand trembled violently. Sarah's limp body in a dirt grave curled her mind with horror. "My little girl's dead."

"It's impossible to think clearly at a time like this," the Father said in his most persuasive baritone.

"I should have called them weeks ago," Rachel muttered.

Ida started out of her chair. Before Anna could act, Rachel shoved her back into her seat and silently mouthed, "Stay right there."

"Did you actually see the bod—Did you actually see Sarah?"

Rachel felt a stab of pain as sharp as an ice pick. "I'm calling 911 right now."

"I'm sorry, child. You were right all along. We should have called them in from the beginning."

Rachel shook her head in disbelief.

"You can't call 911 in rural areas. You'd have to call the Snowville police dispatch during off-hours. The Snowville sheriff would run the investigation. I've met the man. He's an idiot. We'll want the best in on this. I'll call Salt Lake City Homicide and fly an officer down with me in the helicopter. We'll be there before daylight."

Rachel squeezed her eyes shut and groaned.

"We'll get through this, child. I'm so sorry. There's nothing more painful than losing a child."

Punchy with shock and exhaustion, Rachel began to weep again.

"I'll bring you and Anna—Anna's there, isn't she?"

"She's here."

"I'll bring you two down a strong sedative, something to help you sleep."

~

Uneasiness skipped across her nerve endings. Father Goodman had never given her cause to doubt him. She wanted, no, needed to believe in something, but Anna's reaction to his name and the terrified sound of her voice buzzed in her head. "You'll really call them?"

"I swear as God's prophet, we'll get to the bottom of this."

Rachel quietly hung up the phone.

"See, I told you Father would take care of it," Ida sneered.

Anna blinked away the last of her tears. "You didn't *really* believe him, did you?"

Ida lifted an open hand to slap the child, but was blocked midair by Rachel. "Don't you dare touch her."

Ida dropped back into her seat, glowering. "Satan's whispering too loudly in your ears for you to hear or understand a thing." Suddenly she was on her feet, legs apart and ready to fight. "That man you just talked to speaks to God directly. Can you even begin to comprehend your sacrilege?"

Anna looked as if her temper were revving to explode. Rachel's glare told her to save her thoughts until they were alone. She had no desire to talk about the plan she had just hatched, and no desire to give Ida Goodman any more ammunition to use against her and Anna when Father arrived. Her thought was dangerous, but not more than waiting for Father to arrive.

"Ida's right, Anna. I told Father Goodman we'd wait for him and the police, and that's exactly what we're going to do. I've always obeyed our Prophet," she added carefully as Ida stormed away and up the staircase.

Rachel had time to weigh Father Goodman's final words. He had promised, but promised what? Once Ida was out of range, she tugged Anna into the kitchen and huddled close. "I understood what you were trying to tell me in there. We've got to get out of here."

Anna's head bobbed up and down in relief. "What's the plan?"

"We need to let someone know—about everything. It would be harder for us to disappear if people were watching."

"You know he's not bringing in the police, don't you?"

Rachel stared at the dated pattern on the linoleum floor. In the silence, the refrigerator stuttered and hummed. She was turning a hard gaze on Anna as the words came out of her mouth. "I need to know everything."

"There are pictures," Anna's hand automatically covered her mouth like someone else was trying to silence what came next.

"What? What pictures? Hurry, Ida will be back any second and I've got two calls to make."

Anna cupped both hands over her face and began to rock. "I can't talk about it," she whimpered.

Rachel pulled her hands down to the table and held them captive.

"Not this time. I deserve to know."

~

Anna began sweating even as chills ran through her. "He did things to me and the other girls."

"And these *things* are in the pictures?"

Anna nodded. "He said we needed to learn how to be good girls. So—" She swiped the back of her hand across her running nose. "So we would know how to be with our husbands."

"And Sarah? Sarah was in the pictures, too? What was in them?"

Anna said nothing.

Her gaze wandered everywhere but into her sister mother's frantically searching eyes.

"Sarah had the photos, didn't she?" Rachel asked coldly.

"We had to do it, or he would beat us more," she said quietly.

Rachel draped her arm around her and snuggled her close. "I have to know what happened to her." Anna laid her head against her sister mother's shoulder.

"We never talked about it."

"How many girls?"

Anna's body heaved as she gasped for air. "He liked to have us play with each other and—"

"Shh—no more. Never again."

Anna sniffed and tried to smile. "Sarah told me before they brought her here that she hid them at home."

"What was she going to do with them?"

"Get out of marrying Uncle Jacob."

Rachel wearily shook her head. "She actually thought she could blackmail her way out of marriage? Why didn't she tell me? Who did it to you girls?"

Anna used the edge of the kitchen tablecloth to wipe her sweaty hands. "Oh no, I can't tell anybody that. We all swore *nobody* can find out."

"That's why you wouldn't tell me earlier? Because you had promised?" Rachel reached out and tenderly brushed a tear from Anna's cheek with the pad of her thumb. For the first time, she felt the girl was her own child, and if needed, she'd give her life up to keep her safe. As she rose to reach for the telephone, Anna grabbed her hand.

"Israel knows—I told him about the pictures. I didn't tell him who it was, though. He says he doesn't believe it, but I think he really does."

Rachel found a pen in Ida's top drawer near the phone, dialed information and jotted the home telephone number for Charles Carver. Her plan was to alert the one outsider she knew enough to call, then dial the police.

~

Before she had spit out two lines to the stunned listener on the other end of the line, Ida leaped from the hallway shadows, ripped the telephone cord out of the wall, and leveled Donald Goodman's prized 50 mm Browning rifle at the back of Anna's skull. "Do your best not to move, dear," Ida said.

Rachel, nodded, never taking her eye off the barrel. "You're losing it, Ida. Lower the rifle."

Ida curled an index finger over the trigger. Her twisted mouth showed anything but pity. "Heavens to be. Such stories. What will Father do?"

29
CHAPTER

Charlie cinched the belt of his black silk robe, laid aside Patricia Cornwell's *Body Farm,* and went to the door.

"I'd like to offer a solution," Sid said with his index finger held high.

"Sid. What in the...Please, come in."

Sid Burback dipped his head when entering Charlie's home. He still had a full head of ruler-straight, jet-black hair. His appearance and demeanor always reminded Charlie more of a Chicago mob boss than a down-in-the-dirt city editor.

"It's great to see you. This is one helluva surprise." Charlie took Sid's camel cashmere overcoat and motioned Sid into a vacant living room chair, then joined him, settling on the couch. "It hasn't been three days since we talked."

"And I'm heading back home tomorrow," Sid said, studying the immaculate pastel living room doubtfully. "Pretty fancy digs. Cinder block bookshelves, yes, but a *Better Homes and Garden* type?" He scratched through his well-groomed hair. "Charlie, you're an enigma."

Charlie let the comment slide. "Can I get you something to drink? Bloody Mary?"

Sid nodded. "I wouldn't have flown out here if I hadn't heard something in your voice when we talked on the phone that sounded like you—"

"We hadn't even started negotiating, Sid." Charlie waved an arm around. "I've got it pretty nice out here."

The city editor pushed himself out of the chair. "So tell me about that New World of yours we talked about in the hospital." His hands moved as if an orchestra conductor with each point. "You remember, no more all-work-Charlie. Skiing, dating, real friends."

"Yeah, I remember," Charlie grumbled. "You've got to put it in context. Susan walked out on me and there were a few weeks where I thought the cancer was going to kill me. Little things like that can change a guy's thinking."

"How are you doing?"

"You mean the cancer? I'm a testicle short, but they think they got it in time."

"And this born-again life?" Sid said, waving his arms around from living room to dining area. "You enjoying it?"

Charlie shrugged with a frown, his color rising. Marsha Gallenson loomed in his mind. He headed for the kitchen and returned with two dashed-together Bloody Marys.

"I would like to tell you a little story if you've got the time," Sid said.

A smile of wry amusement opened the gates.

"You remember Don Wilson, don't ya?

Charlie nodded. "How is the mayor?"

"Two terms and the third's a cinch," Charlie quipped, his interest piqued.

Sid leveled a shrewd stare at his star reporter. "What if I told you that I just learned that buried under a bunch of tiny rocks is one of the dirtiest schemes in the history of the office? It could not only kill his political ambitions, but also land Wilson in the slammer. What would you think?"

"Where do I come in?"

"Right where you belong—the beginning."

"What is it, and who else knows?" He was starting to feel that old familiar rush.

Sid burst into laughter. "That's the look. That's why I got up before the fish market opens to fly here." He slid to the edge of his chair and clasped his drink with both hands. "Wilson got himself in a real estate deal that makes Clinton's Whitewater look as if it were child's play. He needed money, big money, and fast."

"This is getting good," Charlie said, tensing automatically.

Sid shrugged. "Gets better. But you're not my investigative reporter, so...I really can't be just telling this to anybody."

Charlie mulled over the bait, sitting back, folding his arms. "If I stopped you right now, you'd explode. But in respect to your long trip, finish it, then we'll negotiate."

Sid nodded. "So that means—"

"That means I'm interested in *everything* you've got to say, Sid."

"I got a call from one unhappy contributor to the 'save Wilson's ass fund.'"

"How much?"

"He's raking in minimums of one-hundred grand all over town. You got me, pal, but it's got to be in the millions without a dime making it to the city coffers."

"Political blackmail," Charlie whispered. "I love it."

Sid's gaze skated around the room. He'd done his part.

"The price tag on my Solomon skis has never gotten wet. I haven't been laid or had a beer with someone I could call a friend since I got here," Charlie sighed. "I never even made it through the first draft of my novel. So you nailed me, okay?" Resigning himself to his fate with a much put-upon look, Charlie headed to the kitchen to make another edge-rounding drink, trailed by Sid. Out of habit, he answered the telephone when it rang.

"It's Rachel Zimmerman," she stammered so fast he wasn't sure he heard or could even believe the name. "I didn't know who else to call.

My daughter's been murdered, and I think we're in danger. We're at—"
Nothing. Silence. Dial tone.

"Good God!" Charlie jerked his attention back to Sid. "The mayor's
story is going to have to wait."

30
CHAPTER

The Prophet felt an immediate knot of tension from his stomach to his pounding head. He was caught in a landslide. He set down his daily journal and turned his dazed eyes to the dripping sword-length icicles framing the upper half of his library window.

Should he convene his Council of Seven to explore the next steps, or seek God's divine guidance in how to lead his family out of darkness?

First things first. He needed someone to blame before dropping to his knees. He drew his father out and the lost love of his life quicker than one of his favorite fictional gunslingers.

~

Her hair was like polished gold that never lost its magic. Early Church Prophet and polygamist Brigham Young's blood coursed through her angelic body. Like him, she was descended from God's chosen few. Two generations back her family had fled persecution in the East, bringing along their thirteen children and a devout belief in the Principle of Plural Marriage.

Dorothy Solomon. She resonated in a hidden corner of his soul. Even though God moved his hand in scribing daily journal entries to a spirit he hadn't seen since they were both sixteen, he couldn't harness the perfect devotional words. She alone would be at his side when he ruled his own world, as Jesus had on earth.

Since their first kiss he was no longer the same. With Dorothy had gone every settled thought and feeling, every association he made as a future family patriarch. He had imbibed from her sweet nature much of her view of a monogamous equal-partner life.

But destiny, in the form of Ephram Goodman, came between them.

You heartless bastard. Fury boiled like an evil brew in his stomach at even the thought of his father's name.

The two had vowed to escape from their families' suffocating grip, fleeing to a place where their love could bloom like meadow wildflowers. Throwing down the gauntlet meant, as oldest son, he was giving up Goodman prophet succession plans and tempting God's wrath. For Dorothy it meant letting go of all family, tradition, and a sure path to the celestial kingdom. They had discussed and welcomed tomorrow.

With no more than a small vinyl suitcase overstuffed with one of Donald's long sleeve shirts, pants, socks and her only other dress, Dorothy had slipped away with suitcase in hand to the bus stop rendezvous.

He never saw Dorothy Solomon again. No one saw her again.

Hopelessness fell around Donald that hung deep. He felt cold inside. Brutally cold. Deadly cold. At sixteen he began a secret diary. Soon after, he stopped speaking even a word for nearly a year to the day of her disappearance.

~

His father would shrug off or evade his questions about Dorothy's whereabouts, always a little too easily.

"God has other plans for you," he would repeatedly say. He would become an attorney, a business empire overseer, a God.

By seventeen, Donald Goodman began making his own plans. If God wanted to tag along, that was his choice.

From the day Dorothy vanished, rumors scattered around about her being sent to an out-of-state family in the Order, a common practice for Principle violators. Donald knew all too well how young women were used as barter for land or money. Potential leads grew more distant with each passing year.

One of Donald Goodman's first acts of power as Prophet was to search the entire western states for his Dorothy, but to no avail.

~

Nobody had ever heard of Dorothy Solomon. Even her parents had left the sect years before, claiming they never had a child by that name.

Forty years later Donald Goodman would lay in bed staring into the darkness, envisioning the lone figure with dark nut-brown braided hair, pacing, waiting for him at a bus stop bench. As he imagined stepping down from the bus, something had changed in recent years: the girl waiting for him had Rachel Zimmerman's face.

~

He looked up to see his son Jacob at the door, shifting his weight from one foot to the other as if he had to urinate. "Father, you ready? We've got to go."

Slowly, Goodman turned from the window. His body had broken out into a cold clammy sweat. An image of Sarah's body curled in a fetal position in a cupped-out womb of earth spun crazily in his head. He sank down in his chair and expelled every ounce of breath. He cradled his head in his hands and waited for God's guiding signals.

Moments later he sat up, put the ribbon bookmark in his personal diary, then rubbed his face with his hands.

"Get a tarp and rope," he said. "We'll be needing to cover our sister if she's there when we transport her to her final resting place."

31
CHAPTER

Donald Goodman's fingers teasingly tugged at his Bell helicopter's landing gear for a feather-light landing on a winter-gripped expanse of vegetable garden less than fifty yards behind his Snowville ranch house.

"Hyrum, listen closely." The thundering whirling of blades quieted. He continued as if his second oldest son was a thickheaded child with attention deficit syndrome. "I'll give you about ten to fifteen minutes. No more." His face turned maroon, a signal that one misstep in word or action would unleash a too-familiar beast. "If anything goes wrong, Jacob, you know forensics will sift and dust through every inch of dirt."

"I know," Jacob said. "We won't leave a trace of evidence she was ever buried there."

"Rachel's just acting crazy. There's no body—"

"Shut up, Hyrum," Jacob snapped. "Mom said she'd watch Rachel so she wouldn't call the police."

"Then why was it busy when I called back a few minutes after your mother called?" Goodman demanded. He slid open the cockpit window and blew out a steamy breath. Even a hint of foul play could force the Goodman name into the limelight, muddying three generations of meticulously crafted illusions. He finally gestured a knowing nod.

"You know who she was talking to?" Jacob fumbled for the passenger seat door.

Goodman answered his son with a scathing look. "Get moving."

They stepped out of the helicopter into ankle-high fresh powder. Goodman pulled the legs of his Wrangler jeans further over his cowboy boots and tucked his chin down into his pale yellow lamb's wool collar. "The ground's going to be hard as rock. Use the pick."

Jacob nodded and turned for the barn with Hyrum at his heels.

"Here he comes," said Ida, her eye to the crack in a pair of sheer living room drapes. She let the long-held rifle droop in her hand, the barrel touching the hardwood floor.

Rachel decided not to stir Anna, who slept nestled against her shoulder with an arm wrapped snugly around her waist. "Are the police with him?" Rachel asked softly.

Ida shrugged. She glanced out the window again. Rachel heard the woman's husband was on the top step of the porch, stomping and scraping off the hardened snow. An orange sunrise light washed through the windows, backlighting Ida's haunted look at the sight of the man who had heartlessly sentenced her to the ranch. Rachel could see it all in her eyes: it was easier to worship Donald Goodman as her prophet from a distance. She absently primped, accomplishing not even a hint of change in her frumpy demeanor.

Rachel felt her distress heighten. Her thick black brows tugged together, digging a deep furrow in her wrinkle-free forehead. "A policeman. Did he bring one?"

Ida again anchored the rifle on one projected hip for her husband's full appreciation.

"Sorry I can't greet you at the door, dear," she said, then grinned.

It was all surrealistic horror to be held at gunpoint by strangers with your dead daughter only yards away. Rachel felt it unfathomable to suffer at the hands of a woman she had known and trusted since childhood, and a man who less than a year before sat at the right hand of God.

"The police are with you?" Rachel asked loud enough to wake Anna.

"I'm in no mood for back-talk today," Goodman boomed out, bringing all three women to sharp attention. He smoothly stepped inside from the front door, pulled off his leather gloves and stuffed them inside his coat pocket. Ida and Anna sat in strained silence while he hung up his coat and toed off his boots.

Rachel pulled Anna close. She stared unseeing across the room at Goodman as he and his first wife exchanged looks, then back-turned whispers. "You came alone, didn't you?"

Goodman swept his muscular arms out as if he was clearing a crowd. "Everybody leave the room but Rachel," he yelled, dismissing the scowling glares from the two huddled women.

Ida quickly leaped into action, pulling Anna out of Rachel's grip and scurrying through the doorway into the kitchen.

Once alone, Goodman sat down beside Rachel. She could see his anger melted as quickly as a spring thaw at the sight of her unbraided silky black hair. Rachel wore it draped artfully to the tops of her shoulders. She felt her fiery veneer was in full glistening splendor, though thoroughly exhausted, and utterly unapproachable.

Rachel crossed her arms and began rocking back and forth. "You *really* don't care." Her eyes burned through his stoic shield. "I actually believed you were a prophet."

"You're so confused, child," Goodman responded.

"Uh-huh," she said with no conviction.

"I dropped everything to be here and get to the bottom of this—whatever this is," he said in a dark measured tone. "But I'll warn you only once, never speak to me like that again. Tell me exactly what you *think* you found in the barn." He grew calmer as his intensity skyrocketed, a quality Rachel had seen serve him well as an attorney, and even more so as a prophet over thousands of weaker, questioning minds.

"It's too late," she mumbled more to herself than her interrogator.

"I'm so disappointed you don't trust me enough to help, when that's the only reason I'm here." Goodman pretended frustration, his down-turned lips dramatizing his point.

Rachel steeled herself against her prophet's plea. "Sarah's dead! Murdered! Doesn't that mean anything to you?" She saw something sad, painful in his eyes.

He leaned over and kissed her cheek, not a quick, dismissing peck, but a soft, warm, and intimate pressing of his lips against her skin. The startling move sent quicksilver shivers down her, creating mixed and confused signals. He wanted her. He wanted to touch her, even now. The thought made her stomach turn.

She slammed the mental door on the vision of his aging hands roaming across her skin. His hand moved to her upper thigh, quickening her pulse and sending her common sense spinning off its axis. The hungry look on Goodman's face was enough to make her want to slap him. She slowly rose from the couch. Even with her back turned, she could feel his eyes undressing her. She hugged herself as if trying to cover her naked body.

The prophet always kept her off balance, all knowing and weaving Godly words of wisdom one minute, then the stalking seducer, then the instrument of punishment. Since an early age she had connected with his flurry of inner contradictions, dismissing them as the potent ingredients of a powerful leader. For the first time in her life she wondered who he really was, and for the first time she really didn't care. All she needed to know, she knew.

Don't trust him. Who should I trust? Nobody.

To distract where Father Goodman was trying to lead her, she turned to him, took a deep breath to watch his eyes dance up and down with her heaving breasts, and clasped her hands together. "Anna and I were assigned to shovel out the stalls in the barn. I came back to the house."

"Just slow down. We'll get to the bottom of this, I promise," Goodman said.

"Anna came running back from the barn. She wouldn't tell me what was wrong at first, but we both went out there and—" She felt her throat tighten and reeled, as if she was going to faint. Goodman rushed to her and braced her up close to his chest.

"And what did you two find in the barn?" he whispered.

"I'll show you." Her body seemed to be working independently from her mind. Her mind would never allow her to actually see Sarah's body uncovered, shovel-by-shovelful. Her body was moving away and to the coat closet to rub Father Goodman's righteous face in the horror he let happen to her little girl.

~

Goodman said too quickly, "There's no need for you to see that. I've already got the boys checking it out to see if you and Anna were just seeing boogiemen in the dark. It made no sense to call in the police on a false alarm. We needed to see for ourselves before—"

The front door burst open. Two cherry-faced men in puffy bright parkas stomped the snow from their feet and began the family ritual of tugging their shoes off and placing them neatly on the front door mat next to their father's boots. Jacob nodded to Goodman.

"Well, come out with it. What did you find?" Goodman demanded just as Ida rushed past him with open arms to her oldest son.

"It's freezing out there," she said, pulling Jacob into a tight embrace. "I've warmed up some lentil soup for you boys and Father." She pulled back, her eyes sparkling with love and longing.

Jacob chuckled. "Sounds good, Mom."

Goodman shot a glance over at Anna. "What did you find out there?"

Jacob took off his coat and shook his head as if disgusted with the answer. "I'll tell you what we found, what we dropped everything and rushed out here for—a dead dog."

~

Rachel closed the distance between her and Jacob. "What are you talking about? We saw—"

"You saw King," Jacob snarled, flashing the teeth and eyes of a rabid animal. His face flushed the color of dried blood and his neck veins stood out like tree roots. "My sheepdog I buried out there the same time your daughter ran away. I had wrapped him in an old dress of mother's."

Rachel clutched his arm and dug her nails in. "That's a lie. Sarah was there."

"I…I saw her, too," Anna said. "I dug up her arm and shoulder. It was her!"

Hyrum twisted around and slapped Anna across the face. "Don't you dare call my brother a liar." His arm swung up in the air again, about to descend like a pendulum blade when his father caught it.

"Enough! Everybody calm down."

Hyrum's arm went limp at the order.

"Where did you take the body?" Rachel murmured.

Jacob shrugged nonchalantly tempting her into a white fury. Her fists exploded on his chest as if a pounding war drum. "You bastard!"

Jacob locked her wrists in place while he stoically watched her writhe as if she were a madwoman.

Ida acted at light speed to hold Anna back from leaping into the fight.

"You're liars!" the teenager screamed. "You're all liars!"

Jacob let go of one wrist long enough to whip the back of his hand across her face, sending a burst of blood from her nose. "Don't ever— ever—talk to your Prophet like that again!"

"Jacob!" Goodman yelled. "Don't hurt her."

Rachel glared Jacob down, her anger burning through the haze of defeat. "*You* brought Sarah out here."

"We both did," Goodman snapped. "The girl ran away, Rachel. You just have to accept that."

Rachel pulled her hand free and stepped to the front door closet. "Did you see what was hanging up inside here? Huh?"

Goodman tilted his head in confusion. "What are you raving about now?" he demanded.

She threw open the door and rifled through the men's wet coats. "Where is it, Ida?"

Rachel shot a sweeping glance from the old woman to all the faces in the room. "The coat—Sarah's coat. It was hanging right here." She gathered herself to a state of cool control. "Ida? Anna and I both saw the coat. So did you. We talked about it before you hid it. Where is it, Ida?"

Rachel pulled her glare off Ida and continued to scan the room. "Give my girl a little more credit than to run away without her only winter coat when it's freezing outside."

Goodman eased up beside her. His pupils were black pinpoints, suggesting the whodunit game was over. He slowly held her in place by both shoulders. "We can either restrain both of you, or you can cooperate. It's your choice."

His cold words jolted Rachel back to the danger she was leading Anna into. She nodded while Goodman led her back to the living room couch and pressed her shoulders gently until she wedged against Anna.

"We can't change what has happened. Satan possessed Sarah Zimmerman. Everybody in the family knew it." He put an index finger to his lips alerting Rachel to not dare interrupt. "She has run away, and I'll not hear another word about it."

Anna felt the crimson streak from her nose about to break over her upper lip and into her mouth.

"Ida, get Anna some tissue," Father said.

Ida pulled a well-used handkerchief from her dress pocket and held it in front of Anna's pale face. She hesitatingly accepted the offer.

Goodman shook his head. "There's nothing out of the ordinary here. But there are going to be some changes I've prayed about what will reunite the family again in peace."

Rachel gave him a look that could have frozen fire, and he quickly turned away.

"Now, no one say a word," he stated sharply, demanding absolute obedience.

"Rachel, we'll begin with you. You need to be brought back into the warmth of God's love. He has guided me in understanding my mission in helping you again bathe in the glow of His love. In two weeks you and I will wed on earth and for time and all eternity."

"You said celestial only!" Rachel shouted, rising from her chair. Goodman's sons looked at her with surprise and annoyance for daring to interrupt the Prophet.

"Yes, I know, child. But a lot has happened. You're lost and need all the inspiration I can give you to find your way back on the path to heaven." He smiled. "God still believes in you. So do I."

His eyes and words were laced in the beauty and hope that never failed to seductively pull at Rachel's heart and mind.

Goodman turned to Anna. The tension radiating from her crackled as if static in the air. "You, Anna, will take the holy covenant with Hyrum in less than a week, as will Jessica. The rest of Brother James' wives will be sealed to Jacob and Hyrum in only a matter of weeks."

"I, I don't—" Anna couldn't choke out the words.

Goodman again nodded. "You don't know how to thank me," he interrupted. "I admit the Council entertained some pretty serious consequences." He fixed an eagle eye on Rachel. "And these innuendoes that my boys here, or worse, your own Prophet, could or would have anything to do with—well, it's like accusing God himself."

"Blood atonement's what you both deserve," Jacob spit out.

"The children?" Rachel asked.

Goodman closed his eyes and tilted his head up to the heavens. "Of course they will stay with their natural mothers, but be again blessed with a mother *and* a father."

Rachel felt evil hang in the air as if a foul stench. One of the three men puffing about her like a plumed peacock was a murderer who had long ago lost the boundary between good and evil.

32
CHAPTER

Even though the midday sun illuminated the house with the promise of an early spring, everything had a sinister look.

Rachel paused from heaping chores to glance out at the electric blue feathered back of two Scrub Jays. Their heads were popping up and down in syncopated motion to peck the last dropping from an abandoned sun-bleached pine feeder suspended from a drooping, leafless branch. All the backyard trees were alive with songs, shrieks and squawks. The blended cacophony celebrating the portent of an early spring took on a discordant and unnerving quality. Rachel's heart was shrouded in murky light and gray that even her spirit-freeing birds couldn't lift.

The crisp white framed and squeaky clean windows felt like prison cell portholes with teasing views of an alien world where freedom was as naturally dismissed as breathing.

~

It had been nearly a week since returning from the ranch. All of Goodman's twelve wives were called on duty as cell guards, watching, questioning her every move.

Rachel had set out to distance herself from thoughts of Sarah, but her own home less than a hundred yards away pulled out memories of her living and murdered child as if a magnet. Her since-childhood battle with bulimia had vanished along with her appetite for food and life.

171

From the moment of her arrival in the Goodman house, Father Goodman made two things clear to every woman and child: Rachel Zimmerman wasn't to be trusted, and she was his most prized possession. The second point was gagged down as though lethal drain cleaner.

Rachel turned at the sound of shuffling feet behind her.

"I can't believe Father is actually rewarding her after all she put the family through," second wife Marianne declared. The bone-thin woman moved around the kitchen like a hummingbird, flitting here and there, and resting nowhere. She wore a faded oversized calico dress and an enormous kitchen apron with ties that wrapped around her twice.

"Did I ask for *any* of this?" Rachel grumbled.

Marianne's glazed eyes darted to her two sister wives, then drilled into her usurper. "Why should you get my bedroom?"

"And I'm supposed to feel blessed? Lucky?" Rachel snapped. She shot them all a look of disgust. "You don't even bother to whisper."

"Oh, I've heard," Marianne said. "The way you've been talking about the Father and his sons." She sniffed and hastened from the kitchen island to the sink nearest Rachel. "Your girl runs away and you're trying to get the men in our family arrested."

Rage flooded through Rachel, deep as bone marrow. "You're damn right!"

"Rachel, stop the profanity right now," Marianne demanded. "I have prayed for God to give me understanding and love to welcome you into this family, but I can see now it's no different than inviting Satan himself to share our husband."

Oblivious to Donald Goodman's entrance and balled fist-to-hips stance directly behind her, Marianne fluttered her stringy hand over her heart and took a deep breath. "What is Father thinking?" she muttered bitterly, her features pinching tight.

The eye-rolling dramatics and grimaced silence of Marianne's sister wives made her swallow hard. She pressed the heels of her palms to her temples. "Of course, it's not our place to question."

Rachel could see in Goodman's eyes that he demanded more than contrition. Any wavering from absolute control threatened his domain. Marianne slowly opened her watery hazel eyes and turned to the presence she could feel right behind her. "Good morning, Father," she said in a child's tone.

"Now you women listen carefully. I'm only going to say it once." As Marianne took baby steps back, Goodman moved to Rachel and put his arm around her tensed shoulders. "You will treat Rachel as a respected and loved member of the family."

Marianne's mouth was a thin colorless slash in her narrow face. She offered a strained smile of welcome.

"It hasn't been easy for Rachel, losing her *only* child. Where's your Christianity, women?"

Rachel thought she saw Marianne wince when she extended her hand and patted Rachel on the wrist. She arched her thin brow and nodded. "Father is right, as always."

She looked at Rachel as if she had called her a filthy name, then left the room, flanked by two whispering sister wives.

Goodman waited until the three were well on their way up the entry stairs before he spoke again. "I'll be going out of town after Anna's wedding. I've instructed the women to sew you a beautiful wedding gown. You choose the style, just so it's proper, of course."

A glint of reflecting sunlight caught his sparkling eyes. Father Goodman genuinely wanted her to love him. A shiver ran down her back.

"I haven't been out of this house in days. Could I get the last of my things? I've still got a dress I'm missing that I—" Rachel stopped suddenly.

She could all but see the thought strike him—escape. She couldn't stop the shade of deceit that passed across her face while staring back at him. She passed a hand across her forehead to break his mind reading.

He made a humorless laugh. "Can I trust you yet? Really trust you?"

Rachel blinked innocently and said nothing.

"You don't want to be sealed for time and all eternity to your Prophet, do you?'

"I'm not worthy," she said softly. "I've lost my husband and child. I really don't know what I want."

She wanted to ask straight out. *Did you have anything to do with Sarah's death?* But Rachel held her tongue. She couldn't afford a confrontation. If she even hinted that the rest of her life was going to be dedicated to search and punishment, he would never loosen her chain.

Goodman stared at her, no doubt trying to gain something useful from the conversation. He never seemed to question his powers of persuasion and ultimate worship of his every thought and word. "I've prayed for you." He lifted and shook her single thick braid that hung just over her breast. "Your mind is still playing tricks on both of us."

"I'm not asking to go back to work," she said with slight indignation. "I just need to be able to get out of this house once in a while."

"I would spend a lot of time on my knees if I were you, searching your heart for God's truth." He gingerly let go of her hair and rubbed her shoulder in a non-sensual, parental way. "We live our lives knowing times change, but God's laws don't. Clothes, music, theories of the earth's origin. Church leaders are constantly changing positions based on societal pressures they disguise as visions."

Rachel gazed into her Prophet's eyes. He gave Rachel a questioning look as he fished a common gray-flecked river stone from his pocket. "Do you remember my sermon on how this simple piece of the puzzle helps unravel the mystery of how to live a pure, Godly life?"

"I've forgotten," Rachel admitted.

He opened Rachel's clammy hand and placed the smooth oval stone in the center of her palm, then folded her fingers over it. "When I was a boy my father gave me just such a stone that I've since passed on to Jacob."

"What does it mean?"

"So much that is bad has happened in such a short time, it's no wonder you don't remember. It must seem as though the entire fabric of your life has given way at every seam, allowing all the patterns of your life to disappear." He stood, and with hands locked behind his back began to pace, building inspirational steam with every step.

His hands swept up in swift, fluid motion. "All the great ruins that have survived the ages are made of that simple material God created and that you now hold in your hand.

"A simple stone is more incredible, more valuable than anything the most advanced human mind has invented, or will ever invent. My father carried a stone in his pocket since a childhood vision, in which our Father in heaven told him that whenever he was in doubt of Him or the unchanging timelessness of His words, to rub the stone—an inspirational talisman, if you will."

Rachel opened her hand and stared at the common rock.

He cocked a furry brow. "Still don't see what I'm talking about?"

She shook her head in shame.

"You'll soon be entering into the covenant with me. Do you remember what was said when I sealed you to James?"

Rachel shook her head; her eyes downturned and cheeks crimson.

"We turn to the law of Sarah, whom I recall you named your only child after?"

Rachel slowly nodded.

"Sarah didn't understand God's unchanging laws at first, either. Both she and Abraham laughed at the idea of having a child at their ages. God blessed them both. Sarah, the mother of all of Israel, gave Hagar, her handmaiden, to Abraham as his wife." Goodman's nostril's flared.

"If our way of life is wrong, unlawful, then the whole plan of salvation, through the sacred house of Israel, was a failure." He whirled around and poked an index finger at the book titled *Celestial or Plural Marriage* he had written as a young prophet, shelved between a Book of Mormon and King James version of the Bible.

"The entire fabric of Christianity is without foundation if you can't grasp what that simple stone is calling to you. God's covenant is unchanging, like a rock."

Rachel looked past the power of her prophet's intoxicating symphony of rhetoric for the first time in her life. She saw before her a man who had long ago crossed the line from zealot to madman.

Her mind flashed on the one childhood memory that had first raised doubt about her Father on earth. She had been about twelve when the police raided the compound. Father Goodman was handcuffed and taken away. Not a word of explanation was given to any of the children, and they had no access to news from Babylon. She had only learned what happened months later when eavesdropping on her mothers' whispering while canning mountains of cling peaches for winter. Father Goodman had beaten his son Hyrum on a public street corner so brutally in front of other children and an approaching school bus driver that he was arrested for child abuse. Why Hyrum had gotten the raw brunt of his father's rage or how Goodman had gained such immediate release had remained a mystery she had buried until now.

Goodman paused, raising an eyebrow at Rachel's stormy and distant gaze. "I know everything's confusing for you right now, child. Our wedding is in less than a week, and you'll want your heart and mind ready for your new life. Get back to being our precious Rachel."

He had added the last bit to remind her who she was, how her family history would again right the course of her blood. At that instant she knew that Rachel Zimmerman would have shown a little feisty resistance, but acquiesced to God and Father Goodman's guiding will to lead her along the painful path to salvation. But she had ceased to be that person. The new woman being forged by horror, guilt, and fear was unpredictable, suspicious and most definitely untrusting.

The truth. There would be no new life before she discovered the truth. The pictures were the missing piece that would tie everything together. They were here at the compound somewhere, hidden beneath some loose floorboard or in some corner she hadn't yet discovered, lurking as an evil presence that could be destroyed by the light of day. Sarah had had the courage to attempt to use the truth to save herself from sharing a bed and life with a man three times her age. If Rachel looked hard enough, long enough, dug a little deeper, she would be the one to throw open the doors and blast someone's dirty, dark secret to bits with the blinding light of truth.

33
CHAPTER

Charlie paced Homicide Chief Strickland's sterile, cramped office, shaking so much his coffee cup was jiggling from the suffocating avalanche of terror the Strangler was piling on him.

Tom Strickland rose from a square armchair that was too low for his six-foot-four-inch frame and stretched the kink out of his back. Everything about him was tough, suspicious, all business. Strickland would have fit perfectly in Chicago.

Charlie noticed for the first time that the chief was handsome, in a regular-guy sort of way. His sandy brown hair was combed back from his angular face. He was the kind of guy who didn't care any more about what he ate or about the drab olive suit and statement-free tie he was wearing. His office held no pictures of his wife or commendations. No pictures or personal touches, period. Every government-issued piece of furniture profiled the man: definitely a Type A to the power of two.

"I'll get right to the point," Charlie said, knowing anything less would mean the door.

Strickland leaned down to the base of his chair and pumped the seat adjustment handle twice to raise his seat. "And Fernandez says he never uses my office when I'm on vacation." He shot a glance at the reporter. "Do I really look that stupid?"

Charlie gave a wry smile and shook his head. "It's not you who's stupid."

Strickland bounced on the chair a couple of times to ensure the seat position was locked in place. "You're suggesting someone in my department is stupid? I don't have time for that long of a discussion."

"No, the Snowville sheriff." Charlie scooted on the edge of his muddy brown vinyl-covered metal chair. "Look, we both know the drill when it comes to calling out the cavalry, but I got a call from a woman who said her daughter had been murdered and that she was in danger herself. I've got caller ID, so after she got cut off in the middle of a sentence, I traced the call to the summer home owned by Donald Goodman in Snowville, Utah."

Strickland knew the name. He liked the story. "You seem to be in the middle of every crime in this fucking town. When did she call you?"

"Almost a week ago." Charlie's voice was sharp with indignation. "It took me that long to get to you. The Snowville sheriff said the call was hearsay. Privacy rights, that kind of bullshit. He wouldn't even go out to the house and look around when he found out who it was. Goodman must have that guy by the short hairs."

Charlie threw in the last comment to spice up the kind of dialogue he sensed the classic pulp fiction detective loved.

Strickland's deep-set eyes fixed on Charlie. "Who is this woman? She call you again?"

"She worked as a court reporter at Matheson Courthouse. After the Kingman trial I was chasing her down for a story. She's one of the Goodman Compound wives. A polygamist."

Strickland raised both palms. "Bingo! There it is. You don't touch that subject in this town without physical evidence of foul play the size of an elephant."

Charlie bolted from his chair. "So that's it. A woman's child gets murdered and she could be dead by now herself, and all you do is sit here and talk about politics?"

Strickland's gaze strayed to the officers who stood behind the crazed reporter.

"He said he had an appointment with you, Chief," said a sharp-featured redheaded beat cop.

"Am I under arrest here for trying to report a murder?" Charlie said.

Strickland's bright eyes shone even brighter with temper, even though a boyish grin stretched across his face. "It's under control." The two men turned and left. "So you want me to call this Snowville sheriff and get jurisdictional approval to make a call on the Goodman house?"

"Start with a search warrant to catch them off guard."

Strickland shook his head. "I thought you knew the drill."

"We'll need at least one of your guys in homicide who knows how to approach a crime scene."

Strickland crossed his arms and sat back slowly in the wobbly chair. "I haven't even agreed to make the call, and you're outlining the investigation team. We don't even know if a crime has been committed."

"Can I go, since I got the call?"

"Oh, you'll go," Strickland grimaced. "We'll take the chopper. If there is a killer, his trail's going to be cold as a Montana winter."

34
CHAPTER

Ida Goodman lay on the couch with her gunsmoke gray Persian cat and a full sack of nightmares. She hadn't missed the horror in Anna and Rachel's eyes, as real as her solitude and the winter wind whistling down the chimney.

"You're not going to leave us one day, are you, Lily?" she purred to her cat. "Leave us without another thought?" Lily quivered as if she were shaking off the questions. She was everything Ida envied: independent, full of exuberance and youth, wonderfully athletic, and lover of a good snuggle. But this afternoon even Lily's lulling internal bliss motor wasn't calming her.

"Of course you're not. You wouldn't leave Mommy." She stroked her companion's fur faster and faster while the nightmares started crawling out of their bag.

She scuttled for the barn that day as soon as the sound of Father Goodman's helicopter had faded into nothingness. In a low crouch she had scurried across the barn's dirt floor until she spotted upturned earth at the back of the building. She clutched her chest at what—no—*who* she found.

Images of the lifeless form jammed her mind, leaving just enough room to formulate questions, questions that could drive her mad if she pursued the answers.

The familiar sound of hovering metal blades cut the crisp winter air rescuing her from tugging another nightmare out of the bag.

"Father Goodman's back," she told Lily.

What she had seen in the barn was running hard and fast inside her head. The thoughts were dangerous. Donald Goodman was dangerous. The thought tasted bitterly of blasphemy, as if she were betraying her Prophet to his face, even though the dead body couldn't lie. Still, the possibility of innocent explanations scrolled through her mind—all of them with Rachel Zimmerman front and center as the villain.

With a heavy sigh Ida rose, tucking Lily close to her chest, like armor. "We'd better freshen up before he sees us."

She stood before the mirror, biting her lower lip until blood almost burst forth. She saw herself sitting on the edge of the couch when he last came, reaching out to take his hand. She had grabbed hold and hung on tighter than she meant to, wishing with all her heart he would put his arms around her and just hold her for a while. Rachel had seen it all, the longing that screamed from the depths of her soul for tenderness and compassion, for even feeling she mattered to her family for one moment. She pictured ripping her husband's harlot's pity-filled eyes out of her head.

Ida raised her liver-spotted hand and scooped the tears from her cheeks. She threaded her fingertips into her coarse, graying hair, lowered and flattened her open palm into a comforting position on her cheek. She closed her eyes and imagined the hand was Donald Goodman's, welcoming her back home.

35
CHAPTER

"Ida was Goodman's first wife, one he sent out to pasture, so to speak," Charlie told Sergeant Strickland as he peered out the bubbled Plexiglas window of the Salt Lake City police department chopper. The bird began a descent on a snow-buried unpaved road leading to the house.

"Keep your mouth shut unless I tell you to open it," Strickland said to Charlie.

"What would prompt you to get a search warrant," Charlie said, steering the conversation back on his track.

"You heard me. You have any idea how many cases get fucked up by not following procedure? My guys here know what to do." Strickland pointed to the pilot and pudgy black uniformed officer sitting shotgun. "The search warrant's just the beginning of protecting the public's rights, isn't it, Rifkin?"

"No shit," the officer threw off as though the conversation was all too familiar.

Strickland unlatched his seatbelt upon landing. "Unless there's something subtle like a trail of blood, the do's and don'ts in a search make it hard as hell to smoke out physical evidence."

Charlie had never voluntarily gone to a crime scene, until now. His stomach clenched at the thought of finding Rachel Zimmerman's daughter.

"I won't get in the way," Charlie volunteered.

"Finally, a coherent thought," Strickland retorted.

The four trudged through the snow shoulder-to-shoulder like western gunslingers about to show down outlaws. The door opened before they finished stomping the snow from their boots and shoes. Ida Goodman rocked forward against the screen, clutching a cat in her arms.

"What do you want?" she said.

Sergeant Strickland stepped forward and flashed his badge. "Ma'am, I'm Sergeant Strickland from the Salt Lake City homicide division."

Ida sucked in her breath at the word homicide and pulled the cat even closer to her breast.

"A telephone call was placed from your house that warrants a few questions. May we come in?"

Ida was trying to stall long enough to consider her options.

"We won't be long, ma'am. Just a quick follow-up is all." Strickland's tone was warm, trusting.

~

Ida opened the door and showed the four men into her living room. In passing from the entryway to the front room, Charlie spied a crude dining room table that he quickly surmised had to seat at least thirty. The living room smelled of lemon-scented furniture polish and age.

The two uniformed officers stood near the living room archway as if they were posting guard. Strickland and Charlie sat down beside each other on the couch. Ida positioned herself on one of many high-backed chairs in the spacious room.

"He's a reporter, the *Salt Lake Observer*," Strickland said, responding to Ida's curious stare.

Charlie nodded. "Charlie Carver."

Ida squirmed in her seat as if her back was aching. "Why a reporter?" she asked.

Strickland gave Charlie a 'keep your mouth shut' side-glance. "He received a phone call, traced to this house, from Rachel Zimmerman."

Ida slowly nodded.

"You know this woman?"

"Of course I know her."

"How is she related?" Charlie popped out before Strickland could take his next breath, hoping to make Ida feel as if she was a passenger in a car going out of control.

"She lives with the Goodmans in Salt Lake City."

"She's all right? I need to see her," Charlie asked.

"Of course she's all right. She's a single mother. Sarah was—is—her only child."

"Was?" Strickland snapped.

"Yes, was. Sarah was a rebellious, wild child. No surprise to me that she up and ran away." She wandered to the oval mahogany table, resting her gaze on a recent picture of Sarah atop Buck, a longtime family quarter horse.

"Rachel called me from *this* house whispering her daughter had been murdered," Charlie said.

Ida began squirming again. She turned away from accusing eyes. "Yes, I heard her. Poor woman." Her lips twisted. "She just can't accept that Sarah would run away from her own mother."

Charlie didn't respond to the cynical bite to the comment. He concentrated instead on Ida's face. He was a reasonable judge of body language, and Ida Goodman's facial and body movements were more telling than a mime.

"She also said she feared for her own life," Charlie added.

"Mind if we have a look around?" Strickland said.

"Where is she, Mrs. Goodman?" Charlie demanded.

"She ran away."

Charlie rose and turned Ida around, his hands cupping her shoulders, and looked at her as if their eyes were engaging for the first time. "No, Rachel. Where's Rachel?"

"Father Goodman took her home to be with family." She wiggled away from his touch. She focused on Strickland, who was clearly enjoying the exchange. "What are you here for?"

"Murder! Sarah Zimmerman's murder and possibly her mother's death, too," Charlie said.

"That has nothing to do with me or anybody else in the family. I told you, Rachel's imagining things."

"You have any pictures of the child?" Strickland said, gesturing to the photo table.

Ida folded her arms and rocked her upper torso. "I don't think so."

"Can we search the house, or should I come back with a warrant?" Strickland said.

"Of course. We have nothing to hide," she said too defensively. "If you find Sarah dead in some man's hotel room, I wouldn't be surprised." She finally stopped moving and closed her eyes. "Even God can't always protect us from ourselves."

36
CHAPTER

Anna Zimmerman had learned to hate men at an early age. Her brothers had more than once held her down and felt the first rise of her bosoms without even a reprimand following her pleas for intervention. She scoffed at the teachings that men could one day become gods of their own worlds. If they ruled anywhere, it would be from hell, and she couldn't understand how her own mother and other women in the compound were so blinded by their faith.

Men were the scourges of the earth. She thought so at least twenty times a day. At night, the demons in black, faceless and soundless, cut into her dreams, engendering a terrifying and fatalistic dread of an inevitable future of chained servitude.

She and Sarah had had it all planned. They were going to escape together, live together and die together—if that was the price for freedom of choice. The plan had been perfect, perfect until Israel Goodman had to go and be so understanding, tender, and supportive. Now he floated around in her dreams the same way that she saw bubbles float in a lava lamp in a neighborhood store window.

"They should have to pay for what they've done," Anna declared, wiggling between each straight pin punched into place against the generous contours of her chest. Anna peaked over Rachel's bobbing head at the full-length mirror in the Goodman house's upper bedroom. The patriarch had insisted Rachel remain locked in one of two master suites until their eternal sealing ceremony. "I look fat!" the teenager sighed.

Rachel stepped back to better examine her alterations in the recycled high-neck and floor-length white satin and lace wedding dress Anna would be donning in less than twenty-four hours. Her celestial sealing to Hyrum Goodman was set by Father Goodman within hours from compound touchdown. As customary, the secret ceremony would take place at a meticulously restored, turn-of-the-century, polygamous home in West Valley.

"This dress looks dumpy," Anna grumbled.

"You look beautiful," Rachel corrected her automatically.

"I don't care if they do hear me. I shouldn't have to marry him if I don't want to. It's slavery!"

"Quiet! They'll never let us see each other if you don't start thinking smart," Rachel said.

Anna was still incensed by the way Rachel had pleaded before the patriarch for forgiveness and openly supported Anna's impending marriage to Hyrum.

Rachel pulled her close. "I have a plan."

The room turned thick with possibilities. Anna's eyes locked on the only person she trusted with her life. "You want to escape before the wedding?"

"I want to find those pictures, so we've got something to keep us alive."

"They didn't help Sarah." Anna winced at what she had so flippantly said.

"No, they didn't," Rachel responded with resignation.

"How are we going to get over to your house? They have to be in Sarah's bedroom somewhere."

Rachel nodded. "He's probably been through everything in there."

Anna gaped at her, bug-eyed. "Then we'll run away?"

"I'll tell Mother Goodman I ran out of thread and I've got a match back at my old house." Rachel nodded and began mumbling to herself before looking up at Anna. "You've got to act excited about the wedding to give us some time."

Panic surged through the bride-to-be. "We'll escape before the wedding, right?"

Rachel weighed their best chances. "No. After the wedding, when the happy bride and grateful sister mothers all seem settled back in place."

"I won't let that man touch me," Anna said, stepping gingerly away.

"I wish it could be different, but we've got to do it this way."

"Easy for you to say. You don't have to—"

Rachel pulled Anna to her chest and hugged her tight. "If we get a chance to get away sooner, we'll do it. But they don't trust us yet."

With the wedding in less than twenty-four hours there was no time to wait and see.

Anna dragged herself down Father Goodman's flight of stairs. She felt too numb to react to the buzz of doubting wives expressing overwhelming approval of how pure and lovely she looked in the third-time-around wedding dress. She slipped out of the symbol of ownership and slavery as fast as her hands and wiggles could move, pulling back on her midnight blue tights, calico floral dress, sneakers, and overcoat for nighttime trudging through the snow from Father Goodman's to her new bedroom at her fiancée's house.

Anna flinched as a shadow between the houses sprung to life. "Israel, you scared me to death."

She watched his chest heave more from nervousness than the chilled night air. He looked wan and tragic. "I shouldn't have waited so long to tell you," he said, seeming to talk to himself.

"What? Tell me what?"

Israel's Adam's apple locked as if a grinding gearshift. "I—I love you."

"You think I didn't know that?" Anna swallowed the urge to respond in anger. "Like it's not bad enough I have to marry Hyrum tomorrow, you go and make it worse by—" She huffed and shook her head. She needed time; at least a few minutes alone, to marshal her disappointment that he chose the night before her wedding to confess his feelings. She had been falling into a deep hole of depression for weeks and no one, not even Israel, was reaching in to help her out.

He looked at his shoes. "I want us to run away together tonight—before it's too late." He looked up. His glare was steady, determined.

Anna stepped a breath away and brushed his cherry red cheek with her lips. "You're really serious, aren't you?"

"I was thinking about it long before this wedding was set."

Aware that they could be under the scrutiny of disapproving eyes, she led him to their regular meeting place behind the twin aluminum corrugated grain silos. Nausea was rising up her esophagus at the persistent image of Sarah's dirt-covered corpse.

"You're talking crazy, Israel. They'll hunt you down. Not to mention what they'd do to the woman who took off with Jacob Goodman's son."

"But I love you. We need to be together."

Anna refused to be charmed. "It's too dangerous."

Israel arched a brow at her. "You're not telling me something."

Anna scanned the area to ensure they were alone. "They killed Sarah. Rachel and I could be next if we don't play along."

"Don't talk like that, Anna." He put an index finger to his pursed lips. "Shh, someone will hear you."

"I'm tired," Anna declared, turning back for Hyrum's house. "Good night, Israel."

"Who are you saying killed Sarah? I need to know. Don't leave. I'm serious about us...You know, getting married and running away forever."

"I'm not running away with you. I promise, they would find us."

"You don't trust me," he said.

"There are a lot of things I can never tell you."

Israel slumped in defeat.

"I'm sorry. I really *am*," she said. "I shouldn't be jumping all over you with my problems, but I'm worried about getting you into the middle of it."

He sighed through his nose. "I don't know what I believe anymore. I can't stay here."

She suddenly found herself caught up in the storm of hope he had created. She needed all her wits to keep from folding into his arms and dreams.

"This is a terrible time for us to be talking about this. I don't want to end this with us being enemies," she said softly coming toward him, understanding and open affection on her face. "You're confused, I'm confused." She pulled him close and kissed him deeply.

Israel raised his head an inch or two. "I can't imagine watching you marry Uncle Hyrum, then living with it every day knowing you'll be touched by him—"

"Don't. I don't want to talk about that."

Israel accepted that with a nod. "So you won't marry me?"

Anna kept her wishes to herself. "I'll never forget what you said tonight." She again kissed his cheek and vanished into the darkness.

37
CHAPTER

Rachel's fingers trembled as they gently wrapped around the doorknob of Sarah's room, left unseen since her daughter's murder. She was drawing strength from the word "murder" now. It raised fury instead of loss. She needed fury to survive the nights.

She paused for a long moment before entering. Rachel knew something as normally irrelevant as a pencil or hair ribbon could be the catalyst for horrifying feelings of loss, and unstoppable visions of how she might have died.

You're not going to die for nothing!

Rachel flung open the door. Her eyes darted around the pale yellow bedcover and white cotton eyelet embroidered pillowcases she had handcrafted less than a year ago. Nothing was out of order.

To linger was to think. Her hands moved as fast as her eyes, lifting, uncovering, and opening anything, everything that could have served as a hiding place for the pictures. She ransacked the twelve-by-fourteen-foot room no different than a neighborhood thief, throwing things up and away from her with the subliminal need to create mad chaos.

"Where is it?" she mumbled in manic frustration. "Did he find it?"

"Find what?"

Rachel swung around at the sound of the sharp voice, hastily crossing her arms over her chest. Donald Goodman stood with one hand on the doorknob, the other holding a steaming cup of hot chocolate. His eyes were narrowed in suspicion, his mouth pressed into a thin line.

Without responding Rachel flopped onto the strewn covers of her daughter's bed. Her shoulders sagged as she took a deep breath and defeated sigh.

"What in the world are you doing?" he demanded.

Rachel pressed her palms to her eyes. She ignored him. With everything that had happened or was about to happen, she suddenly figured even his barking demands didn't matter. She would either be dead or free in a matter of days. Either outcome was acceptable.

She lowered her hands. No more tears. Not for a Goodman's pleasure.

"I asked you what you're doing? Every time I turn around, you're in the middle of something that you shouldn't be doing. Anna's wedding is tomorrow, for heaven's sake, and here you are—"

Rachel sprung to her feet; legs spread shoulder width for battle. "I'm what? Embarrassing you over a missing daughter that I find murdered at *your* ranch?"

Goodman's head came up and he regarded her with a piercing stare. "Punishing your family for whatever unfortunate thing may have happened to Sarah isn't the answer, child."

"I'm the only one being punished here."

He shook his head. "What am I going to do with you?"

No, Father Goodman, what am I going to do to you when I get out of here?

The thought was just comforting enough for Rachel to shrink back into nothingness.

38
CHAPTER

Father Goodman's eyes rested on Anna. He spoke of scriptural tenets in velvety tones. "Your husband will be blessed with the authority to call you from the grave to join him, *if, and only if,* he determines you worthy to join him in God's highest kingdom."

Anna stood at rigid attention in the middle of the cleared living room of the fourth generation polygamous home. Her hands were knotted together, as if her compound school principal was reprimanding her.

"Hyrum Goodman, will you accept and cherish Anna Zimmerman as a worthy servant of God and sixth wife to your spiritual and physical needs in this world and the next, if so determined?" Father Goodman asked in deep velvety tones.

"I will," the groom said, barely sparing his bride a glance as the two stood in humbled reverence before their Prophet.

"Anna Zimmerman, will you cherish and serve Hyrum Goodman as your master and spiritual leader, every day making yourself a worthy earthly and celestial partner in thought and deed?"

Anna kept her mind focused on her task, but couldn't speak.

Father Goodman raised his head from his open text and locked a glare on her uncertain eyes. Anna's stomach churned, her face pinched tight. Her mind flashed back to being touched helplessly victimized by filthy minds and cruel hands. The memories bled back into another and another. The man standing next to her was capable of instant, intense rage, which he covered with loose, easy charm. None of the girls had to get close to feel his hungering presence. She remembered the fury on his face when he slapped Rachel at the ranch during her moment of greatest pain and vulnerability. The filthy way he had tried to enter her bed the night before the wedding, grabbing and threatening.

Worthy. The word was sticking in her throat as if a hunk of charred meat.

At least the chameleon in public wasn't unpredictable in private. Being a sexual predator was nothing rare in the Goodman family. She would play his game, then spend the rest of her life destroying every man that dared attempt to enter her life.

"I will."

39
CHAPTER

Anxious, exhilarated, Charlie broke through the scrub oak onto a snow-spotted trail leading to the granite ledge. He smiled back at his cursing photographer, again snagged in the thicket of winter-bare branches. He had no plan in his head on what to do if he spotted Rachel Zimmerman from his high mountain perch opposite the Goodman Compound.

Eddie Walker's one good eye was wide open and conspicuously trained on his mountaineering task master with a look of two parts disgust, one part curiosity. "You're chasing more than a story here."

Charlie marveled on how a man with one eye would choose photography as a profession. Perhaps it was his lack of peripheral vision that sharpened the importance of those objects he *could* see.

"So tell me about her," Eddie said, more collapsing than leaning back against a shaded wall of stone near the cliff edge.

Charlie lifted and rolled the tumbler to adjust the binocular's focus. "I'm not after the woman." At that instant three figures moved, walking between a row of parked cars and heading for the thirty-five bedroom, eleven-bathroom house Donald Goodman called home. "It's Goodman, with probably a son and a woman in a wedding dress."

"You haven't answered my question," Eddie said, scratching the blue-line chin stubble on his bullet-shaped head.

Charlie craned forward, his eyes still beaded on the figures. "There, there she is." He lowered the binoculars and blew out a sigh. Just like that, the frenetic energy was shut off and he seemed to go still from deep within. "At least she's still alive," he murmured.

Eddie stopped waiting for his answer. "I'll put on the telephoto. We've got a pretty good view of the whole layout up here."

Charlie nodded. "It's absolutely incredible to me that this—this illegal world carries on right under everybody's noses without even the slightest fear of the law."

"Interfere with the natural state of things, and you're asking for one mother-of-a-shit storm," Eddie said, turning from a raving complainer to philosopher in a span of moments.

"Maybe, but Rachel was dead serious about her daughter being murdered," Charlie said. He hadn't stopped thinking about the desperation in her voice since she had braved calling him, probably even chancing death over such a covenant violation.

"Who's they?" Eddie asked.

Charlie smiled unexpectedly. "Therein lies the crux of the problem." He put the binoculars back to his eyes. "I need to talk to her."

"You picked yourself the wrong honey, Charlie."

"It won't be easy, but I've got to get in there. Hmm, money. You can't get too much when you've got a community to run."

Eddie moved closer to the edge of the rock. "Your ass is grass if you keep trying to create a story out of this thing. Leave it alone, Charlie."

Charlie beamed. "Who me? I'm just a dumb rich Idaho farmer whose wife up and ran away, just because I wanted to take another wife. I need a prophet and community that understands me."

Eddie wagged his head the way his dog would throw off water. "Oh no, no way. You're not stepping in that hornet's nest."

"And you, Eddie, you're going to help get me in there."

Beads of sweat trickled down Eddie's forehead. "A one-eyed photographer and an idiot wandering right into a murderer's lair? These types are always packing more than hunting rifles."

Charlie narrowed a gaze on the photographer. Was Eddie too wired; too unpredictable, too volatile? He returned to the binoculars, spying Goodman's chopper. "I have to slip in when Goodman's away. You could get in the gate easily. People must be driving in and out all the time."

"Me all of a sudden? No way, man. Liddle's going to hang you by the short hairs on this one."

Charlie dropped the binoculars on the strap around his neck and began to rock himself while his mind was percolating. "Just say you've got an appointment with Donald Goodman. I've gotta know when he's gone so I can get in there and check out this woman's story."

"That's the police's job."

"I tried that." For a long time Charlie stared down at the compound, wondering, scheming, jumpy. He tried to place himself, the twisted farmer, in the charade. What mannerisms, turn of phrases, attitude might be convincing long enough to seek out and speak to Rachel Zimmerman? If discovered, would he be responsible for what harm might come to her? Was he only driven by the instinct to rescue a damsel in distress, or was it the national story? It had always been the story, but this time there was something more. *Definitely more.*

Rachel was a woman engulfed in shadows, strange hues of darkness and brilliant light. Deep-centered purpose and a wild energy had surged through him the moment he met her. He had the rare feeling that if she entered his life, both of their lives would be altered in a permanent way. Was that what he wanted? No, needed? As he glared down the craggy outcroppings of Aspen saplings struggling to hold on a few more days until the first hint of spring, he felt as if he were standing on the edge of an alternative dimension. It was as if she was looking up to the mountains and watching the man about to help change her entire life.

Eddie comically cleared his throat, jolting him back to his present world. "Okay, you got me. What damn-fooled thing am I going to do next?"

~

A pulsing vein zigzagged across Eddie's domed forehead. He stood at the Goodman Compound gate shifting his weight from one foot to the other.

The woman waving her sons off to school on the other side of the gate avoided eye contact. "I have an appointment with Donald Goodman. He lives here, doesn't he?" Eddie stared at her costume-type attire and angelic downturned face, then watched her wheel around the slight opening in the gate before it electronically closed. "Mind if I—"

"No, no you can't come in here." Her eyes met his momentarily, then shot wildly around to see in anyone had witnessed his entry. "Please, leave now."

"I'm just here to see Mr. Goodman."

"He's not here."

With each step he took closer to the young woman, she paced two back. "When will he be back?"

"I don't know. You have to leave." Head down, she shuffled over to the gate opener and pushed the button. "Go on now."

"He'll be gone a few days then?"

"Go! Go!"

Eddie rubbed a hand against his cheek. She reminded him of the woman he shacked up with in Vietnam when he had two working eyes to pleasure in her graceful, silent ways.

"Look, I didn't mean to scare you. I'll leave before anybody sees us." His voice was warm, understanding.

Almond-shaped eyes responded in kind. "Thank you."

Charlie burst into a full belly laugh. "You'd think somebody dropped a snake down your pants," he said to Eddie.

"She, she was so beautiful, man." He blew out a straight puff of Camel smoke.

"You're funny. Giving me all this shit about chasing after some woman, and in less than a minute you're in love with one of them."

Eddie paused, then nodded. "No shit. Go save her, man."

40
CHAPTER

Brooding clouds and distant thunder seemed fitting. Charlie stared at the bizarre setting, suddenly sensing that evil lingered there. Captivity clung to the Goodman Compound as if it were grime.

He flicked off his Jeep's windshield wipers and leaned into the mud-streaked glass to get a better look at the roofs barely visible above the fortress walls.

Charlie tugged on his denim fleece-lined jacket and ran a hand on the back of his head until satisfied his ponytail was snugly in place in its nylon skullcap under the wavy, bronze wig. With one last glance in the rearview mirror at his two-day blue line growth, he turned off the ignition and walked from the congregational parking spot near the main gate.

Rachel Zimmerman's magnetic pull kept drawing him in. He knew it. He would give himself over to the obsession, at least until she was safe.

The wait wasn't long before a man, slightly bigger than Charlie and thicker in body, appeared at the gate.

"What do you want?" he said, his expression dubious.

Charlie leaned lightly against the bars. "This the Goodman's?"

"What's your business?" An open hand popped through the space in the gate. The man jerked back as if a stranger had dropped a hand grenade across enemy lines.

"Sorry, just trying to shake your hand," Charlie said in his best awe-shucks style. "Name's Bill Thackeray, farmer from Lafayette, Idaho. I'd sure like to talk to Prophet Goodman if I could."

"In what regard? He doesn't just see people."

"It's kinda personal."

Without retort, the man turned and began to walk away.

"I want to be one of you." The plea didn't even break the man's stride. "I'd bring a lot into the family if I could get myself some wives."

The man turned at the blunt and strange comment. "Who do you think you're talking to? I have no idea who you are or what you're really after. If you think—"

"I don't think anything. I know down to my bones that celestial marriage is God's way on earth, and I'm going to be part of it whether the Goodmans want me or not." He watched Jacob become aware of him. Charlie made no attempt to move.

"Why us?"

"I have to admit it surprises me that you don't live in a more remote place. Heck, I checked out a lot of groups, but Brother Donald Goodman is God's prophet." Charlie shook his head in the same manner as holy rollers on television. "I just know it, that's all."

The brow-lowered man opened the gate, but still made his emotions hard to decode. "You have any proof of who you say you are?"

Charlie fished out the fake laminated Idaho driver's license that a questionable friend of Eddie's had manufactured literally overnight. "Sure, see? William Thackeray, from Thackeray Farms."

The man gave a quick glance and locked his eyes on the farmer. Then stepped closer and shook Charlie's hand.

"Name's Jacob Goodman. Father Goodman's away for a couple of days, but please come in for a minute, Brother."

Lazily Charlie walked abreast of Jacob to the man's house some twenty yards from the main entrance.

"We have to be careful," Jacob said. "There's a real witch hunt going on right now with the Jacobson trial and the press breathing down our necks."

Charlie nodded. The irony of the last comment amused him. "I heard about that. Dumb little girl's making us out to be monsters."

Jacob paused with an enigmatic expression on his face. "You're a polygamist now?"

"I said my business was personal, but I guess I just have to up and say it."

Jacob's brows popped up.

"My wife left me when I told her God wanted me to take another wife." Charlie swallowed hard and paused for effect. "I lost the other woman, too. The whole thing kinda blew up in my face."

Charlie held his breath when the two crossed the threshold. He sponged in everything in sight for future story reference. "Beautiful spread you got here."

Jacob steered the potential convert through the living room, tidy as a church cathedral. The modest brown and gold velveteen couches and simple side chairs seemed in stark contrast to the opulent size and style of the home. Faded sepia family tree pictures of hard faces adorned the walls along with what looked like scripture quotes. Charlie tried to linger long enough to make out the passages, but Jacob prompted him along.

They passed what appeared to be a hobby room filled with a throng of women all stitching pieces of the same quilt. French doors opened into Jacob's bright window-walled study. The bookcases were lined with hundreds of books shelved alphabetically by subject: business, criminology, philosophy, psychology, and religion.

The lord of the house closed the door behind him and directed Charlie to one of two plaid high-backed chairs. "Father's next orientation meeting is this Friday."

Charlie's stomach growled. God only knew what he was doing in the enemy's lair. "That's where I can sign up?"

Jacob studied him for a moment. He sat down at his desk keeping one hand close to a seemingly self-published paperback book entitled, *Celestial or Plural Marriage*, by Donald P. Goodman. His eyes were still untrusting. Charlie didn't blame him.

"So tell me about this farm of yours."

"Worked it most of my life. Three hundred acres of tree fruit. I grow Bing cherries, cling peaches, Bartlett and Bosc pears." He was running out of names from his neighborhood produce section.

"Pretty tough business to make a living at?"

"My daddy left me well provided for. I do fine. What do you do?"

"I'm a corporate attorney, like my father, but I run the family business side."

"Your father is…"

"Prophet Goodman, of course. You'll stay here for the orientation meeting. It's a pretty intense forty-eight hours, but you'll be a changed man when it's over."

"You got some young women who need a husband? I'm not much of a bachelor."

Jacob shrugged. He expressed no sympathy, and asked for no further details. He leaned toward Charlie and gently patted his knee, without emotion. "First things first."

"Can I see the place? I mean look around?"

He simply stared at Charlie. "Why?"

"I don't know. I'm pretty good at getting a feeling about things in no time flat. You wouldn't need to tell me if I'd fit in after I meet some brothers and sisters."

Jacob bowed his head for a minute. "I suppose that would be fine. I have some work to do. I'll have one of my sons show you around. We can plan on you this Friday?" He didn't wait for Charlie to respond. "It's God's plan that you fit in, too. That's why you should be here."

Charlie looked up at him then, unblinking. "You're right, Brother Goodman."

Jacob leaned over reams of paperwork on his desk and pushed a button next to his computer. "Steven, please come to my office immediately." The page boomed through the house.

In a flash a twenty-something man appeared in the doorway. Like his father, he was dressed in a dark suit and approached the glass doors with his father's brisk no-nonsense gait.

"Yes, Father?"

"Take a few minutes and show Mr. Thackeray around."

"Yes, sir."

Charlie took a deep breath as the two set out to tour the compound. Once away from his father's scrutinizing eye, Steven relaxed only slightly. "What is it you wanted to see, sir?"

"Bill, call me Bill. Just the houses, your congregational hall, and meet some of the folks. How about starting at Donald Goodman's place?"

"Father Goodman," Steven corrected him.

Playing the stupid farmer role and paying homage was starting to turn Charlie's stomach. "Yes, of course."

"I won't keep you long. Your father and I agreed it's best I meet some people if I'm going to join the congregation."

"My uncle and some of the other men are still at work, so I don't—"

"No problem. I'll see everybody at the orientation meetings. I'd like to meet some of the wives and young women."

Steven held himself still for a moment, as if waiting for some silent signal, then guided them out of his home to the Father's house.

After meeting many of Steven's young male peers and three of Donald Goodman's wives, Charlie thought he glimpsed Rachel as Steven whisked him past the kitchen.

"Could I see the kitchen? I always wondered how you could feed such a giant crew."

"We manage easily," Steven beamed. He walked them to the cafe-style open grill set in the kitchen island. Two matronly women looking strangely childish in long braided hair scurried out of the kitchen as soon as the strange man entered. Charlie turned in search of the black-haired woman he had seen just moments earlier. Before he could get a question out, Rachel walked out of the walk-in refrigerator with three cartons of eggs balanced in one hand and a gallon of milk in the other.

"Bill Thackeray, ma'am," Charlie said with an insipid grin.

Rachel's eyes turned to Steven for an explanation of such direct behavior.

"Bill's thinking of joining our congregation."

Rachel's eyes widened and her jaw dropped in recognition of the "farmer." Then she backed away slightly, put the milk on the counter, and allowed the topmost carton of eggs to slide to the floor, where they exploded in a mess of slippery yokes.

"You clumsy woman!" Steven yelled.

"Sorry to shock you, ma'am." Charlie dropped to his knees and began picking up the spilled carton and broken shells.

Steven sharply pulled Charlie up by the arm. "She'll do that."

"It's my fault. I'll help her clean up." He crouched to the floor.

A platter of chocolate chip cookies on the marble-top counter caught Steven's eye. He moved just far enough out of range for Charlie to act. "Are you in danger? You want out of here?" he whispered.

Rachel kept her eyes on Steven while nodding. "I can't go without my daughter," she whispered back.

"I sure am sorry about this," Charlie said again loudly.

"I thought your daughter was—gone."

"Murdered. Anna isn't my birth child." She stood up and surveyed the splatter of egg. "Thank you, Mr. Thackeray. It was my fault, and it's my place to clean. I'll need to use a wet mop to get it all up."

Charlie slipped his business card with his home address and phone number scratched on the back into her limp hand. "Good to meet you. I apologize again for scaring you."

"You're very kind," she said appropriately avoiding eye contact.

Charlie turned his attentions back to Steven. "I really should be going."

Steven finished the last of a second cookie. "You didn't see much, but there will be plenty of time when you come back for orientation."

Charlie glanced at Rachel's eyes with a slight shake of his head. The next move was hers.

41
CHAPTER

The ivory moon illuminated Rachel's bedroom making it easy to count down the minutes on the nightstand digital clock; two-fifteen, two-sixteen. She silently prayed Anna, too, was waiting and would act at the designated time for their final search and escape. Father Goodman was still away, but with Hyrum in the house, Anna's flight could be dangerous.

Rachel slipped on her clothes with the silence of a shadow. The doorknob felt cold, resistant. She quietly gripped tighter and flicked her wrist. Locked, as always at night.

She put her ear to the door at the sound of footfalls on the stairs. The footsteps passed by her door, then fell silent. Catching a moment when someone wasn't up on their way to or from the bathroom or nursing a baby wouldn't be easy.

~

Anna bolted for the front door at the sound of the voice, but in a heartbeat her bed partner, dressed only in his long-sleeved cotton temple garments, materialized from the gloom of the dark hallway and bear-hugged her from behind.

"You little monster," he growled. "I found your suitcase under the bed before we even went to sleep."

"I couldn't sleep," Anna blubbered.

Hyrum cinched his locked wrists tighter until she gasped for air. "You've always been such a little liar. You may be a stupid child, but you're my wife now." He released his hands and locked them on her breasts. "You'll get used to it."

Anna shivered. Rachel would be at the Zimmerman house waiting for her to search Sarah's room before they fled the house forever.

Hyrum poked his head close to her ear. "You've got secrets you're hiding from me." His grip on her breasts went from gentle exploring to punishment.

"Let go! That hurts."

His voice took on a whine. "That's what happens when you're bad. Where were you going?"

"I was just going—"

He tightened his squeeze again until she winced and jerked back in pain. "Please, let me go."

"Who were you running away with? Israel, I'll bet."

"No, it has nothing to do with him."

"It? What's it?" he whispered, easing his grip and moving away far enough to turn her around to watch her eyes.

Anna edged herself out of his grip and stepped back to the wall.

"I won't have a woman who hides things from me."

"I never—"

Hyrum leaped forward, slamming her against the wall. "If you don't like the way I treat you, then start telling the truth." His crazed eyes slacked into dull orbs. "Look, the way you've acted the past few weeks, I've been tempted to take a belt to you. But have I? No. I patiently waited for your tantrums to stop, then married you." He shoved her shoulder back up against the wall. "Then all you do is lie to me."

Anna sidestepped her way in the direction of the living room. Hyrum glanced in the same direction. Black shadowed furniture and streaks of moonlight leeching through the lace curtains cluttered the escape route through the kitchen and the mudroom.

Hyrum's voice was edged with impatience. "Forget it. Even if you did get away I'd hunt you down and beat the tar out of you."

"What are you doing now?"

"You've never seen me mad. You don't want to see that, Anna." His eyes bulged from their sockets. His right hand moved from her shoulder to the base of her throat. "You really don't. Now tell me your secrets."

~

The bedroom door lock was simple to pick with a bobby pin. Rachel hoisted the suitcase from her bed and gave one last look at the digital clock. Two-thirty. She absently nodded, comforted that Anna couldn't have been waiting for her on the front porch of her former home more than a few minutes.

The house keys rattled in her free hand when she opened the door. Her heartbeat pounded in her ears, but that was the only sound she heard in creeping down the stairs and out the door. She vanished from Donald Goodman's life quickly and quietly. She was sure no one even heard the door shut behind her. But then, that may have been due to the pounding in her head. Her eyes darted maniacally at the shadowed shapes in the night. No Anna. Her stomach burned and a wave of weakness swept over her.

No time for delay. She unlocked the door and giant-stepped her way up the staircase to Sarah's bedroom. She had calmed herself enough from midnight to two a.m. to visualize virtually everything in the room to expedite the search. She moved directly to Sarah's bookshelf. Her index finger traced along favorite titles until she reached the complete works of C.S. Lewis, Sarah's most cherished possession. She licked her bone-dry lips and carried the book over to her daughter's bed.

A chill ran up her spine as she pictured Sarah's face seconds before her life was viciously ripped away. Rachel squeezed her eyes shut and held her breath to repress a guttural scream. She drew back the hard-cover of the book as her eyes opened. No pictures. She began turning page-by-page, then thumb flicked through the two-inch-thick book. She wasn't halfway through when she caught the flash of a dingy Polaroid photograph. She sat up, rigid with terror. Her eyes scanned, but couldn't tell who the naked man's lower anatomy in the picture belonged to. "Oh, my God," she muttered in a childish sounding whimper.

~

Starting from page one she turned page by page, uncovering twenty-two, sick-beyond-description pictures. She gathered the photos together neatly as a card player straightening the deck and tucked them into her purse.

The monster had trapped and destroyed Sarah. Now he was trapped himself—on film—and soon in person. Death is an intimate experience, and she was going to make sure he shared it with her daughter.

42
CHAPTER

Charlie shuffled along the carpeted hallway from his bedroom to the living room. With a flick of a switch the brass table lamps filled the room with muted light. The rapping at the door started again. He wasn't imagining it. At four a.m. somebody was paying him a surprise call. He shook the last of sleep from his head just as adrenaline shot through him as if it were battery acid.

He knows where I live. But why would he knock?

He cinched his black silk bathrobe tighter, moved to the living room bay window, and pulled back the sheer just enough to see a diminutive figure huddled by the door. The caller was a woman, bundled and scarfed so well that he couldn't distinguish her hair color or facial features.

"I didn't know where else to hide," Rachel Zimmerman said before he had finished opening the door.

"Please, come in," he responded, stepping out on the porch with her momentarily to see if pursuers were at her heels.

"They wouldn't, couldn't, know I would come here."

He guided her inside, fully aware of her discomfort of being in a strange man's private hideaway.

"I shouldn't have come here. I didn't know…" she trailed off softly while untying and streaming off her scarf and coat, and with Charlie's assistance, hanging them in his entryway closet.

Charlie said nothing, just nodded in appreciation. Just why or exactly when he had become obsessed with Rachel Zimmerman he didn't know, and it didn't matter. Like her, he lived on society's outer perimeter. Something in him had always killed tender emotions. No one knew better than the newswoman who made the mistake of marrying him, only to disappear a year later leaving only a poetic note about his dark heart and spirit lacking inner light. But *this* woman had moved him unbearably from her first words, and they both knew it.

She prowled back and forth in his living room as if a restless cat, running a hand over the furniture trying to ground herself in reality.

"You made the right choice," he said walking past her, then flipping a brass-framed switch beside the fireplace. Flames instantly leaped to life around a stack of Masonite logs. He turned his back to the fire as if it actually released heat.

Rachel stood across the room from him beside a sturdy, overstuffed chair. Her eyes were haunted with anxiety and embarrassment at the sudden realization Charlie was examining her ankle length floral dress and long, pure, straight silk braided hair that rested artfully on the left of her generous chest. She looked frightened, caged, and totally unapproachable.

But even as Charlie saw this, he also saw a hint of a need to be held in protective arms.

"You can trust me," he offered in a sympathetic tone.

Rachel turned her eyes from the affection in his eyes.

"No questions, I promise. Not easy for a reporter."

She nodded and sat down on the green leather couch as if she was waiting for an appointment.

"We'll talk whenever you want. Right now I'm going to fix you some hot milk and start a bath for you."

Rachel rushed a hand to her chest. "No, I couldn't."

"What am I going to do with you?" He pretended frustration, his brows tugging together. "You look exhausted. After a long night's sleep, we'll face tomorrow together." The intimate offer made him pause, then warm to his own words. Sexual electricity filled the air.

Rachel steeled herself against the effect. She took a deep breath and let it out in a gust, leaning back against the couch, too worn out to keep herself upright. "A hot bath would be nice," she sighed.

Charlie instinctively considered pressing for something more before sunrise, but concern for her sense of safety curbed his desires. In escaping the compound, she had thrown down the gauntlet and left herself vulnerable to a near-complete stranger.

He stopped in front of her on his way to the kitchen, close enough to know she could see the desire in his eyes. *Stupid,* he told himself. He wasn't the kind of man to let a beautiful woman escape shared pleasures.

"This place has three bedrooms. Let me show you to yours," he said in an unavoidably sexy tone. With his eyes on hers, he wanted to lean down and kiss her on the cheek. Not a quick, impersonal peck, but a soft, warm, intimate pressing of his lips against her perfect skin, inviting her to return the affection with her lips. The idea began to fog his judgment while sending shivers through him.

"I have the pictures my girl died over," Rachel said flatly.

~

Charlie snapped back in place with the elasticity of a green branch. "Not tonight, tomorrow." He offered her a hand to rise, to no avail. After guiding her to the bathroom and placing a stack of clean towels on the toilet, he slipped away without another misplaced thought or word.

He felt off balance, protector one minute, and seducer the next. She desperately needed to trust someone. One child dead and from the cryptic message he got at the compound, another in danger. Before closing his eyes he chastised himself for such blinding emotions.

43
CHAPTER

"I bet you've never had breakfast in bed," Charlie said, his eyes dancing from the tray of eggs, bacon, toast and herbal tea to Rachel's long, unbundled hair.

"I can't even remember when I didn't fix it."

"I thought it would be the beginning of a fitting celebration of your first day of freedom. I'm working awfully hard on my charm, don't you think?"

Rachel eyes were moist with joy. "What time is it?"

"Ten. I called in. I'm not going to work today."

"You shouldn't do that," she said unconvincingly, then took a sip of tea.

Her profile caught the light from the morning sun, and he was struck yet again by her beauty. She had calmness about her, a mysterious repose, that paradoxically, he felt the urge to disturb.

"First thing we're going to do is buy you some new clothes. Then—"

Rachel set down the teacup and sat straight up. "I didn't come here for this."

He patted her arm. "I know, there are a million things that you need to have happen, but let's just take it one day at a time." He lifted his index finger shoulder high. "One day to sort things out and figure out a plan of action."

Rachel forced a ghost of a smile.

"Nothing wrong with making a nice day out of it. Ever been to Park City?"

Rachel lowered and shook her head.

"I've only been there a couple of times myself. There's a discount shopping center with all the big names. We'll grab lunch at a little place I've heard about in Prospector Square, right next to the ski lifts."

Rachel stopped eating and began both quivering and hugging herself as if she was braving a biting wind. She looked hollow and ill.

"What's wrong?"

"Anna was coming with me. They must have caught her."

She started reciting at a manic pace: Sarah and Anna's objections to forced marriages; the attempted blackmail photos; the barn discovery of her daughter; suspicions that the Goodmans were hiding the body and that one of them was a murderer; Anna's failed escape and what it could mean in punishment.

"Slow down. Take deep breaths," Charlie said.

Rachel's chest heaved at exhilarating mind flashes growing darker by the image.

Charlie shoved the tray aside and pulled her into his arms. "That's enough." He combed his fingers through her loose hair. "We need to take things one at a time. Nobody will see us in Park City. It'll be safe." She cuddled as if she were an attention-craving child in his arms. "You need a little time out before we go to the police."

Rachel ripped herself from his embrace. "No, no police. They'd punish Anna."

"They've got to get involved at some point. With your daughter— gone."

"No police!"

Charlie straightened up and dove into the comfortable role of devil's advocate. "Who else is going to find your daughter's killer and get Anna out?"

"No." Rachel shook her head, her mouth twitching. "She would disappear before they could do anything."

"Then who?"

Rachel's narrowed stare gave him the surprise answer. "What can I do about it?"

Rachel rose from the bed, poked through her purse and pulled out a handful of four-by-five-inch Polaroids. Without explanation she handed them to him. A bit of voyeur curiosity transformed to disgust and fury as Charlie rifled through the pictures. "Good God, Rachel, that's unbelievable." He lifted his eyes to hers. "Your daughter, too."

"She was twelve in those pictures." Rachel covered her face with her hands, then slowly slid her fingers down over her closed eyes, nose, and mouth, finally steepling them as if a child about to pray. With her eyes still closed she spoke. "Sarah tried to use those to stop from marrying her Uncle Jacob."

"You never see the man's face in any of the shots. Who is he?" Charlie tried to hand her back the photos, but she shoved his hand away.

"Anna's too terrified to tell me which Goodman did it." Rachel dragged herself to her feet. "You keep them for me. I—I can't look at them."

Charlie reserved comment, his gaze steady on Rachel.

"You could use them for a story that would destroy the whole family."

Charlie tipped his head and ambled to the bedroom door. "Which Goodman?"

She pulled in a deep cleansing breath. "Anna and the man in those pictures don't know I found them. He'd kill me and her."

"Who? Who would kill you?"

He watched her head turn, hearing her and stomach churn. "I don't know which one yet."

The thoughts Charlie had been trying to hold at bay for the last week crept in. The patriarch's voice in their meeting at the attorney's office had sounded hauntingly familiar. "How many of Donald Goodman's wives have dark hair?"

"What? No way. Father Goodman's no rapist."

Charlie held up the photos. "And what's the man in these photos? A prophet or one sick son-of-a-bitch?" He closed the distance between them. He was crushing something of beauty just to win his point. "You're right." He spoke carefully to strain out any further accusation in his voice, but it lingered the same as a foul stench. "The Strangler's all hung up on right and wrong, good and evil. He confesses to me as though I'm his priest."

Rachel turned on one heel. "Most of his wives have dark hair."

"Doesn't necessarily mean anything," he said, scrambling to cover his bulldozing interrogation. Rage curled up inside him at the thought of the mean bastard he had locked horns with forcing himself on Rachel. He wanted him dead. *Dead and out of our lives.* He didn't feel guilty for thinking it. "We don't even know if he's the man in these pictures yet."

Charlie sat back down on the edge of the bed near her. "I'm sorry for giving you the third degree. It's my nature."

He glanced over at her dowdy dress neatly folded on the dresser countertop. "You really do need some new clothes. We're going to start with a coat that—"

"What's wrong with my coat?"

Charlie got up from the bed, his expression newly energized with joy. "You have no idea how beautiful you are, do you?"

He saw her body stiffen at the brazen comment, wondering if her internal battle was even close to what he felt in her presence. He had subliminally expected heat or cold. She had both in her. He expected power, for she was anything but weak.

Charlie leaned down and kissed her on the cheek before she saw it coming, spilling the tea on her tray. He dragged his mouth away and stared into her eyes, so big, stormy, and shocked. "I'm sorry. I shouldn't have done that."

She looked down at her plate and half smiled. "That's nice of you to say."

"Rachel, when all this is settled I want to be there when you wake up one morning and realize that you've been reborn into a place where the world will be at your feet."

~

Charlie chewed on the intimacy and commitment behind his words as they drove across town and up through Parley's Canyon en route to Park City. His eyes lingered on the sprawl of tight apartment and condominium housing squeezing out the last of the converted coal mining town's natural ambiance.

"It's a shame how everybody has to get a piece of something until what they bought it for disappears," Charlie murmured, turning into the discount clothing complex on the eyebrow of town. "You don't look at one price tag, okay?"

"You shouldn't—"

He held up a silencing hand and sat for a moment, scanning the storefronts. "Levi, Nike, Guess?, Nine West Shoes, Liz Claiborne, everything we need to start you off right."

Rachel heaved a sigh. "Thank you."

He smiled warmly. "The world's about to meet Rachel Zimmerman and wants her to be a knockout."

44
CHAPTER

The faint stench of engine exhaust only slightly interrupted his all-senses fantasy of raping Rachel Zimmerman. Anticipation of his next victim was growing from orgasmic to absolutely liberating. He rammed the accelerator pedal to the floor and the green Chevy Tahoe with the back window sticker reading, "He's coming," lurched around the second-to-last car separating him and ecstasy. Charlie Carver was staring at him through his Jeep's rear view mirror. He was sure of it.

Oh no, Charlie. I want to watch her a little bit longer before letting you know I'm going to suck your girlfriend dry.

He had lost a whole day of work following the two lovebirds from Charlie's house to the shopping center, and now downtown Park City. He dealt with his impatience tapping the wheel in tune to Rachmaninoff's Concerto No. 2 in C Minor as the single lane of traffic crawled to the city center.

~

The straw-blond waiter with a raccoon ski-goggle tan looked as though he was from central casting for Robert Redford's *Downhill Racer*. Charlie glanced up from the eclectic Stein Erickson Pine Lodge menu at the gorgeous woman opposite him with free-flowing satin black hair. She looked striking in her new snow-white fur-lined parka and beige ribbed turtleneck sweater, jeans and sandy-colored artificial fur after-ski boots. With the three dresses, shoes of all types, and a collection of casual clothes he intentionally stopped adding up, he figured he'd spent roughly a month's salary without a moment's regret.

Rachel's eyes widened. Her hands were trembling as she set down her glass of iced tea.

"What's wrong?"

"I thought I recognized one of the men on our Council of Seven," she murmured, then reached up and toyed with the neck of the tight-fitting sweater.

"Is it him?"

"No, it wasn't him." Her eyes continued racing from table to table.

Charlie placed his hand on hers. "Hey, it's the middle of the week. Give yourself a break for a few minutes."

She gently slipped her hand out from under his and turned her attentions back to the menu. They ordered and began eating in a comfortable silence between bites when Charlie's cellular phone rang.

"This is Charlie." He immediately felt a heavy sense of a presence on the other end of the line, an ominous silence. His stomach soured in a now-familiar anticipation. "Who is this?"

"You trying to torment me into hurting you again? I already told you I think that woman you're with is beautiful as an angel." The voice was deep, rich.

Charlie gulped spastically and scanned the room. "What are you talking about?"

"You think I don't watch you? Why did you have to pick her?"

Charlie looked over at Rachel, then around the room. "What are you talking about?"

"Whom do think you're talking to?"

"Donald Goodman!" he said without considering even an ounce of strategy.

Silence again. "You have served my needs, and you will again. I love her new outfit. So tight and naughty."

Charlie shot a glance at Rachel and cupped a hand over the receiver. "I'll be right back." He stood, turned his back to her and lowered his voice an octave as he walked toward the restaurant entrance. "What the hell does that mean, 'you will again,' you sick bastard? Where are you?"

"You two shouldn't wait up for me."

"How did you get this number?" Charlie snapped.

"No more calls." Dial tone.

Charlie took a deep breath and manufactured a smile as he returned to the dining table while continuing to scan the room. Maybe evil created an aura he could see. No suspects. *Are you here*? The twisted monster that raped and killed women and children was watching them at his house.

She isn't safe. I'm not safe.

"Who was it?"

He rebounded with the resilience of youth. "Liddle, my city editor. I told him we were coming up here today."

Rachel shrugged and again looked around the room, glancing out the window at the pelting snow.

"What are you thinking?" Charlie asked.

"Anna," she whispered, peering into the thin mist.

"I'm going to see if Lydia Pearson can stay with you while I'm at work tomorrow. She's one of the three women who created the Women Against Polygamy group that just got...Ah, they got a lot of press attention," Charlie said.

Rachel's eyes were still distant, disconnected, haunted.

Charlie smiled, faking his never-fail charmer. He stood and tucked his loosened beige safari shirt into his jeans, bringing her attention to his tailored build, gym-honed since his early twenties for maximum sports performance. He casually undid the top button of his shirt with his gaze steady on her.

"You can stay at my place as long as it takes to get things settled."

"I don't know."

Charlie shot his hand up in the air. "Remember? No worries, just for today, and maybe tonight?"

"You're a flirt," she said, her eyes inviting the engagement.

"I'll be fixing you a spectacular dinner. That's not against the law, is it?"

She tentatively reached her hand out. Charlie didn't underestimate the courage in such a gesture, taking it gently as if escorting a royal princess to her carriage.

He had drawn her in, making her believe he was stronger than over-the-line temptations. She was beginning to let her shields down. He was beginning to feel suspended between the roles of soul mate, protector, and possible lover.

~

After an Alaskan sockeye salmon and wild rice dinner, the sounds of the night settled around them: wind in the trees, snowplows scraping the last snow from the street, popping and creaking noises common to an older home. Charlie twitched as if he was physically connected to every bump in the dark. Other moments, as the two sat on the couch staring into the fireplace's gas-lit flames, the air around them sizzled with electricity and forbidden sexual hunger.

"What are some of your best memories of childhood?" Charlie asked, continuing his positive theme.

"I don't know. Let's not talk about me right now."

Her implacable expression made him wonder what horrors could be lurking so close to the surface that they created an instantly deep melancholy. He felt her sadness, and for a moment held it inside to meld their souls.

"Me? I grew up in the Chicago projects. Ever hear of them?"

Rachel shook her head.

He chuckled. "Let's just say we were financially challenged. My father slept it off on the couch in the living room every night after work. He died of a heart attack when he was fifty-eight. Guess that's one of the reasons I'm such an exercise and health nut."

He could see Rachel was surprised he had volunteered something so personal.

He tried to picture her as a child of polygamy, seated around an expansive dinner table. But with her free-flowing hair and new casual clothes, he couldn't—or wouldn't.

"How did you go from that to here?" she asked.

"Not nearly the journey you're on."

With downturned eyes she nodded.

He moved one of his hands to her hip, wanting to touch, to devour her, laying claim to a relationship built of more than survival needs. Rachel's breath caught. Anticipation tightened her muscles. Her lips parted slightly. He sensed she was about to tell him no.

"We really shouldn't."

He pressed a forefinger to her lips. "Shouldn't what?" He removed his finger and brushed his lips against hers. "It's too late."

"No," she said softly. "I'm not sleeping with you, if that's what you're asking."

"Of course not." He rubbed her thigh until she started responding in a pulsing motion. "You would have to be totally in love." He kissed her deeply, then moved down to her milky white neck.

"Are you?" he whispered, gazing into her eyes, serious, determined, hungry.

"I don't know how to really *be* with a man."

He slowly moved her to a laying position on the couch while continuing to sensuously devour her lips and tease her tongue, until his certainty sweep them both away and into his bed.

Charlie had come to think of himself as somewhat impervious to a woman's tears. *No more.* Rachel wept, awkwardly pushing away, then lunging to pull him to her bare, hot chest. He held her, rocked her, stroked her damp hair, and cradled her body shivering in ecstasy, all the while telling her comforting words he never expected to say to a woman in his life. He kissed her tears from her cheeks, her jaw, her neck. And then his lips again moved to her mouth, kissing her slowly at first, tasting her pain and despair. Tasting a long-leashed desire.

He didn't know whether he rolled over in her arms, or whether she shifted herself. He only knew he was astride her with kissing that was fast moving beyond the point of comfort. He threaded his fingers through her unbound hair, and her mouth hungrily told him she trusted and needed more. She opened her eyes and stared into his face. Her eyes sparked with confusion and desire.

"I'll stop when you want," he whispered.

Her body tightened around his at the words. He had to force himself not to react, not to take over.

He wasn't surprised that she didn't know what to do, that her movements were clumsy and uncertain. She was frightened of what she was doing, what she was feeling. He knew he could make her do anything he wanted, despite her fear. It made the release of control to her powerfully sensual.

Her skin grew slick with sweat as he drank in her every reaction, every ripple, reveling like a starving man. He entered her slowly, gently, then with her urging, harder, faster. He felt her release, an explosive groan, as every muscle quivered in rigid intensity. Then only their heavy ragged breathing.

"You're incredible," he sighed while holding her still-trembling body. He let her crawl away from him across the sweat-drenched sheets and sink down, curling herself into a tight fetal ball, making no sound whatsoever.

He stared at her for a moment, then crossed the expanse of the mattress, snuggling close to her, until he felt her tight, damp body relax. "You're really beautiful," he whispered.

A moment later she slept.

No more calls.

The killer's soundbite resonated in Charlie's dreams until it forced his eyelids open. A stark vision of Rachel trapped alone with the killer, her screams for mercy, one more vicious blow before death, made him nervously shake. He lay there in the half-light convincing himself he was imagining eyes watching, waiting to attack.

He wrapped his body close around her as if Rachel were a longtime companion. Finally he slept.

CHAPTER 45

Rachel watched Lydia release a sigh of exasperation as the woman continued digging through the stack of paperwork. She unearthed a list of tenants she and her murdered co-founder had scratched out on Burger King napkins less than two days after she and her brood had escaped with nothing but their lives.

"Here it is," she mumbled, pulling it out of casework files and flattening it into a readable surface on Charlie's glass and bleached oak coffee table.

It made Rachel uneasy thinking about it. These women were attracting international press with stories, even if true, that were best kept as family secrets. She flashed on her first day of public school, when boys and girls chided her as a "plyg" and pulled her braids. The woman Charlie had sent to help was also building a coalition of enemies. She winced at close examination of the crusader: she was so rotund that her eyes even bulged.

Where should she draw the line? She had broken the rules by trying to draw the police in, potentially exposing and destroying her entire family. How could Charlie begin to understand that she still found the thought of decimating the world she was raised in devastating? Until Sarah's disappearance she had felt God's presence in congregational gatherings on crisp Sunday mornings, and even at times in silent prayer.

Allegiance to God gave everything purpose and serenity. That was gone now, and a Lydia Pearson was the last person to help her get it back.

Lydia squinted to read the paper before her eyes. "Women Against Polygamy was founded as a political action organization and a coordinating arm for the Utah State Division of Family Services to ensure that women and children have the right to choose, and opportunity to lead a self-directed and supported life." She dropped the paper and propped up both brows. "Kinda rambles on, but you get the picture."

"When did you leave the—"

Lydia's eyes lit up at the prompting. "I had to rummage through garbage cans for almost a year to feed the kids before I got the guts to take off." Rachel knew the kindred spirit was awaiting a saucer-eyed response. Lydia leaned forward on her well-padded elbows. "Not everybody gets to live like the Goodmans."

"I didn't mean—"

"I got your vibes, sister, the second I walked through that door. I'm not your enemy. Charlie didn't want to leave you alone today."

Lydia took a finishing gulp of coffee. "Good stuff. Should have started drinking it years ago."

Rachel straightened slowly, growing more uncomfortable with the woman's every word.

Lydia smirked and sat back. "It's really interesting what usually happens to people—not just teenagers, either—when you give them a taste of the outside." Her eyes turned to the coffee cup. "I don't just mean breaking the Word of Wisdom by drinking coffee, either. They go crazy, drinking, smoking, right off the edge."

Rachel didn't comment, trying her best to be a little less obvious. "I'm a trained court reporter," she blurted.

Lydia nodded. "So I understand." She leveled a stare at the Babylon rookie. "Charlie told me everything, so let's not sit here passing niceties about how wonderful polygamy is, or I won't have a second cup."

Rachel winced. "So what do you think you can do to help?" she said caustically, needing to lash out at somebody.

Lydia's neck veins jetted out the size of sapling roots. "My best friend was just murdered for thinking we can help!"

Rachel put a hand to her mouth, more concerned than contrite.

Lydia stood, reached out, and shook Rachel's hand. "How 'bout we start over again? I'm Lydia Pearson, the name I've adopted, anyway. Here to help get you through whatever, or whoever's, coming after you." She paced the length of the coffee table, nervous energy rising with each step.

"Why did you change your name, when I see your picture in the paper all the time?" Rachel asked.

"I don't know. All three of us did, for the kids, I guess. We wanted to start a new family tree."

"They're still your blood," Rachel said, her face stony.

"The only thing having to do with blood is mine, and they're after it. From the sounds of it, some has been spilled in your family, too."

Rachel rubbed her eyes. "You act like my family's a bunch of psychopaths."

"I'm not the one sitting in some stranger's house, hiding from family who may have killed my daughter. Cut the crap, Rachel, and figure out who's on your side." Lydia plopped back into her seat. "I sometimes manage to piss people off. Guess since I got to speak my peace, I can't seem to shut my trap!"

The comment struck both women as funny. Chuckles turned into hearty belly laughs until they were both reaching for facial tissue.

Rachel pushed a strand of hair off her cheek. "I think it's easier to braid," she said with a peacemaking smile.

"Charlie told me about one of your marriage daughters," Lydia said.

"Anna. She was forced to marry her uncle a few days ago."

"No sweat," Lydia said calmly. "It's not legal in the eyes of the law, so it's not legal. Period."

"How can we get her out of there, Lydia?" she whispered as the fight drained out of her. She shut her eyes as if to wish it would all go away.

"You're in over your head, sister, but I'm going to be your swimming instructor, if you'll let me."

Rachel acquiesced.

"Right now everything has to be jumbled up, with the loss of your daughter and all. You're nobody's child or pawn anymore. You're here because you're tough, and you'd better plan on staying that way."

"I just want to go hide somewhere and have everybody leave me alone."

"And Anna?" Lydia rose and put a hand on Rachel's shoulder. "Just a few days ago I was ready to give up the fight, but we can't. There are too many women and children right now wishing they could go to sleep tonight and never wake up."

"I'm sorry," Rachel murmured. "After I lost Sarah—"

Lydia ran a loving hand over Rachel's hair. "I know," she said softly. "We've all lost precious people and parts of ourselves. You're stronger than you know. I can feel it."

Rachel allowed awareness of nothing but the woman's gentle touch. She reached up and grasped Lydia's hand just as tears lined her cheeks.

Possibly she was going through a temporary delirious grief. Possibly she was losing her mind.

46
CHAPTER

Friday was payday, a day of particular significance to Charlie Carver, man about town, who had just dropped close to a month's paycheck on clothes for not just any woman—*the* woman.

He had replayed the previous night in his head a hundred times before he even made it to his desk. He had made the right choice in helping—loving—Rachel Zimmerman.

His instincts had always been a superior compass as a reporter. But personal life? He hadn't had one in so long that any course had to be the right one. He ignored his city editor's constant whining to get his head, and other parts, out of polygamy and back on the scent for new scandals blossoming. He didn't respond to publisher Glendon Bartholomew's week-old email that they needed to talk.

He also didn't believe in coincidence. The publisher and editor were waving their arms in an overheated battle behind the glass walls of the department conference room, and from the pointing fingers, Charles Carver was the issue.

The possibilities rubbed back and forth until his chafed mind forced his hand. *Careful.* The warning light blinked in his mind. He should have replied to his email. *Too late for that.*

Liddle threw his hands up in the air and stormed out of the room with the singular purpose of making it a threesome. "Charlie! Come in here this minute."

Charlie checked his watch. He was late for an appointment with the mayor. "I've got Mayor Wilson in thirty minutes."

"He can wait." Liddle paced toward the fidgeting publisher, fondly called 'Rug' behind his back because of a black toupee that resembled a beanie atop a gray-flecked arc of hair.

"What's Rug flipping out about?" Charlie whispered.

Liddle grabbed him by the arm and stopped cold. "I told you to stay away from the Goodmans. Polygamy's like a damn tar baby, and you know it."

Before Charlie could charge into his valiant role as crusading defender of women's' and children's rights, Liddle whisked him before his judge and jury.

Bartholomew waited a beat to let the two settle into their chairs, then just stared. The silence was more than disturbing—it was aggravating.

"Well, I'm listening."

Liddle gave Charlie a prompting side-glance.

"What? What did I do?"

Bartholomew planted his palms on the brown laminate tabletop. "I sent you an email more than a week ago."

"I took a day off. And I've been busy."

"You've been busy, all right. Breaking the law and stirring up a hornet's nest all over town."

Charlie had never had a real heart-to-heart with the publisher. It didn't take an investigative reporter to size the man up. He was blunt, tactless, straightforward. A real Chicago bulldog type.

"Lay it out for me," said Charlie.

Liddle swallowed hard before jumping into the fray. "Charlie's from a different world, Glendon. He'd get his ass kicked for not chasing down a story like this one if—"

"You're talking about Goodman, right?" Charlie added.

"Reporting what's happening is one thing. But, Mr. Carver, making things happen, illegal things—"

Charlie was on his feet. "Illegal? What in the hell's illegal?"

"Kidnapping a woman about to be married for one thing."

"Married? Rachel Zimmerman?"

"Calling down the chief of homicide until he finally flies you out on a wild goose chase over some allegation that—"

"*Allegation*? A child was murdered!"

"And who says so? The kid probably ran away. I talked to Strickland." He pounded out exclamation points on the table with his index finger. "He found no trace of any foul play. Just your girlfriend's story."

Liddle leaped between the two crimson-faced men. "Let's settle down. Give Carver a chance to explain." He turned a cold eye to Bartholomew. "You've already heard one side. We're in the business of hearing both." He grabbed Charlie by the arm. "Go on, sit down and fill us in."

Charlie bit his tongue and recoiled back into the chair. He knew Bartholomew wouldn't offer him the same courtesy. "The woman referred to is the mother of the dead child, who recently, along with another witness, dug up her teenage daughter's body in the barn we never checked at the Goodman Ranch. We're getting a search warrant and going back."

"It is the family's responsibility to go to the police with a story like that." Bartholomew shook his head and closed his fists in suppressed rage. "You're here less than a year, and already you've made friends with a serial killer who wants to talk to you before *and* after each killing. Now you're in the middle of tearing apart the family of a man, a good man, one I've known for years—with unsubstantiated stories from a woman Liddle tells me is shacked up with you right now!"

Charlie shot out of his seat with his hands raised. "That's it." He whirled around to Liddle. "Sorry, Theron. I quit."

Bartholomew rounded the table at attack speed. A pulsing vein zigzagged across his broad forehead resembling a lightening bolt. Bartholomew stared at Liddle, then wheeled on Charlie. "A perfect solution, since I was just about to tell you the same thing I told Liddle here a minute ago. You're fired."

The pronouncement hit Charlie with the force of a physical blow, stunning him. He took a deep breath and fell to a dead calm. "You're right. Leaving is a perfect solution. I've got an editor at *The Chicago Tribune* begging me to come back. You know why?"

Bartholomew was steaming, too hot for a retort.

"Because I am the first to get at the heart of dirt and murder in a town as big and crazy as Chicago." Each word was even, dripping in sarcasm. "That's what an investigative reporter does if he's worth a damn."

"And that's why I hired him," Liddle interjected.

The publisher folded his arms, glaring as snidely as an army drill instructor at the two men. "Your game doesn't play in a 'B Market', buddy. Never has and never will."

Charlie stepped to the door, rotating as he opened it. "It plays—at 'A Market' papers."

CHAPTER 47

Night had fallen, Lydia had dashed away to feed and put her brood to bed before returning. Though Charlie had called home, it would still be another few minutes before he returned. Rachel swallowed hard at the combination of disappointment and uneasiness that clouded the back of her mind. Against a gnawing fear, her eyes did a quick scan around the lamp-lit living room, then dining room, and finally kitchen of the two-level house.

"Don't be stupid," she muttered to herself, the nerves at the back of her neck wriggling at the feeling that eyes under the cover of darkness were watching her. Eyes sizing up the curves of her body, her jerky, uncertain movements, before tasting, then devouring her until she was only a cold corpse, like Sarah, left for Charlie to find.

Entering the hall of barely familiar surroundings, she fumbled along the wall for a switch, then blinked against the glare of four small bulbs arranged in a brass and frosted glass floral cluster.

Her first thought was of Charlie's old house, creaking and making the same sudden noises as the family ranch house. The thought reeled her back to her constant nightmare: Sarah's lily-white arm lying motionless in its humus grave.

She drifted down the hall and into the bedroom where she and Charlie had made love, her brain stumbling to make sense of contradictory visions and information.

Suddenly she heard a muted shuffling sound outside in the direction of the front door. Her pulse picked up the rhythm of fear. "Charlie, is that you?" she called, her quaking voice a vocal extension of the goose bumps pebbling her arms. She froze in place awaiting a response. The only answer was an ominous silence that was louder in her eardrums than noise.

She stepped over to the bed, held her breath, kneeled and shot a quick look under the bed. She stood and backed away slowly, deciding not to open closets. Her hand trembled as she reached out to steady herself on the bedroom door handle. She held her breath while continuing the ghost hunt through a sheet of tears.

"Charlie?" she called once more, her heart accelerating at the now sure knowledge she wouldn't get an answer.

Her gaze drifted to the staircase that led to the second floor. Maybe the sound came from upstairs. Her heart beat faster. *Maybe somebody's already in the house.*

The front door. It's not locked, or is it?

She stalled, then ripped through the hall to the entryway, partially shadowed by the light emanating from a sole living room table lamp. She took an uneven breath and reached for the handle.

"Too late."

The words were no different than a pair of shotgun blasts in the still of a graveyard. Rachel wheeled around, a scream wedged in her lungs. She caught a glance, his eyes inflamed in fury, his mouth set in a grim, compressed line. His rising hand was big, with blunt-tipped fingers. Then she felt the biting sting and saw white light from the blow to her face.

Before fading away to darkness she heard him speak again, his voice melodic and rich. "Surprised?"

CHAPTER 48

Charlie pulled the Jeep Scout to a stop and let the engine percolate and wipers swoosh while he tried to stop his head from spinning, bursting with recreations of the newsroom battle and what it would, could, mean to life with or without Rachel Zimmerman.

He had to stop the excessive images for awhile. He had to shut down all his engines, or he would explode. He had to stop being a self-righteous reporter who never took direction. The difference between him and other newspapermen, he knew, was that he could only do things one way—his.

He wouldn't feel any guilt or regrets, even though he was bursting at the seams with it.

I'll have to leave her right when she needs me the most. Leave her. Stop the images! Stop everything for now.

Charlie pictured Rachel sleeping in his guest bedroom. Once matured to the outside world her brightness would be blinding, intoxicating. His love for her was so deep, so overpowering, it was starting to scare him and put his own judgment in question. He lowered the power window and looked to see if any lights signaled a welcoming return. Total darkness. It scared him most to think of what he would do if he lost her, too.

He killed the engine and staggered to the front porch. He blew a plume of frosted air in his hand, but couldn't smell his breath. As he neared the house, the air felt tinged with menace, danger. The front door was slightly ajar.

He had to lower his chin and concentrate to swallow. "Rachel?" he said in a hoarse voice. He carefully pushed the door open fully with his swaying fingertips. "It's me."

Charlie moved through the entryway into the living room, where he flicked on a table lamp. While he got no response, he took in a pent-up sigh of relief. He had been to enough crime scenes to know the place would show some sign of chaos if something had happened. He headed toward the larger of the two guest bedrooms, the one he had designated as her sleeping quarters if she didn't want to again celebrate their union in his bed, then shook his head. *Let her sleep.*

He went to the kitchen, turned on the bright ceiling lights and squinted, then pulled the ground coffee beans from the refrigerator and filled the automatic brewing machine. He scrounged for a dry bagel to soak up some of the still-accelerating alcohol rushes. The house felt as it always did when he passed through the front door—alone.

Just a peek. I won't wake her.

He started for the bedroom, passing the shadowed dining room en route. He stopped and shuffled back, shaking his head to clear away the thick-as-molasses effects of the scotch. His stomach turned at the site of the overturned captain's chair nearest the living room.

"Shit," he muttered, trying desperately not to make any premature deductions.

The serial killer's threat reverberated like a pair of two-ton church bells. *You served my needs and you will again. Get out of my head, you bastard.*

He drew himself up and hurried toward her room. *Easy to knock over a chair when you don't know a house. She didn't turn on all the lights when it got dark. Went to the kitchen from the living room, through the dining...*

Charlie narrowed his eyes at the sight of Rachel's bedroom door left wide open.

"Rachel, you asleep?" he said quietly. The silence hung in the air. Nauseating spurts of adrenaline coursed through his veins while his pulse roared in his ears in the strangely disembodied silence. He bit down on the tip of his tongue at the sight of the empty, neatly made bed.

"Rachel," he loudly groaned between his teeth. In a frenzy he ran from room to room finding nothing out of place. He leaned back against the hallway wall to stabilize his whirling mind and emotions.

Lydia. She went out with Lydia. He heaved a sigh of relief, went to the kitchen phone and punched out her number.

Busy line. Sandwiching the receiver between his shoulder and his ear, he rifled through the city phone book under the heading police homicide and called Lydia again. The phone hadn't trilled twice when she picked it up.

"Yes?" The voice was tentative, scared to death.

"Lydia, it's me, Charlie Carver."

"Oh, I thought you were somebody else."

Charlie scrunched his entire face into a look of suffering anticipation. "Is Rachel with you?"

"What? She's not there?"

"I'll get back to you." Charlie slammed down the phone.

His brain buzzing, Charlie staggered back to the front door and turned on the chandelier. He dropped his head and closed his eyes lamenting his selfish indulgence in self-pity that had allowed her abduction or murder. His eyelids locked wide open as he lifted one foot, then the other. He had smeared one of them, but he saw two more. No, three splatters of blood.

The madman's ominous words echoed in his mind again. He dropped to his knees, more in nausea than inspection. His mind shuffled possible scenarios while gritting his teeth to hold down a belly full of scotch. He knew better than to touch evidence at a crime scene—and it was a crime scene.

~

"Doesn't look good." Sargent Strickland rubbed a hand across his eyes as he fixed a gaze on the normally smart-ass reporter who was trying to direct the scene investigators where to wave their black light wands for latent prints. "Hey, Carver, let them do their fucking jobs."

"If you guys would pull your heads out of your ass we could have—" Charlie cut himself off short, jerking his gaze away from the color rising in Strickland's face to continue surveying the room for more clues that his now stone-sober mind could detect.

"Use the powder for hell sakes! There should be new prints on the overturned chair in the dining room," Charlie called out in the direction of the black-mustached policeman wannabe-junior investigator tagging and snapping photos of the blood droplets.

Strickland motioned for the reporter to join him, alone, in the living room. Once in range he prowled a little closer to the reporter. He looked into Charlie's eyes, his glare shrewd, predatory. "I never asked what color her hair was." Charlie could tell he read his thoughts in a heartbeat and leaned down into him. "Get a call from your friend yet?"

No retort formed, no words came out of Charlie's dry mouth. He finally got it out. "Asshole."

A wry smile of amusement curled up the corner of Strickland's mouth. "I thought we'd take turns."

"I know who he is," Charlie blurted out, his resolve hardening.

Both men's fists spasmed at the sound of the phone ringing.

"If that's him, hold him longer this time. We haven't been able to get a bead on the son-of-a-bitch," Strickland said, then nudged Charlie's shoulder to act fast.

Charlie looked at him sideways and waited.

"Hurry up, damnit. You could miss him!"

"What would it help?" Charlie said at last. "He's only calling to torture me."

"Keep him talking." Strickland shoved the reporter toward the kitchen. "Get in there."

The fire went out of Charlie abruptly. He rubbed his hands over his face and along his ponytail line while taking his time getting to the phone. He reached out as if handling an explosive as he put the receiver to his ear.

"It's Lydia. Is Rachel back yet? I'm really sorry, Charlie. I shouldn't have left her to get the kids to bed."

"*I'm* the one who shouldn't have left."

Charlie glared at Strickland and shook his head. "I found drops of blood. The police are here right now."

"Those monsters probably beat her up before taking her back to the compound."

Charlie's head pounded with no mercy. Strickland stood perched close by. "No. I'm being tracked by that bastard who's been killing everybody."

"They've got their own law, Charlie."

The knowledge served to only darken Charlie's mood, if that was possible. "You mean Goodman?"

Charlie watched Strickland wince at the mention of the name.

"I can only tell you I wouldn't be surprised if she just disappears," Lydia added. "It doesn't mean she's dead, Charlie."

"Doesn't mean she isn't, either," he snarled and pounded the phone down.

Strickland waited for Charlie to cool off a little. "So who is the serial killer?"

"Serial killer and Rachel's—" Saying it could make it a reality. He wasn't ready to let it solidify.

"I'll get a search warrant this time."

CHAPTER 49

Rachel sat in a rocker by her bedroom window, staring out from her locked prison at the fifty-foot pine trees as they transformed from shadows to vague, then crisp shapes in the rising sun. It was the start of another day without Sarah, and now without Charlie Carver. She couldn't imagine how she was going to live through it, if, in fact, the Council of Seven and Father Goodman allowed her to live. She was ready, even welcomed blood atonement if the alternative was life in *his* bed, those nine clawing fingers, and blind servitude.

The night of making love to Charlie whispered in the back of her mind. The visions were as smooth and comforting as warmed honey.

She glanced over at her twin bed and pictured him sleeping, sprawled face down in the center of the bed, his arms flung wide over its edges, claiming the entire mattress as his own. Since Jacob had brutally dragged her back to captivity, she had tried to imagine what Charlie was going through from the first moment he found she had vanished again from his life.

She closed her eyes and saw them each in separate cars, frantically waving out the back window at each other as the drivers widened their distance until they could no longer see each other's eyes, faces. In her mind's eye, she reached out to him mutely, but he was fading back into the foggy mystery of a forbidden world.

Loneliness clamped over her, tightening her chest, her lungs, her heart.

God, take me away from this. I don't want to live anymore.

The knock at the door shattered the eerie silence. "Rachel, I need to talk to you," Donald Goodman's voice boomed out. Her breathing stopped at the fumbling sound of a key being found and inserted. "You hear me? I'm coming in."

She pressed a hand to her broken, taped nose, holding back a cry of fear. "Please don't come in." She watched the now-turning knob hesitantly.

Everything had been so different when she was a child. Father Goodman had been, at least seemed, different. He had always favored her, showing pride and bragged about her from when she entered puberty. Just his presence gave her a sense of personal validation, real self worth. He was aware of her distant and demanding parents and captured the opportunity to be supportive to the point of family resentment. She had grown up proud, feeling genuinely loved and respected, even her resistive antics.

Now the man about to enter her private cage she viewed as selfish, bitter, possessive, and resentful of any signs of independence. A man consumed by the need to acquire and control.

Ignorance had been at the core of innocence. Panic closed over her throat. She forced herself out of the chair and went toward the door and paced a rectangle in pale light that fell from the window onto the wood floor. She forced herself to think, to scheme, sparking ignition of her survival senses. Every ounce of her being was trembling. It took every fiber of strength to confront and conquer her demons, the most beastly just entering the room. Gritting her teeth, she fought against cowering in the corner. *You don't own me. You don't own me. You don't own me.*

She was back in her midnight blue, little girl tights and calico dress. Her hair was braided and twisted into a bun on the crown of her head. On the back of the opening door was a slightly distorting narrow mirror, made more so by a bizarre reflection of her youth. The cold floor seemed to seep through to her heart.

"Why didn't you answer when I called for you?"

Rachel jerked backwards at the sound of her master's voice.

"There's nothing to say."

In the pale light of the room, Donald Goodman looked gray, older. Lines of disappointment and anger were etched deeply into his face beside his eyes and mouth. A sigh leaked out of his lungs in seeing his favorite back in proper attire.

Rachel wanted, needed, to get back something of herself, but he had left her nothing to control or oversee, not even Anna. "I don't care what you do to me. I can't live like this anymore." With each step he made closer, Rachel backed up until her body was pressed against the cold corner walls.

He gave a bitter laugh. "A kicking bronco right to the end." He backed away and sat on her bed. He patted it for her to join him. She reluctantly walked over and sat down.

"Now, that's more like it." He gave an exasperated sigh. "What am I going to do with you?"

"Let me leave. I won't bother anybody here again."

"You're so lost," he said, flinging an arm up in the air. "Do you have even the slightest idea of how you've upset our family?"

The question died as a wave of rage surged through her. "My only family's dead."

"That's absurd." He stood and turned his back on her. "You've taken advantage of me—of all of us. I've made allowances for your rebellious behavior for years because you've always been special to me." He swung around to face her.

"All these years, but you're nothing like her."

She looked into his dejected eyes, her expression a plea for under-standing. "Like who?"

"I'm sorry," he murmured. "For both of us."

His statement hung between them as the moment grew more taut.

"What have they, you, decided to do with me?"

Goodman looked away as Rachel started to cry. "Our celestial marriage would have been a thing—" He was stopped by a knocking on Rachel's bedroom door. "What?" he demanded.

"The police are at the door, Father," a quavering woman's voice responded.

Goodman pulled Rachel roughly up from the bed. "What's this about now? Your boyfriend get the police?"

~

The pressure had built up behind Charlie's eyes to the point of resembling an overfilled balloon. He was bearing the full responsibility of Rachel's probable death, and Goodman was going to pay for it. Two officers flanked Charlie and Strickland in Goodman's entry. They were newer to the force, less jaded than Strickland was, and more revved for an explosive confrontation.

Since discovering the drops of blood, Charlie's imagination had been running wild with confusing evidence. *His* killer's bodies were always surgically clean of cuts, even bruising, except around the neck. He took pride in never spilling blood that might disturb the twisted, but artistic signature. Some kind of consistent pattern usually bubbled up after any first few serial murders, and this killer was no stand out. His victims were all strikingly beautiful, usually under thirty, Caucasian, flawless complexions. They were perfect cover girls made even more alluring by his post-strangulation positioning of arms, legs, and splayed dark hair.

Blood droplets. No body. Inches of room for hope, maybe, but enough that Charlie's raw instincts dismissed Strickland's quick-to-judgement assessment. Charlie pictured Rachel anxiously awaiting her loving protector's return, opening the front door without hesitation. He cringed at the thought of her surprise and helplessness when the attacker brutally beat her and dragged her away. He felt himself inside Rachel Zimmerman, allowing her to finally trust and feel safe with a man, then tumbling back down into the depths of male-dominated captivity. Strickland's voice brought him back.

"You really think Goodman's our man?" Strickland slipped on a pair of scholarly-looking reading glasses and gave the search warrant a final once-over.

"I think you're full of shit, Carver," he side-mouthed, just as the patriarch descended the stairs in a black suit, stark white dress shirt, and maroon tie.

"What are you people up to now? Harassing my poor wife at our ranch. I've talked to the governor about this, and he's not happy," Goodman said.

Strickland's eyebrows rose above the rim of his glasses. He took them off and curled one hand into a fist as if he was going to throw a baseball slider. He waved the search warrant in front of Goodman's face, then handed it to him. "I apologize for not obtaining one of these before we took the time and expense to beeline to Snowville. Our search might have been more productive for both of us."

"Meaning?" Goodman said.

"We have a few questions before we look around. And this time we will look around." Strickland glanced over at Charlie's more-than-satisfied expression, then whipped his head in the direction of the living room.

Goodman bit down on his reply and led the group to the designated spot. Strickland was baiting the power mogul and he was taking it. Charlie eased himself into a chair, now feeling no need to engage.

"We'll start with Rachel Zimmerman." A slight grin washed across Strickland's face. "Where is she?"

Goodman bulleted a dismissing glance at Charlie, then returned a cool stare to his interrogator. "Other than responding to unfounded and misdirected questions, let me ask you a question. Why are you harassing my family with matters that are strictly domestic and no business of the police, let alone homicide?"

Strickland's grin curled into a smile that was nothing short of feral. He vaulted off the couch and leaned into Goodman. "Rachel Zimmerman. She lives in this compound, correct?"

"And?" Goodman responded, waving on a further explanation.

"She is missing, and we—"

Instead of the continued flare of temper, Goodman stood back and regarded Strickland with a look of surprise. He turned to three women hovering in the nearby formal dining room. "Ask Rachel to join us," he told the women in a voice rich as black velvet. When the women left, Goodman's smoldering eyes turned on Charlie. "You're behind this. I hope you have deep pockets, because one more word and I'll squeeze every last dime out of you for defamation of character."

"I'm glad she's still alive," Charlie said, unaffected by the bravado of the threat.

"How did she get here?" Strickland asked.

"She wanted to come home, where she belongs." Goodman folded his arms. "What's this really all about?"

Strickland pulled out a small pad from his shirt pocket, flipped over a couple of pages, and was about to speak when Rachel entered the room.

Charlie's lips pursed, trying to hold back his fury at the sight of her taped nose and still-swollen shiner under her right eye. "Rachel! What in the hell did they do to you?"

She offered a little shrug that knotted Charlie's stomach. "I walked into a glass door and...I broke my nose."

The room fell to a dead silence. The words, so casually spoken, made faces flush and tempers dim. Strickland tipped his head a little to one side, amazed she would actually think the feeble answer would do.

"When? Before or after they beat you to a pulp and dragged you back?" Charlie demanded.

"You heard what she said!" Goodman yelled.

"Come with us right now, Rachel. We'll get you out of here."

"Officer," Goodman said. "This man's been infatuated with this poor woman, who is still suffering from the tragic loss of her husband and her daughter running away." He walked over to Rachel and lightly tucked an arm around her shoulders. "There are laws against stalkers, and all you've accomplished by invading my home is one heck of a nasty lawsuit."

"Let her speak for herself," Charlie said. "Come on, Rachel, now's the time to get it all out."

Rachel looked down at her laced, flat-soled, black shoes. Her cheeks colored as she tried to speak while being now tightly held.

Charlie stepped up to Goodman and started to pry her free, but the man's powerful free forearm shoved him back.

"Get that man out of this house, Strickland. Right now!"

Strickland rose and attempted to contain Charlie, an effort as futile as trying to get a champagne cork back in the bottle.

The front door opened and a tall young man with angry dark eyes bolted into the living room and leaped between his father and Charlie. "Get out of our house," Hyrum Goodman yelled.

Charlie stepped back, never losing eye contact with Rachel's blood-drained face. "Don't let this happen, Rachel. You can leave with us right now." He watched her face as she struggled to respond.

Strickland heaved a deep sigh and tucked his notepad with dates and approximate times of the serial killer's murders back into his pocket. "All right. I've seen enough. If you're not going to press charges, ma'am, there's nothing more we can do to help."

"Get the hell out of my father's house!" Hyrum shouted. He turned and left as quickly as he appeared.

Strickland gave Donald Goodman a dismissing glance and eased his way close to Rachel, then lightly tugged her free from Goodman's supposedly comforting arm. Goodman moved away. "If there's anything else you want to tell us about your missing daughter——or what really happened to your face—then please call. I'm Sergeant Strickland." He pulled out his card and placed it in her hand. He motioned to the two officers standing behind him. "Let's go."

Charlie shook his head in disbelief. "Goodman, I know who you are and I'm going to get you."

"What is that supposed to mean, Mr. Carver?" Goodman shot an instructing finger up. "Be careful with your words. They could hang you."

"How about you being a sociopath, a pervert, a murderer of young women, a ruthless controller of people's lives? One sick son-of-a-bitch."

Goodman faked a smile. "Perfect. A room full of witnesses. You've just clinched my case, Carver. I'll see you in court." His eyes were filled with dark portents. "And that's the last time I want to see you. Step on my property again, and I'll shoot you for trespassing."

Rachel failed to raise her head. Realization dawned with a thick thud in Charlie's stomach. "It's Anna, isn't it? He's threatening you with—?"

Rachel blinked at the sound of Anna's name and looked up with a telling flash of her eyes. Strickland didn't miss it.

Charlie beamed at the untangling of the puzzle, an expression that crashed in the next instant.

"Remember what I said, Miss Zimmerman," Charlie said.

Goodman hovered behind Charlie and Strickland, too wired to stop moving. He paced, his face flowing with zeal or fever. He pulled a meticulously folded handkerchief out of his suit breast pocket and handed it to Rachel to wipe away cresting tears.

"This is no more or less than you could expect from people so far from God's calling," he said in a fatherly voice. He leveled a gaze on Charlie that had turned far more powerful men to ashes. "Don't let him into your heart and mind, Rachel. He's possessed by darkness that's making him mad."

Charlie nodded. "You're absolutely right, Goodman, if the God you're talking about condones slavery, murder, and perversion. I'd have to be crazy to follow him."

Goodman was turning purple from his throat up. He stood toe-to-toe with Charlie as if he was about to exorcise a demon. "Now leave this house and never return."

Strickland's jaw tightened to the quality of granite. "You might be through with him," he said, tipping his head in Charlie's direction. "But I'm not through with you." One corner of his mouth kicked up. He slowly retreated and walked out the door with Charlie and his officers at his heels.

The homicide chief waved off the blue-and-white and settled next to Charlie, then pulled out a slightly crumpled pack of cigarettes. "Down to smoking one a day. Sometimes more." He lowered his window, lit up, and took a to-the-toenails drag. "This is a more day."

50

CHAPTER

The voice registered with a jolt. The last three days had been a blur of being forced to take one Valium, then another, until everything in her new bridal bedroom had taken on round edges.

"Anna, open the door. It's Israel."

"I'm not supposed to talk to you," she murmured from the edge of her bed.

He tapped on the door again. "Open it quickly, before somebody sees me."

Her thoughts returned to how things had been before she shared a bed with her uncle-turned-husband. She wanted Israel to remember her as a virgin, fresh with dreams they shared over stolen moments, and hopes for a different tomorrow as innocent as their kisses and words of lifelong love.

She brushed a tear from her cheek. She glanced down at her lap, feeling shame for allowing the monster to ride and toy with her as he pleased. Bile rose in her throat as she absently rubbed herself between her legs, as if she was trying to rub out a soiled spot.

"Unlock the door. I'll only stay a minute," Israel pleaded.

She drew a deep breath and composed herself, primping in front of the door mirror to create a contented façade. She unlocked and slowly opened the door.

"What do you think you're doing? I'm married now."

He shook it off, frowning. "Don't *ever* talk about it—him—again." He led her by the arm to the bed. "Now please, don't interrupt me." His gaze was assessing, scrutinizing. "You drunk or something?"

"No, course not. They're making me take pills." She sat perkily as if a child who knew the answer. Her hair came loose from its twist as she worked to at least appear coherent. "They're afraid I'll hurt myself."

"I've got a plan."

Anna moved away from him, shaking her head. "You'll get us in trouble. You've got to get out of here before Hyrum catches you. He'll be home from work any minute."

Israel pursued her across the room. "That's why you've got to listen to me." He pulled her back to the bed. "Are you too screwed up to understand me before both of our lives are ruined?"

"I'm listening."

51

CHAPTER

Rachel clasped her hands in prayer, hanging on every sculpted image their Lord on earth forged for his standing-room-only congregation. This was why he was worshiped as more than a man. The very air around him vibrated with inspirational energy. As on every Sunday, he and his six council members were dressed in white robes, symbolizing the purity of walking in God's footsteps.

"So who is the enemy?" Donald Goodman asked rhetorically. "You may not be *the* enemy outside these fortress walls, but you're *an* enemy just the same if you adopt, even in your heart, what the outside would have you believe." He paused for effect, then stared over the pews at the lone Rachel Zimmerman, obviously socially ostracized from his flock. "And there are enemies right here among us this morning." The unadorned worship and activity hall was suddenly abuzz with whispering.

"Am I the enemy? Some would have us think so. Prophets have always been called out as the enemy by the masses. Christ, Moses, Abraham. They, too, were the enemy." He raised a balled fist, hammering it on the podium with each pounding thought. "If you don't embrace God's order on earth, sacrificing and serving, you, too, are the enemy and will never, never ascend to His highest kingdom."

No longer. Rachel was no longer moved or impressed by Goodman's guilt-laced rhetoric.

She thought of the children's story about the emperor's new clothes. The emperor stood naked before a child who was the only one to see, or to admit it. Rachel no longer cared a lick about family acceptance or being the patriarch's favored one. She didn't care who he was when it came to his multi-million dollar empire. She cared about *what* he was, and she had made up her mind on that before his son had beat her face in and brought her back to the compound. Donald Goodman was responsible for the death of her child, a self-deceived murderer and slave trader who had to be stopped.

The double doors of the chapel flew open. "The Zimmerman house is on fire!" Jacob Goodman bellowed out at the top of his lungs. Rachel was the only member of the congregation not to gasp or react in any way other than to lower her head with a wry smile.

Burn. Please, God, let it all burn to the ground.

"I'll help you out of here," a balding man with dough-soft golden eyes offered Rachel amidst flailing arms and churning legs.

"I'm fine," she announced. Maybe too fine, she suddenly realized. "Better go help get that fire out."

He shrugged and joined his wives and family in the crowd thronging out the doors.

Donald Goodman clapped and raised his hands. "Slow down. We don't need any unnecessary harm here. The fire's next door, not in here, folks." His calming words floated over the shoving crowd with no effect. He shook his head in disgust and retreated into the inner sanctum behind the speaker's stand with his church leaders.

~

Seven inches of fresh-fallen powder hadn't deterred the raging fire, which spewed flames out of windows on lower and upper floors.

Rachel moved away from the gawking crowd, turning her eyes to two figures bundled in winter coats nearing the open gate.

There would be no fourth generation ascension to the patriarch. Israel had not only crossed the line; he'd burned it to ashes. Now there would be three escapees.

52
CHAPTER

Rachel had almost begun to relax as the bus rounded the corner of Fifth North and South Temple, just a mile walk to her last chance for at least a temporary safe haven. When the three stepped off their rendezvous bus, her gaze swept the area, seeing her surroundings in a far more critical light than when she first fled to Charlie's house.

Lydia Pearson's house had seemed like the perfect refuge less than twenty-four hours before. It now struck her as a stupid choice. The woman had just barely escaped being blown to bits, and had repeatedly told Rachel in their first meeting of sleeping with all the house lights on for fear of a deadly figure darting out of the darkness and killing her, or worse, her children.

They had been trudging through a Sunday morning snow flurry past an abandoned brass foundry. As the burgundy early model Continental purred up alongside them, she cursed herself for not walking where shadows and shrubbery could offer cover.

The smoked glass driver's window silently dropped, and white blinking eyes set in a broad-smiling tar-black face appeared. "You good folks want a ride? Snow'n like the devil out there."

A deep imprinted prejudice struck Rachel, courtesy of Father Goodman, who had told his flock that dark skin traced back to God's mark of punishment on Cain. This, coupled with a learned fear of men, especially in Babylon, made each swallow dry and hard. Rachel jumped back, the dry ankle-bracing snow shooting chills through her.

"No, thanks," Israel said unconvincingly in a quivering tone, while securing an arm around Anna.

The man nodded. "Suit yourself. Just trying to be friendly." The car eased away and turned the corner.

"He could have hurt us," Anna said, snuggling closer to her proud, nodding protector.

"I wouldn't have let anyone hurt you."

Rachel's eyes flashed with impatience as she forged ahead towards Lydia's house. "You kids don't know what you're talking about. You were scared because he was black."

Israel chuckled. "And you weren't?"

She hesitated, then nodded, pulling her coat collar closer at the sudden gust of icy wind. "I can't think of anything I'm not afraid of right now. We're criminals, you know. Arsonists. Father Goodman could do anything to us, and who would know?"

Anna closed her eyes and put her head on Israel's shoulder. At the tender sight of the young innocents, a single tear spilled over Rachel's lashes. It felt as if their world had come to an end.

~

Lydia had been a collector of ceramic teapots since she entered puberty. Vegetables, a hippo, an elephant, a panda bear, houses from fairy tale cottages to Elizabethan Tudors, cuddly animals, a tree with a drooping branch for a pouring spout.

Even a hairline crack or indiscernible chip would have made her frantic at one time. Things had changed. When she left she had wrapped the survivors of her collection, one-by-one, in aged newspaper sheets.

She called them survivors because her former husband would jab argument points through her heart by snatching one of the teapots out of their glass ornamental cupboard, and hold it hostage until he had her pleading attention. Then he'd lightly release his fingers as they both watched it explode into pieces on the kitchen floor. Of course, she learned the first time he did it to lower her head and clean it up, or there would soon be two broken pots.

The clock on the kitchen wall ticked one minute to noon. The room was sunny, with beveled glass-fronted cabinets and butter-scotch plaid wallpaper. Lydia was completing her long overdue burial of the last bitter memories of *him* at the small wood nook table when the doorbell rang.

With her brood at Sunday school, she was alone, and anticipation wound taut inside her, doubling with the next trill from the bell.

Her mind gushed with possibilities: a fiery and unpredictable abandoned polygamous husband bent on vengeance or recapturing his human property; a screaming woman with her pursuer a breath away; ordained and blessed Fundamentalist men with weapons in hand carrying out an act of blood atonement. An apparition from hell would have been less threatening than the tornado of broken families funneling through her front door since the creation of her organization.

She had heard Woman Against Polygamy referred to as a bunch of whining hags no man in his right mind would lay claim to, but the women and children who graced her organization and home door were usually the treasured jewels who demanded something more. The group on Lydia Pearson's doorstep fit the latter description perfectly.

"Heaven's sakes, you just seem to pop up everywhere," Lydia said with a smile in her voice while shooing the three into her living room. "The kids are at church." She glanced around the room and softly laughed. "I'll bet Charlie never warned you. The place is a mess."

She studied the pain and confusion swimming in Rachel's eyes. "Gimme your coats and have a seat. I'll get us some hot tea to warm your bones."

Rachel tugged off her coat and backed to the couch. "It got out of control," she whispered while nodding to herself. "It's as if we're in a car with no brakes that's going faster and faster, and nobody can stop it."

Lydia gestured to the young man near the pooling morning light at the living room window, teasing and whispering to a girl beaming in wonder and appreciation for his heroic act.

"Who's he?" Lydia asked.

"Only the son of our next patriarch. He set the compound on fire as a diversion for the three of us to escape."

Lydia dropped down into a chair. "Oh, good heavens."

Rachel thought she should thank the woman for harboring every imaginable crisis under her own roof, but no words formed in her mouth. She couldn't help feel the sting of irony that the one man who had dedicated himself to her safety offering her sanctuary in his own home, was now the least safe to entangle in her life.

Lydia looked through her. "You girls aren't going to be safe until they get that boy." She gave Rachel a somber glare. "I never saw you. Goodman will go to the police and put a warrant out for your arrest, I would bet, cutting off any chance for the Division of Family Services to help us out. Does that reporter, Carver, know you've run away again?"

Impervious to the sudden unease in the room, Rachel smiled at the mention of his name. "He's done so much for us. I can't bring him in any further."

Lydia tentatively nodded. "That's one way to look at it." She got up and began shuffling between mounds of teenager's clothes, stereo equipment and schoolbooks on her way into the kitchen. "Not the way he would look at it, from what I've seen."

She pulled Charlie Carver's *Salt Lake Observer* business card out of her telephone directory.

"Charles Carver, please. Newsroom."

After a brief silence an all-business reporter answered. "Carver no longer works for the paper."

"Since when?" Lydia said.

"I said he no longer works here." Dial tone.

Lydia stormed back into the living room. "Rachel, do you have Charlie's home phone number?"

"Why? I told you—"

"He's been fired, and I'll bet a month's tithing it has something to do with you."

Color flared across Rachel's cheekbones. "I memorized it." She stood, followed Lydia into the kitchen, and picked up the receiver. The phone at the other end only chirped once.

"Yeah, this is Charlie."

The static of a bad connection crackled over the line. "It's Rachel. I—we—escaped."

"Are you all right? Where are you? I'll be right—"

"Have you still got the pictures?" she asked in a strangely detached voice.

"Yes, yes I do. They're at the office in—-oh, shit!"

"What?"

"I got so pissed off at the publisher when he canned me the other day I didn't even stop to clear out my desk."

"You've got to get them!"

"Where are you? I'll call Strickland and—"

"No! I'll explain when you get here. We're at Lydia's. Jacob Goodman's son, Israel, is here with us, too. They won't just lock us up this time."

Charlie's words faded into the background as a vision of Sarah in an angelic glow reached out for her mother to join her. Feelings of loving warmth, wholeness filled her. She hung up the phone, leaving Charlie behind in mid-sentence.

53
CHAPTER

Charlie didn't blame Rachel for losing her nerve. Considering what Donald Goodman and family had put her through, it was a wonder she hadn't put a gun to her own head. He sat and watched her pathetic attempt to map out a future for Israel and Anna, vocally committed to marrying and starting a new family.

"You went to school, public school, longer than Anna," she said, coaching a reassuring response out of the fiancé.

Israel sat erect. "Senior. I would have finished high school this year."

"Still can," Charlie remarked.

"We'll change our names and move somewhere else," Rachel said.

"No need for that," Lydia added. "I know I took a chance, but that's all I do anymore."

"What did you do?" Charlie asked, arching a brow.

"Kent Wynngate, director of Family Services, has been great in helping find temporary and permanent homes for our families. I called and told him everything."

Charlie was on his feet. "They'll arrest all three of them."

"Give a girl a chance," Lydia said with a little swing of her well-padded hips.

"I've already got a family lined up in Las Vegas who will take all three of you in like family." She steepled her fingers and arranged her features in a humorously contemplative demeanor. "Israel here's going to learn to be a journeyman carpenter. The benefactor has his own construction business."

"Lydia, you're underestimating Father Goodman," Rachel said. "He'll find us. I'm too old to be adopted anyway," Rachel said flatly.

Charlie's eyes locked in for effect. "I'd adopt you."

"Charlie, I figure those pictures you told me about will give you some kind of security," Lydia added.

Anna fell silent, cowering in Israel's arms, then moved away from his security to the other side of the couch, holding her arms tightly to her sides.

"What pictures?" Israel asked, still celebrating the news.

"Lydia's right," Charlie stared hard at Anna. "We've got to know who the man was in those pictures right now, if—"

Anna popped to her feet. "Hush up about that. I knew I shouldn't have said anything."

Israel's smile disappeared. "What pictures?"

"Tell him, Rachel," Charlie said. "He has to know at this point."

"You said nobody would have to know. Don't tell him anything!" Anna yelled.

Rachel flinched at her understandable belligerence. "Things are different now. They could kill us."

"Who? Father Goodman?" Israel shouted. "That's ridiculous."

Charlie went to Anna and sat beside her. She lifted her head, her lower lip trembling. "It was Donald Goodman, wasn't it? The man in the pictures."

Anna whimpered, tears glittering in her eyes.

"It was that son-of-a-bitch, wasn't it?" Charlie added just above a whisper.

"I heard that," Israel yelled, jerking onto his feet, face turning red with rage.

Charlie rubbed Anna's back. "We've got to know, so we've got something to trade your safety with."

"Nobody needs to know," Anna sneered.

"We do," Rachel said, sitting on the other side of Anna. "I need to know, for Sarah." Giving her no chance to refute the statement, Rachel cupped Anna's trembling hand in both of hers. "Just nod your head. Was it Father Goodman?"

Anna looked up with a wounded look, then shook her head.

"It wasn't? Who then? Who, Anna?"

"What pictures?" Israel persisted.

"Your Prophet violated young girls and took pictures of them. It's what cost Sarah her life."

"That's ridiculous. Blasphemy. My father warned me about you people." He backed away from the three of them as though he smelled imminent danger. "I can't believe I burned down one of our homes for people like you."

Charlie bounded to his feet, making the young man gasp.

"Don't hurt him!" Anna screamed and clung to Rachel.

"Of course I won't hurt him. I'm going to the office to get those pictures before they're found, if they haven't been already."

"You've actually got them?" Israel said.

Anna began to cry. "Everything's ruined."

Rachel held Anna closer and gave both men a warning look.

Anna turned her face up to Rachel, her big brown eyes swimming in tears. "I'll tell you." Rachel's eyes dilated.

The room fell silent while Anna eased away from the comforting embrace, wiped away tears and evened jagged breathing. "Israel, I'm sorry." She rushed an open hand to her tightening throat.

"What? My father? Not my father. No way!"

Without allowing himself to question the safety of it, Jacob Goodman's son ran out of the house and kept running.

54
CHAPTER

The threat of a migraine had nested behind Donald Goodman's right eye, making it tick in a constant rhythm. The aspirin he had taken since receiving the late night call from Charlie Carver demanding an immediate meeting was stubbornly refusing to stop the thick, growing pain. He needed something stronger, but had never given in to the temptations of caffeine, as scripturally prohibited as alcohol. He rubbed his forehead and stared at the neatly positioned casework on his desk until it blurred into a collage of meaningless abstract shapes.

"A Mr. Charles Carver is here, sir," Goodman's secretary said, nervously bobbing her head as if a pigeon waiting reprimand.

Charlie appeared at the threshold behind the secretary until, with the tilt of a head, Goodman signaled him in. "You've upped your ante to a highly personal level," he said coldly to the heathen bully. "Aiding in burning down homes, sheltering runaway children."

Charlie took a seat without offering a retort.

"You think this is a game, Mr. Carver?" Goodman whispered.

"We both know why I'm here," Charlie said. "To trade the pictures for the safety of Rachel, Anna, and Israel."

Goodman ground his teeth. "Israel's back home where he belongs. He told me about the outrageous things that you claim my son did. I'm afraid you lost that chip."

Charlie watched Goodman's eyes as he pulled a stack of Polaroids from his brown tweed sports jacket. He waved the pile up and down with cocked brows. "Here are my chips."

Goodman's left eye twitched when he smiled. "Those aren't chips," he lied. "They're evidence I'll be using when I rip you to shreds for defamation of character."

"So why did you drop everything and meet with me?" Charlie said casually.

"To put an end to all of this," Goodman snapped.

"Wrong answer," Charlie said. "It's the end of your sick little empire."

"Let me see those," Goodman growled, stretching across his desk to snatch the photos. Charlie watched his adversary's one normal blinking eye, seeing the attorney's mind at work trying to fit all the pieces together into one, clear attack strategy. The man tensed his broad shoulders even more as he settled his hands on one end of the pictures.

Charlie flicked the stack of pictures across Goodman's desk. "I've made inter-negatives."

Goodman's nostrils flared. His eyes were ablaze with determination. He rifled through every picture without a word or hint of revulsion. He returned to his burgundy leather swivel chair, never breaking scrutinous examination of the photos. Charlie watched facial features that had once been sharp and handsome mutate into tensed thin lips locked at the gum-line of graying teeth. The lips turned into a grimacing frown. Goodman's shoulders drooped while he slowly released his rage. "This is horrible," he muttered to himself.

Charlie shook his head in disgust. "It is. And you let it go on for years."

"I didn't know. I would have—" Goodman sat back and squeezed his eyes shut. "Those poor children."

"Sarah Zimmerman was using those photos to blackmail your son out of marrying her. He killed her, and buried her in *your* barn."

Goodman shot out of his seat. "You can't tell who's in these pictures." With a violent flick he sent the photos careening off his desk to the floor at Charlie's feet.

Charlie held his ground looking him in the eye. "You want to talk to Anna?"

Goodman's mouth twisted with delusion. "She'd do that?"

Charlie nodded. "If that's what it takes to convince you, she said she'd tell you everything."

The instant the words came out Charlie wanted them back. He had never dared broach the specifics of what was done to her and the other girls himself, let alone expect her to look her Prophet in the eye and describe to him his son's perverted acts. He bit his tongue, but it was too late. The outrageous offer was out there, hanging in the air to be considered and possibly even acted upon by Donald Goodman. Charlie felt as though he had not only violated Anna, but also Rachel's trust.

What an idiot. How could I be so stupid?

Appalled at his blunder, Charlie prayed the man would have the good judgment to not subject one of his children to another terrifying and humiliating experience.

Goodman stared at his accuser, at the uncompromising, rigid set of the shoulders. Clearly the reporter wasn't bluffing. "What are you going to do with those pictures?"

Charlie breathed a deep sigh of relief at the response and replied with his best poker face. "Destroy Jacob Goodman on a court stand."

"What do I have to do?" Goodman asked.

"I can't stop what's going to happen to your son. He's got to pay for what he did to those girls. And what he did to Sarah Zimmerman."

"Wait a minute! Don't try to tie him into that, too. He's never hurt a soul," Goodman said unconvincingly.

"Why did you hide the body then?"

"You haven't got a thing tying Jacob to Sarah's disappearance." Goodman's right eye blinked like a warning light. His eyes went dark, as though a light switched off inside him. "My boy's no killer."

"I don't think either of us have an idea of exactly what he is."

CHAPTER 55

Killer. Child molester.

The horror of Carver's indictments burned in the back of Donald Goodman's mind as he awaited his son's arrival from work. He stared at the one Polaroid he had slipped under his paperwork without Carver seeing him. He desperately wanted, needed, to believe the next prophet of the Goodman Empire wasn't capable of such atrocities.

Time and distance from the reporter's scalding eyes was slowly rebuilding his faith in his son's total innocence. Somewhere there was a key piece of information that would unlock all his unanswered questions since acting as architect in snatching and hiding Sarah Zimmerman's body.

Donald Goodman wanted to believe the answers would come from the other side of the fortress walls: an evil plot crafted by Rachel Zimmerman and her soulless lover, Charlie Carver. Crossing swords with Donald Goodman had already cost Carver his job. He had personally seen to that. He pulled out a clean legal pad, scribbled down Carver's name, and began constructing phase two of the meddling reporter's destruction. At first his actions had been professional; this time revenge would be personal, discrediting Carver on his favorite turf, the courtroom floor.

God set these demons behind me.

Goodman's fear settled on his youngest son. Hyrum, was the child with the violent temper and secrets, not Jacob. He didn't bother to hide his appetite for young women and his obsession over Rachel Zimmerman. Jacob, always the calculating, cool-headed son, was both centered in God and his father's direction since he was a towheaded boy. Goodman's stomach rolled at the thought of Hyrum's probable reaction to his father's probing. He always chose to play the persecuted innocent, but Father Goodman knew better. By the time Goodman realized the questions should begin with his youngest, not oldest son, Jacob was in his office perched at the edge of his seat.

"What did Carver say?" Jacob asked.

Goodman sat back and fluttered his fingers together. "What happened to Sarah?"

"How should I know?"

Goodman leaned forward with the demeanor of a prosecutor. "You took her out there for correction. You were the last of us to see her alive." He leaned in closer. "What did you do?"

Tension gripped Jacob by the temples as painful as a pair of tongs, clamping tighter and tighter. "I didn't kill her! I swear I didn't, Father."

"What happened? Tell me, son, right now. I have to know everything." *Damn you Jacob, you're hiding something.*

He tossed the Polaroid to Jacob, who caught it in mid air, righted it, glanced at the golden haired child of twelve performing oral sex on an unidentifiable adult male. He turned his eyes away from his father.

Goodman knew his overwhelming power over his oldest son. Their relationship was mortared between God's laws and truth. "Look at me, son. Jacob. You can't lie to me."

"I swear to God, Father, I didn't kill her."

Goodman shook his head sadly, wearily. "But you know who did. And you know who's in those pictures."

"She was possessed by the devil. We all knew that."

"You're talking about Sarah now, aren't you?"

"Yes. I started back for the city, but it was late." Jacob paused to compose himself and his story.

"What did you do to Sarah before you left?"

"I beat some obedience into her," he said callously.

"So you beat her. Badly? Enough for her to die?"

"Absolutely not, " Jacob replied, his voice shaking in indignation.

"There's more, go on," Goodman said with a surrealistic detachment.

"She thought I was going to punish her again and climbed out her window." He lowered his head, averting his father's piercing stare. "The fall from the roof killed her." Donald Goodman had to wait a full minute before answering. He could see his son wasn't about to match stares. This was a confession, not a confrontation. "She caused her own death, but I thought it best to bury her and let everyone think she ran away." Jacob hunched over on one elbow with an open hand clasped over his mouth.

"It was an accident."

Goodman lowered his hand. "And the pictures? Who's in the pictures?"

Goodman's stomach churned again as he imagined Jacob victimizing innocent children. "Don't hide anything from me, son."

Jacob replied, measuring his words carefully. "I couldn't tell you that."

"Couldn't or won't?"

Jacob's face pinched tight. "I don't even know what you're—"

"You're lying to me Jacob, and you're bad at it." Goodman reached out his three-finger and thumb claw of a hand to again examine the photo. Once in hand he moved the Polaroid close to his eyes. "That's...I can't see the face, but that's Nora."

Jacob bolted to his feet. "You think I would do such a thing with my own daughter?"

"Who did then? Anna Zimmerman says it was you. She's ready to say it in court."

Jacob dropped into the chair, his eyes dilated in cold speculation. "They burned our house, brought in outsiders to destroy us." He shook his head and gave his father a dark, smoldering look. "Talk to the Council and tell them God has led you to the right, the only answer. That can only be blood atonement for Anna and Rachel."

A red haze filled Goodman's vision. The luxury of paranoia and conjecture were gone. Jacob Goodman, his royal-blooded and beloved oldest son and next family prophet was a child molester and the second-degree perpetrator of Sarah Zimmerman's death. The cold facts made the hair on the back of his neck stick up.

He suddenly felt as if he had been living in a fog of self-delusion. The monster that sat indignantly before him suggesting cold-blooded murder of more innocents had come from his own loins.

"It's all we can do at this point," Jacob said. "We have to think of the family."

Goodman winced at the last statement, dished out as if he were a righteous, caring son. Goodman felt rumpled and ragged. He sighed. As badly as his son was pressuring him to act in self and family defense, he couldn't escape the mountainous weight of accountability to his Father—in heaven.

Donald Goodman's chin slacked. "Your own daughter," he mumbled. His mind faded back to a carefree summer day and the gurgling sound of the Provo River. The Provo was always their place, father and son, where they shared stories of the past and hopes for the future. Jacob loved to fly fish, claiming God himself had blessed him with the power to always come home with the biggest rainbow or cutthroat trout. A boy, unlike all his others, who not only took his father's counsel, but also sought it for everything from the right girls to marry to key business decisions. He had become the backbone of Goodman Enterprises and was acknowledged and honored by Goodman's entire congregation as his spiritual and business successor.

Donald Goodman sat silent, propping his head in his hands to veil his shame. His son had only seen him cry once, when his father died. But today, and for days to come, his heart would be ripped from its cavity and tears would flow like spring rain.

"Do you have anything more to say?" Goodman stood and moved heavily around his desk.

"I didn't mean to hurt anybody. I swear to God, father."

Goodman called on anger to save his sanity. He grabbed his son by his shirt and lifted him to his toes. "You swear to God. How dare you try and bring God into what you've done to all of us?"

"Damn you!" Jacob said and easily broke his father grip.

Goodman moved so close to Jacob his son couldn't escape him. His voice broke as the tears fought for release and the frustration choked him. "Jacob, I've always watched over you. You were my favorite."

"Yes, and you put everything on me. Let Jacob do this or that. Jacob will take care of it. Your father was an attorney, you're an attorney. Of course, I have to be an attorney. Of course, your oldest son has to take your place as the Prophet." His eyes blazed murderously. "Well I'm no prophet, and Father, neither are you!" He tipped his chin up so Goodman had no choice but to look at him. "Look me in the eye and tell me you're really a God on earth."

Goodman's nostrils flared and lips tightened with suppressed fury. "You are no longer my son. You're nobody. You never existed."

"You've never once asked me what *I* wanted. Me! Not you, me!" He sidestepped his father and started for the door. "I've been afraid of you my entire life. Not any more. I'm glad to leave."

Father Goodman could see his son, who had always desperately sought his approval, and wanted to reach out and hug him. Nothing would ever be the same. A voice came, low and eerie in the back of the patriarch's mind. *Make them suffer unto death.*

56
CHAPTER

"Brother Thomas, will you please get me a wet towel?" Donald Goodman asked his lifetime friend and most senior member of the church leadership, Council of the Seven. "I've got a nasty migraine."

With a cold washcloth banded across the top of his forehead, the Prophet offered an opening prayer in the back chamber of the Goodman Compound congregational hall.

"Brothers, I have a grave matter that requires an immediate decision." Goodman's eyes shifted from one nodding set of eyes to the next until all understood the gravity of the emergency meeting. "First, let me say that what I'm about to share with you and the decisions we make will never leave this room."

He lowered the cloth and bowed his head. "God, give me strength I alone don't possess." His transcendental glare riveted his followers. "My son, Jacob." His right eye kicked into erratic blinking that forced him to patch the eye with the soothing cloth.

"There's no other way to say this. Jacob's been taking our young girls to my summer house for years and molesting them." He took a deep breath.

"How young? My girls?" Brother Steven interjected.

"No, only Goodman Compound girls, including his own. Some of them younger than twelve, from what the photos showed."

He watched their faces grow ashen before continuing. "I don't want to ever go into what he did, but he scared them into secrecy until one of my flock had the courage to use pictures of his horrible acts to try to escape marrying him."

Brother Thomas, sitting directly to his right, patted his Prophet's arm. "Why, Father, do you have to share these painful family concerns with us?"

"There's more." Goodman shuddered at Brother's Phillip's quivering words. "James Zimmerman's death wasn't an accident," Phillip finished.

Goodman pushed the chair back from the table and rose, working at containing his temper. "My son's no murderer."

Brother Phillip recoiled, clasped his hands together as if in prayer, and lowered his head.

"Speak up, Brother," Thomas said.

Ephram Mine manager, Brother Phillip waited for his Prophet's amazement to simmer. "Jacob sent James into a mine shaft we had shut down weeks before."

"That's nothing," Goodman said.

"Yes, Father, I know, but Jacob thought everybody was off shift and gone. I was there, though, when he—"

"When he what?" Goodman demanded.

"When he dynamited the entrance of the tunnel, then claimed it caved in. I heard the blast."

The room fell deadly silent. "Rachel," Goodman muttered thin as a whisper. He dropped to his seat, clamped his eyes shut and returned the cloth band to his eyes. He rocked back and forth in the high-back chair without a word.

"Who will take your place, Father?" Brother Thomas asked.

"Not Hyrum." He lingered on his own words. "Israel, when he's ready."

Just as his Council was about to adjourn, he sat up. "Jacob took off. Find him and tell him everything's going to be all right." His tone was cool, icy. "Tell him I'm not mad anymore and want to see him."

Without exception, all nodded in understanding.

~

At the whirling sound of helicopter blades Ida Goodman dropped her teacup, splattering its contents over the lap of her worn cleaning dress. "Heavens. It's him."

She lumbered to the entry hall mirror and patted her already perfectly bunned hair. "Never calls. Just shows up out of the blue," she said.

Goodman hurled himself through the door and tugged his first wife to the couch.

"Can I get you something to eat?" she asked, forcing a smile.

"I have to get right back, but there's something I have to talk with you about."

Ida Goodman adjusted in her seat, flabbergasted he considered her inclusion in any matter worth his personal time. "Yes, Father, what is it?"

"Remember in the early fifties when our clan in Colorado City was broken up by the state?"

Ida flinched. " Of course I do. My mother was taken to jail and my youngest sister was sent to an orphanage." She swallowed hard at his pained expression. "What's this about? That Rachel and Anna again? Have they—?"

"Sometimes we have to be strong for the family." He stood up and turned away from her curious eyes. "We have to protect ourselves so the outsiders don't try to destroy us again."

"What are you trying to say, Donald?"

"In time you'll understand. Like Abraham, God's asked me to trust in Him and do whatever He requires—no matter what He asks." He turned, and as he did his eyes narrowed into a warning gaze.

~

Impervious to his son's unease, Donald Goodman pulled him into his arms and embraced him, right in front of the gawking women and children who filled the living room. "Good to have you back, son." Before Jacob could respond, Goodman's gaze skated past his son to his helicopter pilot, flagging him at the door. "There's our chopper."

Father Goodman felt his son tense as he released his embrace. "Where are we going?"

"I thought it best we just dive right back into the business." He lightly slapped Jacob on the shoulder. "We need to get our minds off of everything. Sound good?"

"Sounds good," Jacob said tentatively.

As they passed over Utah Lake, Jacob nudged his father awake. "What operations do you want to visit first?"

"Oh, I thought we'd start with the Ephram Coal Mine. Production's been lagging for months."

"What do you mean?"

"You're not getting anywhere. I thought that maybe I could give a fresh perspective. You know, shake things loose."

"That's *my* job, Father."

"I know, I know. It's the only business in your portfolio that's holding up profits. I just wanted to see it for myself. Brother Thomas is planning on us."

"You called him and didn't even tell me about it?"

"Frankly, Jacob, I didn't know if you'd ever come back."

Jacob turned to the view out the window. The hour flight passed without another word spoken in anger, pity or reprimand. Without a word at all.

~

"We should make a good half a mill this year," Brother Thomas said while the mine cage doors closed and he punched the down button.

"More like six hundred," Jacob said.

The cage clattered to a stop at its one-hundred-foot base.

Jacob stepped out first. "Since the Jacobson trial the state's been snooping around everybody's business, so we upped the working age to eighteen." He tugged on his father's sleeve as he passed. "That's why production's been lagging."

Goodman tipped his head in understanding. "Thomas, lead the way."

The three were soon crouching to make passage to a higher vaulted tunnel. Jacob turned and pointed to the pick diggings to his far left. "Kills your back. The kids can stand straight up," he grumbled.

"I'm glad we got them out of this hell hole," Thomas said.

Goodman held up his hand to ward off a rebuttal.

"I'm just stating the facts," Jacob said.

Once they were able to walk upright Thomas doddered at the entrance of the furthest left mineshaft. "We should open this sucker back up. It's loaded with coal."

"Isn't that the shaft where James was caught in the cave-in?" Goodman asked rhetorically.

"It is," Jacob responded.

Thomas shook his head. "We cleared it all away. Good as any of 'em now."

"I'm not going in there," Goodman said. "Stay out of there, men."

Thomas shrugged "You're the boss."

"No, I'm the boss!" Jacob crowed. "Let's have a look at it."

Thomas waved him past while never taking his eyes off Goodman.

Jacob trudged past his mine manager, mumbling to himself. His rage at his father's snide remarks only made his temples pound harder.

"Don't go more than a hundred yards," Thomas yelled into the black hole. He looked at his watch and back up at his prophet. "I've timed it. Another thirty seconds."

Goodman plodded over to him. "I'll do it."

Thomas plucked the dynamite ignition plunger out of the nearby wheelbarrow.

"He's your *own* son, Father," he whispered.

"You're all my sons and daughters," Goodman said flatly.

CHAPTER 57

Charlie jangled the change in his pockets and blankly rolled his eyes across his kitchen. "No more crap from you, Goodman, or your perverted clan."

"We're not a clan," Donald Goodman said in round pear-shaped tones. "We're a religious sect, no different than the Latter-day Saints, except we never abandoned our prophet's words and beliefs. Put Rachel on the line."

"She doesn't need any more of your religion or threats."

"Mr. Carver, you will shortly get your job back for no other reason than the call I just placed."

"What are you getting at, Goodman? Killing her daughter and chasing down Rachel and Anna make you a good guy now?"

"Please, Mr. Carver. It's critical I speak to her."

Charlie reluctantly held out the receiver. "It's Donald Goodman."

Rachel grabbed the phone out of Charlie's hand. "Leave us alone or—"

"Silence!" Goodman's voice was tight and biting. He paused for effect before proceeding. "I'm not going to repeat myself, so listen carefully."

Charlie watched Rachel's facial muscles twitch. Even the sound of her Lord's voice still humbled her. "Yes, sir."

"First I want you to know I knew nothing of what Jacob did. I share in your suffering more than you can imagine."

"Easy to say when your son's safe and my child's dead." Rachel's throat wrenched tight. "That monster killed Sarah."

"I know, child. And he's now paid for his sins. He died in a mining accident less than twenty-four hours ago."

"You're just lying to protect him," she snapped.

After an uncomfortable silence, Goodman cleared his throat. "No, his death is on my head, God forgive me. Sarah's death was an accident. He came back when Ida was asleep, and I guess, thinking he was going to beat her again until she gave up the pictures, she climbed out the window and fell off the roof. She died almost instantly of internal injuries."

Her voice degenerated into a childish whimper. "And you just buried her like some farm animal."

"I couldn't—wouldn't—allow myself to think about anything but protecting family from a police raid." She heard raspy uneven breathing. "I'm sorry, Rachel. God has already punished me. My oldest son, my favorite."

"You stole the body when you dragged me back from the ranch and lied to my face about sending word out to the family to find her." Rachel swallowed the lump in her throat. "Everything has been a lie."

"Enough! Remember who you're addressing, young woman. Here's my offer. I will place two hundred thousand dollars in whatever bank you want to get you and Anna started in Babylon. I will arrange for you to get your job back at the courthouse. I've already got Carver's job back. No one will bother the two of you again."

Rachel stood trembling, paralyzed. "Where's Sarah?"

"We will never speak to you again," he continued in a cold lawyer's voice, "and you are never, never to contact anyone in the family again."

The connection turned sharply hot. "Where is she?"

"Well, Hyrum exhumed the body, moved her to our funeral home, placed her in our most expensive coffin and buried her. A magnificent cherry marble tombstone is at the carver's awaiting your instructions before setting it in place."

Rachel steadied herself as she forced back bile. "This is supposed to make everything better?"

"With the plot purchased for you beside Sarah at the most peaceful, and expensive site at Sunset Lawn, I couldn't think of anything else. My son's already been put to death, for heaven's sake!

"Rachel, I have to tell you something just as painful to me. Sarah's death was a tragic accident, your husband James's wasn't."

"I hate you. I pray there is a God so He'll send you to hell."

"Jacob blew up the tunnel that your husband entered," he said soberly. "I guess none of us ever really knew him."

"You created him in your image, you dirty-minded bastard."

"And I destroyed him with my own hands."

"You're not getting off that easy, Goodman," Charlie said from the living room phone receiver that he had silently picked up to monitor the man's threats and promises.

"Still the deceiver," Goodman spit out.

Rachel slammed down the receiver, turned mad eyes to Anna, and raked her fingers through her hair. She had no tears left, not even for Sarah.

Charlie slipped up behind Rachel and gently folded his arms around her. "I've got some better news," he said.

Rachel pulled away and faced him. Her fixed gaze was blank as a porcelain doll's painted eyes.

"After Marsha, I've been terrified you were next. If it was Jacob, and there's no reason not to think it was, the girl at the cemetery two nights ago should be the last. I thought the Strangler was Donald Goodman all this time, when his son sounded just like him. I believe Goodman killed his son, do you?"

"What girl? Another one?"

"She was found at Capital Cemetery, naked like the rest of them with her arms spread out on a tombstone as if she was making angel wings in the snow."

CHAPTER 58

As he drove past the downtown Gallivan Ice Skating Pavilion, it was nearing dusk with temperatures near zero, but the setting sun was still licking the tops of twenty-story buildings. The sky had been bright, almost a blinding blue. Beautiful. A sky full of hopes and a better tomorrow.

The pathetic leech reporting his spiritual journey and his new teasing whore were ripe for plucking. Today was truly going to be *the* perfect day.

He thought about the affectionate, naively trusting wife he had kissed at the birth of the day and the forthright, solid children he was raising, making days like today even more like polished gold.

There was pride, too, in being tagged in the press as a "criminal genius, without an ounce of conscience or remorse."

"An extremely dangerous sociopath, whose personal religion is as twisted as his mind," were characterizations that hack reporter Charles Carver had concocted after he harvested his fifth soul. Carver's views came up short, pitifully shy of the dynamics of light and darkness in his psyche that flipped like a switch without even a warning. His deeply flawed soul craved company for the light and purity only found in the female of the species. With each conquest he purged the beautiful essence out of each of *his* women. Soon his trek into darkness would be over. The black haired woman sitting on the skating spectator bench like his guardian angel would be the last. Soon he, too, would walk among the angels.

I am a good man. Remember that. You're a good man about to reach perfection.

His thoughts lingered on how gently he made love to each of them, satisfying their deepest hungers. Strangling hands gripped the steering wheel as he turned down the concrete parking ramp and eased the metallic forest green and beige trimmed Chevy Tahoe into a first floor corner space. *Perfect spot*: a single draped-in-shadow stall isolated from flanking parking spaces by roped off areas piled with chunks of concrete. He took a chest-deep sigh and nodded in satisfaction.

After tonight, even God won't be able to resist me.

~

"How sure are you about Jacob being your serial killer, Charlie?" Rachel asked. "You said this man always does things with these women before he kills them." She shook her head at the thought of Jacob Goodman being able to set romantic webs. "It can't be the same man."

"With the exception of his age, he perfectly profiles a serial killer from what I've read about in the FBI's Behavioral Science unit whose studying these freaks. He's white, married, and feeling repressed from his overbearing father, and a mother being allowed no voice in the family. With one unplanned exception, every murder he planned, organized and executed in the same pattern. Want me to go on? He's the Strangler, all right."

"It's freezing out here." Charlie shoved up his parka sleeve and looked at his wristwatch. "It has been twenty minutes." He glanced at the red and green neon sign lighting Chio's Italian Restaurant across the four-lane street. "They'll be calling our name any minute. I'm getting hungry, aren't you?"

"What exactly did Father Goodman say?"

"Let's not talk about that tonight," Charlie answered.

Rachel scanned the shoulder-to-shoulder crowd of mostly families. "I feel like he's watching us."

Charlie tore his eyes away from Rachel's flawless face. "You probably will for quite a while. You and Anna are safe for now." He gently touched the tip of her nose with his gloved finger. "You're going to accept Goodman's bundle of guilt money and start a new life."

"*I'll* decide what I'm going to do!"

Charlie threw his head back and laughed. "See, you're already starting."

Rachel shivered and wrapped her scarf tighter around her neck. "I just feel his eyes on me."

"Female intuition?" Charlie said with a slight diversionary smile.

"They told us it would be forty-five minutes. Can we watch the skaters a little longer? People stare at me in public places," Rachel said.

Charlie chuckled. "And you think that even though you're out of those calico dresses, they won't stare anyway?"

Rachel's crimson cheeks went a blush darker.

Charlie gently clasped her hand in his. "They're staring at the same thing I did from the first time I saw you in the courtroom." He took in the first glint of stars. "You just don't know what a knockout you are, do you?"

Rachel shook off the compliment. "Maybe we should go to the restaurant."

Charlie motioned to the portable concession stand on the opposite side of the rink. "I'll get us some hot chocolate."

Rachel clutched his arm and snuggled closer. "Don't go."

"You're right, come with me."

With one eye peeled for any strange men lurking near them, Rachel shook her head. "No, you're right, there's nothing to be afraid of anymore. Go ahead."

He rubbed her arm in a warming gesture. "It's got to be below zero." He took one last look around, comforted by the chatter and laughter of parents and children. "I'll be right back."

~

He worked the leather glove over the pair of paper-thin latex gloves with his teeth, then rummaged in his gray overcoat pocket, fingering the bottles of ether, ammonia and two thin cotton washcloths. He ascended from the dim recesses of the parking ramp, easily assimilating into the throng of families and young couples. They would soon be a couple, too. For about an hour.

He had never killed a man before. But what man didn't deserve punishment? Lives full of ulterior motives, hidden beastly instincts, and stone-cold hearts. After tonight he wouldn't have to suffer another day and night as a man. He would be man and woman, God's perfect creation.

I shared my deepest feelings. My guilt. I don't want your essence, Carver. I want you dead.

Of course, given even a moment alone with her, and with pleasure he would leave Charlie Carver to wallow in his pathetic life, but no such— *Wait! He's leaving her alone to get her something at the food stand. Oh, what a perfect day.*

~

Rachel continued to crane her neck, raking the area for any suspicious-looking men or Jacob Goodman's shock of cropped blond hair. A forty-something man, square-shouldered and bull-necked as a marine, silently slipped up next to her when her head was turned the other way.

"Excuse me, ma'am."

Rachel yelped. Her arms sprung straight up.

The stranger jerked back. "Sorry, just wanted to know the time," he said sheepishly.

Rachel raised a quivering arm while looking around the man for Charlie's appearance. "It's six o'clock."

"Something the matter, ma'am?"

Rachel shifted her weight back and put a gloved hand to her forehead. "No, no. I'm all right." Sobs of frustration and fear caught in her throat and choked her. Tears blurred what sight she had in the moon-slivered night.

He's dead. Jacob's dead.

The thought brought her back to Sarah. She hadn't cheated death. What made her mother so different? She was violating everything she had been taught since childhood. Her mind flashed on Charlie caressing and feather-kissing her breasts. *Fornication.* Snippets of sermons and damning scripture pounded as if background drums in her head while she tried to rationalize her act of truly making love for the first time.

Her heart fluttered and throat tightened at the idea that she had joined in cheating Sarah out of a normal life.

The engulfing vision of her own impending death stunned her, and she wanted to stand away and stare at herself, this woman dressed in Babylon clothes, ready to live with a man she had only shared a bed with one night. It was as if she was having an out-of-body experience, as if this person hiding from herself were someone she only knew in passing. Her instinct for Anna's preservation and new life spurred her back to reality.

"I'm sorry to scare you, ma'am," the clear-eyed stranger blurted out. "I'm an investigator with Salt Lake Homicide. We've had a tail on Charlie Carver since the serial killer started calling him."

Rachel's brows tugged together, trying to comprehend what he was leading up to.

She flinched when the tall man with tight-cropped blond hair and riveting jungle-green eyes reached out and softly clutched her arm. "You'd better come with me right now."

"Why? What did I—"

"It's Carver. He's been stabbed," he winced and shot a quick look around the area. "Ambulance is on its way."

Rachel scrambled to her feet and began running in the direction of the refreshment stand. The detective was at her heels.

"Hold on!" he yelled.

She turned and gasped for air. The salty taste of tears made her lick her lips and sniffle. "What?"

"You could be in danger. Stay with me."

"The Strangler's dead." The word "dead" barely crossed over her lips when she knew she had made a monumental mistake.

The detective tilted his head in aggravated curiosity. "What? How do you know that?" He rubbed his well-defined chin. "Carver. He was wrong, ma'am, unless somebody else was after him."

The detective took Rachel by the hand, then tucked her arm in his. "Stay close."

As they started rounding the outer corner of the rink spectator area, the detective took a sharp right turn in the nearby direction of the underground parking lot.

"Why are we going there?" Rachel said through rattling teeth.

"That's where we've got him. We've got a blue-and-white down there with him until the ambulance arrives."

Rachel shook her head while her face spasmed in confusion. The breath started coming raw in her throat. His eyes were wrong: haunted. She tried to coyly, then overtly, pull her arm free, but he only gripped it tighter.

As soon as they started down the darkening cement ramp she lunged free, but after only a few wildly running steps, she tripped, taking the full force of the tumble on her outstretched gloved hands.

"What's wrong?"

She abruptly looked in the direction of the thin male voice. Two hair-bleached, grunge-dressed men in their early twenties instantly let go of each other's hands.

"I'm sorry, Rachel," the man in the gray overcoat at the base of the ramp muttered. "She didn't mean a thing to me."

Rachel was back on her feet, bolting in the direction of the only other people in the garage. "Help! He's trying to kill me." She darted behind a

Buick sedan and started to low crawl around its front bumper to the Ford Explorer parked next to it.

The man in the gray coat planted closed-gloved fists on his hips shaking his head. "Come on, honey. They'll think you're serious." He looked up to the two gawking witnesses and stopped, acting as though he needed a breather. "Women!" he announced again, wagging his head. "They're impossible."

"No shit, man," the one with the ring in his nose spouted. The two rejoined hands and laughed their way up the ramp.

The hunter's voice had a hollow echo. He walked deeper into the belly of the garage and at the sound of shoe soles sliding along concrete he crouched perfectly still, as if a panther about to pounce. "There's nobody down here but us, beautiful." He waited, but heard nothing. "I saw what car you were hiding behind." His voice was playful, inviting.

Rachel popped up and started running, panting for the ramp leading to the second level down. Once in the open he had no trouble grabbing her from behind. She threw her head back and caught another look at his face, set in angry lines that were exaggerated by the shadows of the gloomy garage. He rushed the ether-laden cloth to her face. The struggle didn't last but a moment before she flopped limp in his hold.

He smiled at the floral scent of her hair, but his eyes were dead.

~

"Damnit," Charlie muttered to himself while tipping his wrist to spy the time. It was just approaching six-fifteen p.m. The line at the refreshment stand had eaten up all their time. He zigzagged through the crowd, juggling the cups of hot chocolate while searching for wherever Rachel had moved to get a closer look at the skaters. He scaled the aluminum bleachers and scanned the throng of bundled bodies one-by-one. "Rachel." He said it softly at first, then with each hammering heartbeat raised his voice to a near-panic calling.

"Rachel! Over here." Nobody's head turned. The chocolate slipped from his hands. A sickening wave of terror welled up from his belly. Convinced he had scrutinized everybody on the side of the rink where he left her, he broke into a full run, shoving through the crowd until he had completed his mad dash around the oval.

Oh, Jesus! Where did you go? Damnit, Rachel. Answer me.

"Rachel!"

The nose ring wearer turned around and waved Charlie over to him at the rink's edge. "Hey, some guy was chasing down a woman named Rachel in the parking garage over there, if that helps ya," he yelled as Charlie approached him.

"You sure her name was Rachel?" Charlie snapped.

"She really ate some concrete when she was trying to—"

"Carver," an intensely groomed middle-aged man yelled over crowd heads.

Charlie shoved past a family to get to what had to be surveillance.

"Dennamire, FBI. We've been shadowing you for weeks. We nearly nailed him in Park City after he called you on your cellular, but he got away."

"Where's Rachel? Have you seen her?"

The agent tugged the squawking walkie-talkie from his belt. "Anything?" The agent nodded and started to break into full stride for the parking garage with Charlie at his heels.

"What is it?" Charlie yelled.

"He's on the move. Just left the garage."

Charlie jogged up along side the agent as the two entered the garage. "What kind of truck?"

"Chevy Tahoe, dark green. He just turned left on State Street. Same truck as the one we chased in Park City. It's gotta be him."

Charlie rocketed to his Jeep before the agent reached his Ford sedan. His tires screamed as he vaulted ahead of the agents' car and two Salt Lake City police cars. He bulleted along State Street at sixty miles an hour, banging on his brakes to stop from crashing into a mass of cross-street traffic. A dark green Tahoe had just made it through the light at legal speed. Charlie jumped out of his car and climbed on his roof to track the sports utility vehicle. It was moving inconspicuously slow.

"What the hell are you doing?" the FBI agent yelled out of his window from two cars back.

Charlie hopped back in the car and lurched between cars, barely missed getting broad-sided by a horn-blasting furniture delivery truck. He slowed down to just above the speed limit when the Tahoe was only five cars ahead of him in the same lane. The vehicle suddenly jumped lanes and turned right. Charlie was locked in until the four cars to his right moved forward or turned. Nobody was turning. He was trapped "Damn, you saw me," he mumbled, slamming his palm on the steering wheel.

The Strangler hopped lanes and in a flash turned into Liberty Park, traveled straight to the back of the public pool area at the center of the inner-city playground and parked under the dark shadow of a fifty-foot pinion pine.

Rachel choked on the nostril-biting smell of ammonia as her eyes began to focus. Her scream in seeing the carnivorous face looming over her muted to a high shrill. The duct tape over her mouth didn't allow for much more than her ears popping from the pressure.

"I see we're awake. Good."

Her eyes became full moons as she lifted her head enough to see her near-naked body. He had secured her wrists and ankles with women's nylons to metal rings anchored into the plush carpeted cargo space floor. She moved her mouth from side-to-side, but couldn't budge the tape covering it.

"That's right. You're all mine. Like the panties?"

Rachel could lift her head enough to see the purple and gold lace French-cut panties. She shook her mane of hair wildly and tried to scream again.

"Victoria's Secret." He glared down at her silky smooth curvaceous body. "Now it's our little secret. Symbolic really. I'm liberating you from those sexless temple garments. Setting your spirit free to join mine." He ran his thick latex covered hands across her bucking stomach, then cupped her firm breasts and sighed. "I am so blessed. Those bruises on your face. They're going to have to go. Why ruin such a perfect picture?"

"I really hate to do it this way." The creature put an index finger to her taped mouth and ran it slowly, like a crawling spider, over her chin, down her neck, between her breasts and down her panties until it found warmth. Her hips bucked in every direction at the hideous feel of his violating finger.

He leaned into her lips and lightly kissed the tape. "I would love to taste your lips and tongue while we share your essence. I brought some make-up. We'll touch up those bruises a little later.

"I've been told I'm a good lover."

She nodded in numb horror.

"Will you be good if I take off the tape? It goes right back on if you scream."

Again she tried to physically act out surrender.

He unbuttoned his shirt as if he were a dollar-a-beer bar stripper and again put his hand between her legs. "You're getting warmer. I can tell you want us to share, oh, everything."

Delicately, very delicately he pulled up the tape so it wouldn't leave ugly red marks. Just as he lifted the last edge of it off her face she gulped air furiously and let out a long guttural scream, stopped only by the claws tightening around her neck. When he could only hear her raspy jagged breathing he released his grip.

Just as he reached over to grab the roll of duct tape, the Tahoe's back window exploded into shards of glass. He roared a hysterical growl at the sight of the landscape boulder near Rachel's feet.

Charlie reached through the hole and yanked open the latch. The double doors flew open. The Strangler instantly threw himself on

Rachel's outstretched naked body, rolled back, and kicked in Charlie's face with rocket velocity. Charlie flew backwards, arms spread wide open. The back of his head bounced off the asphalt as if it were an inflated ball.

The Strangler was out and scrambled up and away before Charlie could get to his knees and feet. He wiped the spurting blood from his nose with the back of his hand. Pure adrenaline put his wobbling legs in motion.

He threaded his way through a thicket of bushes and trees just in time to see the killer touch down on the curb on the other side of the four-lane street. He flashed a glance up at the red light and blazed across the danger zone between speeding cars. The Strangler vanished around an alley corner with Charlie battling to keep pace.

The killer was almost close enough to tackle when he stopped and whirled around, wielding a knife. The tip of the blade grazed Charlie's chest. Before the blade could cut flesh again, Charlie kicked the Strangler between the legs. He let out a primal groan and dropped to his knees just as they both heard the shrill of sirens.

The Strangler put the blade to his own neck. "Too soon, you bastard. God won't take me now." He slit his own throat, just below his Adam's apple.

59
CHAPTER

Even before his eyes opened in the morning, awareness was upon him. He imagined Rachel in a provocative wedding dress, himself, slowly lifting her veil to seal a life together. Suddenly Rachel was there beside him, surrendering to a big yawn, then stretching, arms out, with hair and fingers splayed. He felt a brief flutter of total exuberance, but then he woke fully, and it was gone.

He was alone in bed and would remain so until Rachel charted her own course, felt the wonder and strength of independence. The conscious thought wasn't so bad. In fact, it filled him with a warm purpose.

Chicago Tribune, New York Times, forget it. Today, after whipping the girls up a fresh fruit yogurt, cinnamon raisin English muffins, and herbal tea for breakfast, he was off to patch up some emotional wounds. Watching Glendon Bartholomew's face as he coughed out his reason for rehiring him was going to be precious. The call had been no surprise, despite what Donald Goodman claimed to have arranged. He'd made a point of giving accolades to the *Observer* for making Charlie Carver a new Salt Lake Valley household name. The gush of cameras and ink were still flowing over his dramatized role in saving the girl and bringing down the bad guy. A long-established and respected commercial photographer, church and family man, Borg Erickson, was now immortalized as the Salt Lake Strangler.

Charlie slipped into his guest bedroom where Rachel was still in slumber and eased up the blinds. He went to her bedside and stole a moment, staring at the only women who had ever completed him. *Ironic.* He'd never known a person with more pieces missing.

~

"The sun is out," he said softly and kissed her bare shoulder.

Rachel absently pulled the covers up to her chin. "So it is."

"Do you want a big breakfast? You name it and it'll appear."

Rachel teasingly smiled. "You're starting to make a habit of this." She put her index finger to her lips and tapped. "Let's see. My favorite is homemade oatmeal. You know, where you grind the oats yourself."

"Sure. I know I shouldn't be in a lady's bedroom," he playfully tugged at her blanket, "but I was just wondering if you'd like to make a habit of something else?"

For a split second she thought he was serious, and then they laughed together.

After breakfast Rachel predictably announced that Lydia, in conjunction with Family Services, had arranged temporary housing for them in Salt Lake City. A small place, but a beginning.

"Are you going to take the money from Goodman?" Charlie asked.

Rachel shook her head, her eyebrows scrunched together. "That...That asshole!"

"Son *and* father," Charlie said.

Grabbing their coats, Charlie hustled her to the front door. "We're going out for a few minutes," Charlie yelled in the direction of the kitchen. Israel Goodman poked his head around the corner. Anna's arms were wrapped around him from behind with her chin resting on his shoulder. "Where are you going?"

"Where are we going?" Rachel asked, still reeling in anger at the mention of Donald Goodman and sons.

"Sunset Lawn, of course."

~

After kneeling hand-in-hand at Sarah's gravesite, the two spent the morning walking. They followed any street wide enough to have a sunny side, going to any shop for diversion, simply looking. Charlie surprised her with a single crimson long-stemmed rose, accompanied by a loving kiss on the cheek and tight hug.

Charlie ambled hours past his appointment time with his publisher, watching the people, dawdling listlessly as if robots low on battery juice. When Rachel finally gained an appetite, he bought them fish and chips and found a bench at a downtown park aviary.

"We can skip talking about anything," he said gently to Rachel, "but I would like your opinion on what I should write, if anything, about the Goodmans."

She ate for a while before answering. "I don't know. I don't want to see it go on."

"I think we ought to blow the whistle on the whole damn thing—polygamy. Force the state's hand to do something about it," Charlie said.

Rachel lowered and shook her head. "I don't want his money," she said. "I only want him and the rest of the world to leave us alone."

CHAPTER 60

"What is it with you?" Theron Liddle exploded once Charlie was settled back at his workstation. "Are you nuts in some complicated way I haven't figured out yet? You've got the front page of the paper with free reign to rip polygamy apart from one end of the state to the other." He sharply shook his head. "You were going to quit over it, for damn sakes. Don't you see how crazy this is? What an opportunity."

Suddenly Liddle was calmer. "All right. So some people are going to get hurt. If we don't stop it now, generations more women and under-age girls will pay the price with their freedom." He rounded Charlie's desk, examining his face owlishly. "Isn't that what this country's all about? Freedom of choice?"

Charlie shrugged and looked away. "I told you, with Jacob dead we've got no case."

Liddle perched on the edge of Charlie's desk and shoved up his unbuttoned sleeves, old beat-reporter style. "You know how long I've wanted to do this story." He threw his arms up in the air, still searching for the bare-fisted investigative reporter he thought he hired. "What's your problem? She's broken away from them. Hell, Charlie, what do you think the fourth estate is all about? It's our responsibility to right what's wrong when we can." He leaned in close and whispered. "And from what bits and pieces you've told me—"

"I told you off the record, Theron."

"I know, I know, but buddy, this is a Pulitzer Prize winner." He stared down at outstretched palms. "This kind of inside exposè comes along once in a lifetime."

Charlie drummed his fingers on his desk. Liddle was scraping at his core. Carver couldn't deny what he had spent his life defending: Truth at any cost.

An insipid grin crept over Charlie's face.

Liddle stood, patted him an "atta-boy" on the back, and shuffled off to his page makeup man for a humdinger of a lead story.

Charlie reached over and eased open his desk drawer. He scanned his station area for probing eyes and lifted the Polaroids out onto the center of his desk.

One-by-one he tore them to pieces.

ABOUT THE AUTHOR

Lon LaFlamme is a former AP wire service and daily newspaper reporter. He was CEO of one of the largest marketing communications companies in the western U.S., receiving numerous national advertising and public relations awards. LaFlamme has served as marketing professor at the nation's largest private university. He divides his time between Seattle, Washington and Salt Lake City, Utah.